Praise for Curiosity House: The Shrunken Head and Lauren Oliver's Liesl & Po

'Stupendous and stupefying! A riddle wrapped in a mystery inside a Shrunken Head. If you aren't curious about *Curiosity House* somebody must have pickled your brain and put it in a jar. Read this book immediately.'

Pseudonymous Bosch, *New York Times* bestselling author of the *Secret Series* and *Bad Magic*

'Step right up! Step right up! Mystery, murder, curses, and sideshow freaks! Or are they superheroes? There's only one way to find out . . . Read *Curiosity House*! You'll be glad you did!'

Adam Gidwitz, *New York Times* bestselling author of the *A Tale Dark and Grimm series*

'An absolute delight . . . The story is packed with mystery, murder, adventure, humour and magic, but above all it is a beautiful evocation of loss, tempered by the gradual blossoming of friendship, trust and hope. Although aimed at younger readers, the lightness of touch and the tenderness of the message could make grown men weep.'

Daily Mail on *Liesl & Po*

'A gorgeous story – timeless and magical.'

Rebecca Stead, Newbery winner for *When You Reach Me*

'*Liesl & Po* by Lauren Oliver brings much-needed magic to an increasingly neglected age group . . . there are some exquisitely drawn characters . . . it's books like this, with its classic quest plot, intertwined with lyrical metaphysics, that can set a child up for life.'

Telegraph on *Liesl & Po*

32

Also by

LAUREN OLIVER

FOR YOUNGER READERS
Liesl & Po
The Spindlers

FOR OLDER READERS
Before I Fall
Panic
Vanishing Girls

The Delirium Trilogy
Delirium
Pandemonium
Requiem
Delirium Stories: Hana, Annabel, & Raven

FOR ADULTS
Rooms

CURIOSITY HOUSE

~THE~ SHRUNKEN HEAD

LAUREN OLIVER & H.C. CHESTER

HODDER

First published in the United States in 2015 by HarperCollins Children's Books, a division of HarperCollins Publishers.

First published in Great Britain in 2015 by Hodder & Stoughton
An Hachette UK company

First published in paperback in 2016

I

A CIP catalogue record for this title
is available from the British Library

ISBN 978 1 444 77721 5

Printed and bound by Clays Ltd, St Ives plc

Hodder & Stoughton policy is to use papers that are natural, renewable and recyclable products and made from wood grown in sustainable forests. The logging and manufacturing processes are expected to conform to the environmental regulations of the country of origin.

Hodder & Stoughton Ltd
Carmelite House
50 Victoria Embankment
London EC4Y 0DZ

www.hodder.co.uk

L adies and gentlemen, boys and girls: step right up and don't be shy. You must not—you absolutely *cannot!*—put this book down.

Yes, I'm speaking to you—you, with the chewing gum and the smudgy fingers. Don't try to pretend your fingers aren't smudgy. They are leaving marks even now. It's okay. Smudgy fingers are quite allowed in the museum.

What museum, you ask? But surely you've heard already. You see, within these pages is a museum, and within the museum is a story of wondrous weirdness, of magic and monsters . . . and of four of the most extraordinary children in the world.

Ladies and gentlemen, please don't push! The doors will open soon enough; the page will turn. I assure you, there is room enough for everybody.

And now, for the rules:

All grown-ups must be accompanied by a child, and disbelievers will be clobbered on the head with an umbrella. Gaping and gawking are strictly encouraged, although pointing is, as always, considered rude. Coat check is on the left, popcorn on the right. Please do not litter, and do *not* feed the alligator boy.

And now, ladies and gentlemen, boys and girls, children of all ages: welcome to Dumfrey's Dime Museum of Freaks, Oddities, and Wonders.

COME IN, PLEASE. ST P OUT O THE RAIN.

It had been raining for three straight days, and even the regular customers were staying away. On Thursday, Thomas had the idea of posting a sign on the doors of the museum. By Friday, several letters had blurred away, and the others were running toward the bottom of the page as though attempting a getaway. By Saturday afternoon, the note had turned to a sodden piece of pulp and, driven by the winds into the gutter, was carted away on the underside of a busy man's leather-soled shoe.

Thomas was bored.

It was only April 20, and he had already read all the

books Mr. Dumfrey had bought him for his birthday on April 2, including *The Probability of Everything*, which was nearly a thousand pages long, and *A Short History of Math*, which was even longer. So he spent the morning in the attic, playing DeathTrap, a game of his own invention. It was like chess, except that instead of using a checkerboard, it relied on the patterns of a threadbare Persian rug, and instead of pawns, bishops, and knights, the pieces were various things pilfered from the exhibits over the years: a baby kangaroo's foot, which could only jump spaces; a dented Roman coin that could only be spun or flipped; an old shark's jaw that didn't move but conquered pieces that came too close by swallowing them; a scorpion tail that paralyzed other players so they lost a turn; an armadillo toe that could be used by any player, depending on who was in possession of the armadillo shell.

As usual, Thomas had no one to play with, so he had to do both sides.

He flipped the coin and sighed when it landed faceup. That meant he had to move the Egyptian scorpion tail back three swirls in the carpet.

"You should take the armadillo toe."

Thomas looked up. Philippa, the mentalist, was sprawled across a daybed, watching him.

"What?" he asked. He and Philippa were both twelve, but her dark, almond-shaped eyes, her straight fringe of black bangs, and her sharply pointed chin made her appear much older.

Philippa sighed. "If you move the scorpion there"—she pointed—"you can take the armadillo. Tail takes toe, right?"

Thomas saw that she was right and felt annoyed. "I didn't know you were playing," he said. He had grown up with Philippa, but they had never been close.

Philippa shrugged and picked up her book—*Mystics, Mind Readers, and Magic*, which Thomas had also read and found exceedingly stupid—then rolled onto her back. When she wasn't looking, Thomas swiped at the armadillo toe with the scorpion's, sending it skittering off the rug.

He had won again. It would be more exciting if he hadn't also lost.

He stood up, feeling restless. It was uncommonly quiet, the kind of day that made him feel lazy. Sam was sitting in one of several armchairs in the common area, his hair mostly concealing his face, as it had been ever since he'd discovered his first pimple. An issue of his favorite magazine, *Pet World*, was open in his lap.

Monsieur Cabillaud, the children's tutor, was snoring. Having exhausted himself earlier that day in an argument with Philippa over who was to blame for the Thirty Years' War, he had promptly taken a nap on the sofa with a textbook covering his tiny head.

Phoebe, the fat lady, had retreated to her bedroom. Smalls, the giant, was working on his latest poem and had spent the whole morning repeating "the swallows fly like shadows across the sky" and "like shadows the swallows fly across the sky" and "across the sky, like shadows, swallows fly" and shaking his head.

Danny, the dwarf, had gone next door for a drink. Hugo, the elephant man, was working on a crossword puzzle in the corner. Betty, the bearded lady, was carefully combing and braiding her beard. Goldini, the magician, had been puzzling all afternoon over a new trick but so far had succeeded only in vanishing three quarters somewhere under the sofa cushions. Rain lashed against the large windows, and the glass seemed to be slowly melting into liquid.

The radio was reporting news of another washed-out baseball game. Then the advertisements came on.

"Ladies and gentlemen, boys and girls . . . step right up and don't be shy! Down at Dumfrey's Dime Museum is a world of wonder, of wondrous weirdness . . ."

"Turn it down, please," Philippa said primly. "I'm reading."

Just to spite her, Thomas stood and turned the radio *up* a few notches, even though he'd heard the ad a million times at least.

". . . our brand-new exhibit, guaranteed to knock your socks off and spin your head around in its socket! New York's only shrunken head! Straight from the Amazon! Delivered only yesterday!"

"Pippa's right, Thomas," Betty trilled in her sweet voice. "I've had enough talk of that silly head. Uglier than sin, if you ask me!" She swept her long brown beard over one shoulder serenely, stood, and switched off the radio.

In quick succession, like an echo, bells on every floor of the museum began to ding. That meant someone was at the doors.

"I'll get it!" Thomas said. He didn't bother with the stairs but threw himself into the air duct, whose cover he kept loose for this reason.

Unlike some of the other performers—Danny, Betty, Andrew—Thomas looked completely normal. He was a little short for his age and a little skinny, too. He had a smattering of freckles across his nose, which was stubby, and straw-colored hair that never managed to lie flat. He had vivid green eyes that were, more often than not, trained on a book about mathematics, science, or engineering.

But he wasn't normal—far from it. Thomas could bend his nose to his toes. He could flex his spine like an anaconda. He could squeeze himself into a space no larger than a child's suitcase. His bones and joints seemed to be formed of putty.

Now Thomas shimmied down the narrow duct, counting the floors, and sprang free of the grate in the lobby, completely unconscious of the fact that he was sporting a small mass of lint on his head.

Mr. Dumfrey was already opening the doors, saying, "No need for all that fuss, Thomas. I have it."

Just then, Thomas had the strangest sensation that reality had hit a snag, as though he were watching a play and one of the actors had skipped several lines. Afterward, he was to remember that moment for a very long time: the thin girl standing on the stoop in the rain, with the narrow face and wild curtain of dark hair, and the scar that stretched from her right eyebrow to her right ear, dressed in clothes three times too big for her and clutching a rucksack in one hand; and Mr. Dumfrey, his large, kind face so pale, it looked as though his head had been replaced with a pile of bread dough.

"It can't be," he gasped.

The girl frowned. "I heard an ad on the radio. You got a head here, don't you?"

Dumfrey recovered somewhat. He swallowed loudly. "We have the only shrunken head in all of New York City," he said grandly. "And the finest collection of freaks, wonders, and curiosities in the world."

The girl sniffed and looked around the dingy lobby, where Andrew, the alligator boy (who was actually pushing seventy-five and walked with a cane), was playing solitaire behind the admissions desk, and several buckets had been set up to catch the rain where it was dribbling through a leaky window. "You looking for another act?"

"That depends," Dumfrey said. Thomas noticed he was still gripping the doors, as though worried he might fall over. "What sort of act?"

Thomas did not see the girl reach into her pocket. He saw only the glint of metal in her hand, before, with quick, fluid grace, she rounded on him. He felt a wind whip past him, heard the thud of something on the plaster wall behind him.

Two high points of color had appeared in Dumfrey's cheeks. He stood, eyes glittering, staring at a spot directly behind Thomas's head.

Thomas turned.

Embedded in the wall, practically to its hilt, was an evil-looking knife, staked directly in the middle of a small ball of lint.

"You're hired," Mr. Dumfrey rasped.

The girl smiled.

The new girl's name was Mackenzie but she insisted everybody call her Max.

Initially, when Philippa heard a new girl had been hired, she was excited. She wasn't the only female resident of the museum. There was Betty; Phoebe the fat lady; and the albino twins, Quinn and Caroline (who despised each other). There was also the cook, Mrs. Cobble, and Miss Fitch, the costume maker and general manager, whom nobody liked.

But none of the others *really* counted, because they were old. She thought maybe she'd at last have someone to talk to.

But one minute with Max changed her mind.

"Humfrey seems nuttier than a box of peanuts," was the first thing Max said. "He looked at me like he'd just swallowed a toad."

"His name is Dumfrey," Pippa said. "And he isn't nutty. He's a genius."

"Oh yeah?" Max dumped her rucksack (dirty, Pippa noticed) on top of the narrow bed next to Pippa's, which had until this day remained empty. All the performers lived together in the portion of the attic not dedicated to the common room or the washrooms, of which there were two. A mazelike formation of old furniture, folding screens, and clothing racks had been arranged to subdivide the space and give each performer privacy, although many of the residents nonetheless had to share their sleeping quarters to accommodate all the beds. "Then how'd he end up saddled with this dump?"

Already, Pippa was regretting her new roommate. "This *dump*," she said, "is one of the very last remaining dime museums in the world. It's a wonderful and historical place." Pippa was losing patience. "Why did you come, anyway?"

Max flopped down on her back, seeming not to care at all that she was dirty and the bed was, or had been, clean. "I heard an ad on the radio," she said. "I've been looking for somewhere I can get comfy." She kicked off her boots and wiggled her toes. There were several large holes in her socks. She sat up on an elbow, sniffing. "What's that smell?"

"Your feet," Pippa responded.

"Not *that* smell." Max rolled her eyes. "The other one. Like—like—like cat boxes and meatballs."

Pippa stiffened. "That smell" was the candle Pippa liked to burn before each performance.

"Sandalwood," she said. "Brings luck."

"What do you need luck for?" Max said.

Pippa smoothed a wrinkle from her coverlet. She didn't like the way Max was looking at her. She didn't like the way Max spoke, either—like one of the street kids who tried to sneak in and try to steal coins from the cashbox, when there were any. "I get stage fright," she said carefully.

"Stage fright?" Max repeated, as though she'd never heard the words. She propped herself up on one elbow. "For real? What's your act, anyway?"

Pippa lifted her chin. "I'm a mentalist," she said stiffly.

"A menta-what?"

"A mentalist," she repeated. "I know things. About people. I can . . . sense them."

Max stared at her. "Like . . . you can tell what people

are thinking?" She looked suddenly afraid. "Can you tell what *I'm* thinking?"

Heat crept up Pippa's neck. "It doesn't work like that," she said quickly.

She couldn't possibly tell Max the truth. That her gift was *real*—not like the tricks that street performers did, with their setups and sleight of hand, their fake volunteers and their cheap frauds. She really was a mentalist—she just couldn't control it. Although sometimes she could feel other minds, pushing like alien blobs against her own, the only thing she had ever consistently been able to decipher was what a person was carrying in his coat pockets or in her handbag or—occasionally!—what kind of undershirt a person was wearing. And even that was blocked sometimes—like when Pippa was scared or angry. Or when she had stage fright.

That's why she needed the candle.

Max was obviously unconvinced. She crossed her arms. "How does it work, then?"

Fortunately, Pippa was prevented from replying by Potts, the janitor. He lumbered past the Japanese screens, hat pulled low over his eyes, without bothering to tap or even cough.

"Downstairs with you," he said. As usual, he spat out

14 ☞

the words, as though they carried their own particular bad taste and he had to get rid of them as quickly as possible. "It's six o'clock already. Almost showtime."

Dumfrey's Dime Museum was, from the outside, easy to miss. The four-story brick building, originally a combination art school and gallery called the New York Cultural Academy, was sandwiched between Eli's Barbershop and the St. Edna Hotel, like an awkward middle child getting squeezed to death by its two prettier, more impressive siblings.

Inside, however, the museum was unlike any other in all the world—at least, that's what was written on the illustrated guide to the museum available for purchase at the ticket desk. (*Welcome to Dumfrey's Dime Museum*, the guide said, *a Museum Unlike Any Other in All the World, Featuring the Largest Collection of Oddities, the Strangest Assortment of Freaks, and Novel and Astounding Exhibitions Comprising More Than One Thousand Curiosities from Every Portion of the Globe!!!* And for those who still doubted it, an enormous banner stretched above the lobby repeated the information.)

In addition to the coat check and refreshment stand—which sold gumdrops, caramel-coated popcorn, and root beer—the first floor housed two exhibition spaces. One was the Odditorium, where the live performances took place. The other was the Hall of Worldwide Wonders, which contained more than one hundred items hand-selected by Mr. Dumfrey, including an Eskimo seal-hunting spear, the headdress of a pygmy witch doctor, and a carved wooden platter used by Polynesian cannibals; and a large, open gallery of glassed-in exhibit cases, containing everything from a tiny doll-like figure floating in a jar of alcohol, said to be a genuine changeling baby from the British Isles, to a mummified cat found in King Tut's tomb.

Tucked next to the Hall of Worldwide Wonders was a smaller room dedicated to special exhibits; inside it was the staircase that led down to the kitchen in the basement, and a bedroom concealed away behind a false bookshelf where the cook, Mrs. Cobble, slept.

On the second floor was the Gallery of Historical and Scientific Rarities as well as the Hall of Wax, which Pippa tried to avoid. She had never been able to stomach the curious blank look of the modeled faces, all of them fashioned by the famous sculptor Siegfried "Freckles" Eckleberger, whom Pippa had known since she was a baby. She loved Freckles but hated his wax figures; they were too real, and she could never shake the idea that they might come to life at any second and reach for her. In particular, she despised the chamber of horrors, where visitors could see famous crimes reconstructed in wax. Max, on the other hand, immediately declared that the statue of Lizzie Borden clutching an ax was her favorite.

In the tableau of Adam and Eve was a small door concealed behind the Tree of Knowledge; this led to the costume room and Miss Fitch's quarters, dominated by ancient sewing machines, heaps of fabric, and racks of costumes for performances both past and future.

On the third floor was the Grand Salon of Living Curiosities. Beyond the Authentic Preserved Two-Headed Calf!, whose second head was constantly having to be reattached with adhesive, a small door marked *Private* gave access to the performers' staircase and to Mr. Dumfrey's office. This last room was cluttered with various items removed from or rotating out of the exhibits. It was not uncommon to see Mr. Dumfrey scribbling off a note with the pen that Thomas Jefferson had once used to sign the Declaration of Independence. Then came the attic on the fourth floor, crowded with box springs and wardrobes, creaky beds and overstuffed armchairs, where the performers lived happily among dozens of pieces of stump-legged furniture and cast-off oddities, including, in one corner, a moth-eaten stuffed grizzly bear rearing up on its hind legs.

There had once been many other dime museums in New York City, and across the country—each of them declaring its own collection the most renowned, the weirdest, the most extraordinary.

But times and interests had changed. Money had run thin. People had lost interest in the weird and the wonderful; they preferred the kind of entertainment that was easily enjoyed and just as easily forgotten. Slowly, the other museums had shuttered their doors.

By the time our story begins, Mr. Dumfrey's Dime Museum of Freaks, Oddities, and Wonders truly did live up to its published promise: it was unlike any other museum in the world. And it was the only place on earth where four extraordinary children like Thomas, Sam, Pippa, and Max could fit in.

The nightly performance began punctually at six thirty. The rain had stopped three quarters of an hour earlier, and either the change in weather or the advertised shrunken head, or both, had worked their magic: there was a crowd of nearly two dozen in the audience to witness *Dumfrey's Living Miracles and Wonders!*, as the show was labeled on the distributed handbills. This was more than three times the usual number, and Potts,

grumbling the whole time, had to bring up extra folding chairs from the basement.

Pippa always watched the early acts from the wings,
safely hidden behind heavy velvet curtains that had
been recycled from a funeral parlor. As usual, her collar was pinching her. Pippa hated the dress Miss Fitch
forced her to wear. It managed to be as shapeless as a
sack and too tight in all the wrong places.

But at least, she thought, it was better than Sam's
costume: frayed khaki shorts and a ripped white
undershirt, as though he was the sole survivor of a des-
ert island shipwreck.

"What's he do?"

Pippa hadn't heard Max approach. She turned
around and saw that Max, too, had been outfitted by
Miss Fitch. She was wearing black leggings and leather
boots, along with a tasseled leather jacket that had been
used at one time for a short-lived cowboy act featuring
a two-headed horse.

"He's the strong man," Pippa whispered.

Max nearly choked. "Strong man? No way. He
couldn't win a fight with a string bean."

"Just watch," Pippa said.

Sam always started the show. Now, he shuffled miserably onstage, hands shoved deep in his pockets, hair

hanging over his eyes, like a prisoner moving toward his own execution.

A quick murmur went through the audience, and there was a faint rustling, as nearly two dozen people consulted their programs. This couldn't really be Samson Jr., Strongest Boy Alive? This pale, miserable, speckled, scrawny thing, like an overgrown newt, who stood sullenly, blinking on the stage . . . ? Perhaps there had been a typo or a change in the program.

But then Mr. Dumfrey's voice rolled out over the audience. "And now . . . ladies and gentlemen . . . boys and girls . . . I give you the most amazing, incredible, unbelievable, and inconceivable Strongman of Siddarth!"

Max snickered as Smalls the giant and Hugo the elephant man wheeled out a large block of stone on a dolly. Mr. Dumfrey invited audience volunteers onstage to test it, touch it, sniff it, taste it, and the stone was declared real and solid. All this time, Sam stood slightly apart, looking mortified.

When the audience members were satisfied, Mr. Dumfrey trumpeted: "Hold on to your seats and sit tight on your hats, ladies and gentlemen! What you are about to witness is a superhuman, a supernatural, a superfluous—"

He did not get any further. With an exasperated look, Sam stepped forward and drove a fist straight into the stone. There was a thunderous crack as the stone cleaved straight down the middle and split in two.

For a second, there was utter silence from the audience. Then applause: a smattering at first, then cresting to an appreciative roar.

Sam turned so pink, it looked as though he'd been dipped headfirst into an oven. He rapidly hurried off the stage.

"See?" Pippa whispered to Max. Max was doing her best to look unimpressed, and only shrugged.

Next was the magician, the Great Goldini. He seemed to be speeding through his act. Before she knew it, he had successfully withdrawn an ace of spades from the purse of an ancient woman in the front row, whose face looked like it would crack in half when she smiled. He had extracted a rabbit from a hat, and then, with a wave of his wand, transformed it into a gopher. Even though Pippa knew the secrets behind Goldini's tricks, she was still impressed, especially since they didn't always go so smoothly. Just a few days earlier, the magician had reached into his hat for a rabbit and pulled out an ace of spades, while the gopher somehow ended up in the pocket of an unsuspecting audience member.

For his final trick, the magician sawed his assistant, Thomas, in half. And as usual, Thomas looked absolutely miserable—Miss Fitch insisted that the magician's assistant *must* dress as a girl, and Pippa could see him glaring at the audience from underneath the thick fringe of his wig's bangs, as though daring anyone to laugh. Sadly, until they could find a replacement who was as good at managing the illusion, which required him to squeeze his whole body into a wooden container barely larger than a breadbox, Thomas was stuck in the job.

After Goldini came Caroline and Quinn, the albino twins, who performed a perfectly synchronized ballet, although as soon as they retreated backstage, they began arguing furiously, each accusing the other of having been off tempo. Then, a parody: Smalls the giant and Danny the dwarf also performed a dance, which never failed to produce a laugh, especially when Danny sprang into Smalls's outstretched hand and executed a graceful pirouette on his palm.

After that came the stately procession of Hugo, the elephant man, and Phoebe, the fat lady; Betty, the bearded lady, and Andrew, the alligator boy. Although they did nothing but walk across the stage and stand for a minute under the spotlight, the audience gasped and tittered nervously. It was always particularly momentous when Betty, who emerged from the wings backward, swaying her hips, spun around to reveal her long beard, crimped and tied with a bow.

And suddenly the stage was cleared and the lights were dimmed and it was Pippa's turn.

"Don't choke," Max whispered.

Pippa wanted to respond, but her voice had turned suddenly to sand in her throat. The spotlight was up, and the old gramophone, concealed behind the scrim, began to warble faintly. That was her cue.

As she stepped into the light, there was another gasp. The dark fabric of her dress, embroidered with hundreds and hundreds of reflective, diamond-shaped chips, was dazzling. The effect was supposed to be of jewels, although Pippa knew that the dress was made of tarlatan, sequins recycled from the gown worn by last year's "mermaid," and tiny glass pieces.

Pippa launched into her prepared speech: "Where I come from, we speak not with our tongues but with our hearts and our minds." She ignored the very audible snicker that came from the wings. She had to focus. Otherwise, she would block. "With our minds," she repeated significantly and raised both arms.

She closed her eyes as though to signify that she was

busy looking deep into the mysteries of the universe. In the darkness, she heard a rustling sound, the scuffling of shoes, a sneeze, a short yip of surprise and then an apology—the usual sounds. When she was satisfied that the silence had gone on long enough, she opened her eyes again. "Can I have an audience volunteer?"

"Oh!" The old woman in the front row looked alarmed when Pippa's eyes landed on her. She was fanning herself energetically with one of the illustrated guides. She had a ferociously noble-looking nose, with nostrils that quivered like a frightened bunny's, as though they were besieged by terrible smells from all sides. "Not me, please. Oh, no. I could never."

"I'll do it." A man stood up from the second row. Pippa felt a rush of gratitude. Picking the audience volunteer was the worst part—she hated the moments of ticking silence, the awkward laughter, the protests.

The man made his way quickly to the stage. He was tall and had a thin mustache above a very pleasant, toothy smile. An honest face. That was a good thing: for whatever reason, Pippa could think her way into the pockets and purses of honest people more easily. She supposed that liars had all kinds of blocks up.

"The name's Bill Evans," he said, putting two fingers to his hat brim. "Reporter."

Pippa felt like smiling back, but she couldn't. It would be out of character.

"Thank you, Mr. Evans. Your job is very simple. All you have to do is stand still. Close your eyes, and open your mind. And I will tell you what you have in your pockets."

Actually, it wasn't necessary for him to close his eyes. He didn't have to stand still, either—he could be dancing a jig, for all she cared. But it was all part of the show.

"In my pockets?" Mr. Evans instinctively put his hands in his trouser pockets, as though worried that Pippa would steal something with her mind. "I'm afraid you'll find them disappointing."

"That's for us to decide, Mr. Evans," she said, and the audience tittered.

She closed her eyes and took a deep breath, fighting back a wave of panic. This was it. The moment it came—or didn't. Focus. Deep breaths.

She felt a huge, stubborn pressure—that was his mind, bumping up against hers, elbowing her off. She was surprised. Harder than she thought. She tried once again to think her way into his fingers, into the fabric lining, into the fabric itself. It was like pushing through layers of treacle and sludge.

"Well?" Mr. Evans sounded amused. "Can I open my eyes yet?"

"A minute, please." Pippa fought a wave of panic. She was going to choke—in front of Max, in front of everyone. "The workings of the inner eye won't be rushed."

"Whatever you say, little lady," Mr. Evans drawled, and Pippa heard a chuckle from someone in the audience.

Just then, she got it: a break in the folds, a separation in the tissue, and she wrapped her mind comfortably around the objects the man was carrying. She opened her eyes.

"A money clip," she blurted out.

Mr. Evans smiled, showing all his teeth. "Anyone could have guessed that."

"A silver money clip engraved with the initials WDE, and containing exactly seventeen dollars."

Mr. Evans's smile faltered. He reached slowly into his pocket, extracted his money clip, and counted the bills slowly.

"She's right," he announced to the audience. This was greeted by a low murmur and scattered applause.

Pippa wasn't done yet. "Also," she said loudly, and the applause died away, "a roll of breath mints, containing four mints; three quarters and one nickel; a cigarette case; a set of two keys, one brass, one iron, held together on a silver key ring; a notebook; and two pens, one running very low on ink."

By now Mr. Evans's face was pale. "I'll be scratched," he said. "She's right about everything!" The audience broke out into full applause. Mr. Evans leaned in closer, so only she could hear. He whipped out the notebook and one of his pens and began scribbling in it. "You read the *New York Screamer*? No? Best paper this side of the Atlantic. Check page six tomorrow. I'll give you a write-up."

Pippa couldn't stop herself from smiling then. She took a short bow as the audience continued applauding. She even heard several murmurs of "Good show," and "Excellent. Very excellent." The old woman in the front row had redoubled her fanning and was staring at Pippa openmouthed, as though she were enchanted.

Pippa cast a triumphant glance toward the wings. Even Max looked impressed, although as soon as she met Pippa's eyes, she scowled.

Pippa practically floated off the stage. Max was preparing to go on.

"Don't choke," Pippa said to her.

"I never do," Max replied.

Pippa resumed her usual spot in the wings so she could watch Max's performance. She had to admit,

Max was good. Better than good. She had a gift like Pippa's—like Thomas's and Sam's, too—an ability that didn't seem learned but was just *there*. Her hands moved so quickly, they were a blur. She hit the exact center of the tiny red bull's-eye of a target pinned to the wall on the opposite end of the stage, then threw another knife that split the handle of the first one. Then she split a grape midair. She diced a whole tomato by tossing four paring knives simultaneously.

"Impressive—extremely impressive."

Mr. Dumfrey must have been watching the performance from his typical position: the right wing, third leg. Pippa, standing in the second, heard his voice quite clearly despite the heavy cloth between them.

Miss Fitch responded with much less enthusiasm.

"Mmm," Miss Fitch said. "Terrible manners, though."

"Well, who can blame her?" Mr. Dumfrey dropped his voice, and Pippa leaned closer to the velvet to hear him. "I'll tell you, Evangeline"—Pippa was momentarily bowled over by the mention of Miss Fitch's first name, which she had never known—"that girl must have had it very hard. All those years . . . I thought she was dead! And then she lands like a fly onto the doorstep. Can you believe it? Now I know all four of them are safe—"

"Let's hope they're safe," Miss Fitch replied darkly.

Pippa's curiosity was piqued. But at that moment Mr. Dumfrey and Miss Fitch moved off, and she lost the thread of their conversation. She was quickly distracted.

Danny the dwarf—who was *technically* an inch too tall to be a real dwarf but kept his knees bent permanently to conceal the fact—toddled onstage, wearing a Panama hat. He took his place in front of a small wooden post, looking extremely unhappy.

Max crossed toward Danny and placed a single lima bean on the flat top of the hat.

She withdrew a sharp blade from the belt around her middle, long and slender as a dagger, sharp and glittering in the light. She turned to the audience and lightly pressed her finger to the knife's tip. Instantly, blood welled up.

The ancient woman in the front row muttered, "Mercy."

All this time, Max hadn't said a word. Her face was expressionless, calm. But Pippa could see her eyes were blazing. She was having fun, Pippa realized.

Max pivoted so that she was facing Danny. She held the blade loosely in her right hand. Danny's face was now practically as green as the lima bean balancing precariously on his hat.

Max moved so quickly, Pippa nearly missed it. One second she was still. The next she had flung out her right hand and there was a whoosh of air and a small ping, and the blade had pinned the lima bean to the wooden post board behind Danny. He had not had time even to flinch.

For a moment, there was stunned silence. Danny removed his hat with a flourish, took a little bow, and collapsed to his knees. The audience burst into thunderous applause. The old woman in the front row was fanning herself so furiously, the brim of her hat fluttered. Pippa noticed Bill Evans scribbling away in his notebook.

Max gave a short bow, then turned and abruptly left the stage, smirking.

As she passed, Pippa said, "Good job."

"I know," Max responded, without even looking at her.

Then it was time for the big finale. Mr. Dumfrey himself took the stage, and Potts appeared immediately after him, scowling, and pushing a wheeled glass case covered by a heavy velvet drape. Underneath it, Pippa knew, was the prized shrunken head from the Amazon.

In reality, she knew that Mr. Dumfrey had found the head on a dusty back table of a hole-in-the-wall collectible store in Brooklyn, just behind the collection of broken clocks. The head was not even all that shrunken—it was certainly bigger than Monsieur Cabillaud's head by at least two inches around—but of course advertising a smaller-than-average head from a junk shop would not have had the same effect.

In the stage lights, Potts's face, which was pitted with acne scars, looked like the surface of the moon. No sooner had he wheeled the case into position than he clomped off the stage, muttering. Dumfrey, however, came alive on the stage—like a strange variety of flower that blooms underwater.

"And now, ladies and gentlemen, boys and girls, a special treat," he said. "An object so horrifying, so terribly grotesque, so murderously macabre, it will blow holes in the brain of any civilized man! It will make you shiver and shout, and send you home praying for protection! Never before seen on the shores of this or any God-fearing country . . . I give you . . . the shrunken head of Chief *Ticuna-Piranha*!"

With a grand sweep of his hand, he whipped off the velvet drape, just as the spotlight brightened and fell on the single object on display there: the shriveled, blackened head, teeth bared as though it were grinning. Thick tufts of wiry hair sprouted from it; feathered earrings hung from ears so shriveled, they resembled dried apricots. Around its neck, or what remained of its neck, was a bone necklace.

It didn't actually look all that impressive to Pippa—just kind of gross and sticky, like a rubber ball charred in a fire. But it had the desired effect. Several people gasped, and someone screamed. A flash went off.

Then there was a heavy thump and another scream, this time long and much, much louder.

Suddenly, everything was chaos. Pippa was nearly toppled by Hugo, who came running onto the stage, yelling for someone to call a doctor.

The lights in the auditorium came up; Pippa saw that the ancient woman in the front row was lying facedown on the floor, directly on top of her very noble nose.

"I about swallowed my tongue when the old balloon sat up," Max said. "I thought for sure she'd croaked."

Philippa shot her a look. "Don't sound so disappointed."

Max shrugged.

"It's too bad she didn't, in a way," Thomas said thoughtfully. He was still covered with dust from the vent, which he had used to travel between floors to report on the progress of the police and hospital workers as they loaded the old woman, whose name was Mrs. Weathersby, onto a stretcher. "The probability of someone dropping dead from shock is one in forty million. It would have been kind of exciting."

"Thomas!" Philippa said.

The four children were gathered in Mr. Dumfrey's office on the third floor, where they had been ordered to wait by Miss Fitch so they would be out of the way.

"Have any of you ever seen one?" Max asked. Seeing Philippa's expression, she rolled her eyes. "You know, a stiff? A body? A dead person?"

"I saw the magician hold his breath underwater for seven minutes," Thomas piped up. "He *looked* dead."

"That's not the same," Max said.

"Have *you*?" Philippa demanded. Max colored briefly.

"I known plenty of dead people," she mumbled.

"But have you *seen* one?" Philippa pressed.

From the way Max's lips went tight, Philippa knew that she had not.

"I have," Sam said suddenly from his position in the corner, where he was pushing crumbs of bread to Mr. Dumfrey's pet cockatoo, Cornelius, through the bars of its cage.

For as long as Pippa had known him, Sam was the quietest person she had ever met. He could go for days without talking. She remembered the time, a few years back, when he was sick with chicken pox and had lain in bed for a week without saying a word. Finally, Thomas had asked him what chicken pox felt like. "Itches," he had replied.

Hearing his voice now, she practically tumbled out of her chair.

"What did you say?" she squeaked at him.

"I have," he said. As usual, he wouldn't make eye contact, and looked everywhere—the piles of yellowing papers on Mr. Dumfrey's desk, the shriveled big toe of an albino orangutan floating in an alcohol-filled bottle on the bookshelf, the hissing radiator—but at Philippa. "Seen dead people."

"Where?" Max said, and her voice held a challenge. "When?"

To Pippa's deep surprise, Sam turned his eyes to Max calmly. "When I was little," he said. "I don't like to talk about it."

"I don't believe you," Max said.

Sam shrugged. "That's because you never saw one. If you did, you'd understand."

A moment of tense silence settled on the group. Max and Sam continued staring each other down. Max looked like she was considering whipping out one of her knives and trying to puncture Sam with it.

The door flew open, banging hard against the wall

and rattling the various shelves. Cornelius the cockatoo squawked loudly.

"They're gone! Gone at last!" Mr. Dumfrey stood in the doorway, mopping his face with a handkerchief. "I tell you, children, I thought they would never leave. Between the questions, and explanations, and questionable explanations . . ." He exhaled loudly. "Well. This calls for a celebration, don't you think?"

"A celebration?" Philippa repeated.

"My dear child," Mr. Dumfrey said as he crossed the room and filled a kettle from the tap in the corner, then plunked it down on the electric hot plate perched precariously on an overstuffed leather stool. "Mrs. Weathersby did us a tremendous favor this evening. One look at the shrunken head, and she was struck down with terror! She collapsed under the fierce gaze of its eyes! And to think that *Bill Evans* was right there to witness it . . . really most convenient. He used to be one of the best of his kind, you know. Broke the story of the great stock market crash even before the stockbrokers knew about it! Of course, his name doesn't mean what it used to. He got into some trouble because of his fondness for the—*you* know." Mr. Dumfrey whistled and made a drinking motion with his thumb and pinkie finger. "But even so. Most exceptionally fortuitous!"

As he spoke, Mr. Dumfrey reached for the tin of cocoa powder but grabbed instead a tin of cyanide—once used as evidence in the infamous Morrison murder trial—in his distraction.

Thomas scrambled to his feet and plucked the cyanide out of Mr. Dumfrey's hand, replacing it with the correct tin. Mr. Dumfrey patted him on the head absently.

"I thought the old lady had ate something bad," Max said. "And that's why she keeled over."

"Eaten, my dear," Mr. Dumfrey said, now setting down five mugs on his desk. "You thought the old lady had *eaten* something bad. And she did—trout, she told me, from Corrigan's Chophouse. Poor thing. No wonder she dropped so fast. You can get food poisoning just from reading the menu!" Mr. Dumfrey roused himself and smiled. "Ah, well. But the point is *they* don't know that, do they?"

"Who's they?" Philippa asked. She loved Mr. Dumfrey dearly, but his mind, it seemed to her, was like one of those Chinese knots that Thomas often worked his way out of in his solo acts: strings all over, everything a tangled mess.

Mr. Dumfrey's eyes grew dreamy and unfocused. "The public," he said in a hushed voice. "The vast and hungry public. They need us, you see. They're starving. They're dying! They hunger for the tiniest spark, the kindling to their imagination, the stories to light their brains and hearts on fire!" By this time, the kettle was shrieking, and the sound roused Mr. Dumfrey from his reverie.

"And by golly, we'll give it to them," he said cheerfully. *"The Curse of the Shrunken Head*. It has a nice ring to it, doesn't it? I thought so. And so did Bill Evans. Now be a good girl, Pippa, and help me spoon out the cocoa."

"Cocoa, cocoa, cocoa!" Cornelius repeated, ruffling his feathers in a satisfied way.

4

Sam woke up the next morning to an unfamiliar sound. At first he thought it must have been raining, a terrible rain that sounded like fists pounding on glass.

But no. It couldn't be raining. Sunlight was filtering through the attic windows, lighting up dust motes revolving lazily in the musty air and skating over the jumble of bookshelves and costume racks, bureaus and old trunks, scattered clothing and squashy clothes. And then he realized that the sound was not coming from the attic but from one of the lower floors. Having never known rain to fall upward, he sat up carefully, intending to go investigate. Mr. Dumfrey's latest gift to him, *The Illustrated Guide to Pet Care and Management*, slid off his lap.

On the other side of the bookcase, he could hear the new girl, Max, snoring. He thought the noise was kind of cute. Like a baby pig in hay—or at least what he imagined a baby pig would sound like. He considered telling her that, then immediately thought better of it. Sam didn't know much about girls, but he figured that most of them wouldn't appreciate being compared to a pig, even a baby one. Especially not Max.

She was quite a girl, Max was.

He changed clothes, pulling on a pair of his softest pants and a T-shirt and deliberately avoided his reflection in the standing mirror wedged next to his bed. He didn't want to see how many pimples had sprouted overnight. He combed his hair carefully forward with his fingers.

The rain that wasn't rain was still ongoing. If anything, it was even worse.

Just as Sam was shoving his feet into a pair of beat-up canvas shoes, Thomas burst through a grate in the floor, nearly toppling him. Sam reached for the chest of drawers to steady himself and accidentally ripped out a huge chunk of wood. Great.

"You've got to see this," Thomas said. His eyes were

shining. Even his freckles looked more pronounced, as they did whenever he got excited.

Sam exhaled and unclenched his fingers, and saw the wood had become mere splinters and sawdust. Double great. At this rate, Mr. Dumfrey was never going to let him have a pet *termite*, much less a hamster or a dog.

"Sorry," Thomas said, without sounding at all sorry. "But it's worth it. Trust me." He started to disappear down the air vent again.

"I'll take the stairs, thanks," Sam muttered. But Thomas's head had already vanished, so Sam wasn't sure he'd heard.

Sam was always very careful on the stairs, especially the performers' spiral staircase that ran up and down the back of the building. It was much steeper than the big central stairway used by the public. Once, several years ago, he'd been annoyed about his costume and had gone stomping to his room, and accidentally put a gaping hole in four different stairs. Dumfrey had been decent about it, which made Sam feel even guiltier.

"I know you're very strong, Sam," he had said, sighing, while polishing his wire-framed glasses. "And I know you don't mean to break things. But you must try and be more careful. The museum really can't afford the repairs."

It was true that Sam never intended to break, smash, crush, shatter, or destroy anything; and yet break, smash, crush, shatter, and destroy things he did. Chairs and countertops, glass vases and picture frames—they splintered under his weight and in his hands.

Years earlier, a small bird had flown into one of the museum windows just after they were washed. Sam found it on the front steps, gasping for breath. He had wanted to save it. He had wanted to take it upstairs and repair its wings with tiny splints, and feed it from an eyedropper. He would never forget the expression on Mr. Dumfrey's face as he burst from the front doors.

"For heaven's sake, my boy, don't touch it! You'll pulverize the poor thing. Let Danny do it, or Goldini."

He was skinny for his age and he knew he didn't look strong. But it didn't matter. The strength wasn't in his muscles. It was in his skin, his fingertips, his blood. He could feel it flexing at the core of him, in who he was.

It had been with him forever. He carried it with him in his earliest memories.

In *the* earliest memory . . .

He pushed the thought away quickly. He would not think about what couldn't be changed—that's what Mr. Dumfrey had told him. He tried as hard as possible to ignore the fact that he was different, even in a place where different was normal and normal was odd. Thomas had once approached him about it. "You're like me and Pippa," he'd said. "A freak among freaks." Sam had glared so hard Thomas had muttered an apology. For nearly a month afterward, Sam had ignored Thomas completely.

As he corkscrewed past each successive floor, the drumming noise got louder. By the time he'd reached the ground floor, and the main hall of exhibits, the sound had swollen to a dull roar.

He entered the lobby and stood, dumbstruck, staring.

His ears hadn't deceived him. The noise that had sounded to him like dozens of fists *was*, in fact, dozens of fists—pounding on the glass doors, rattling the handle.

"Isn't it amazing?" Thomas once again popped up next to him, seemingly from nowhere. This time, however, Sam was too dazed to react. "Isn't it *improbable*?"

Even as Sam watched, he saw that people were pressing their faces to the doors, smudging the glass with their breath, hollering to be let in. And Dumfrey was standing on the other side of the glass, still dressed in slippers and his tattered scarlet robe, trying to mollify them.

"Very soon, very soon," he was saying extra loudly so he could be heard through the glass and above the roar of the crowd. "Ten o'clock is opening hour. You'll see it on the posted sign. Don't worry, don't worry, there's room enough for all of you." He squeaked and leaped backward as a very determined-looking man gave another rattle of the handle.

"Vultures," the alligator boy muttered, scratching the tip of his scaly nose. He, too, had come downstairs to investigate, along with the magician.

"Dear me," Goldini said. "That's quite a crowd, isn't it?" Goldini fumbled in his bathrobe for his glasses but produced nothing but a plastic flower and a series of multicolored handkerchiefs.

"Need help, Mr. D.?" Thomas asked.

Dumfrey squeaked in surprise and spun around. "What on earth are you *doing* down here? Get upstairs, get upstairs, all of you. It ruins the effect to see an actor before the performance, don't you know that? Thomas, tell Potts to open up all the exhibits. Is Miss Fitch awake? Dear me, dear me. What a crowd! What a glorious crowd! You'd think it was Thanksgiving and we were giving away free turkeys!" Dumfrey's round face was shiny and his eyes sparkled with pleasure. "Sam, make sure Monsieur Cabillaud is awake and dressed.

We'll need him to man the ticket booth. And make sure he brings the extra strongbox. It looks like we're going to need it!"

"What do you think's going on?" Sam asked Thomas, after they'd left the lobby and the noise had receded somewhat. He had a bad feeling. All of those people—they'd tramp through the museum, leaving rubbish behind them: apple cores and ticket stubs and bits of tobacco. They'd point and gape at him and ask to see his muscles. He preferred the museum quiet, as it always had been in the past.

Thomas obviously felt differently. He was grinning. "I don't know," he said. "But whatever it is, I hope it lasts."

Sam's prediction was correct: the crowd did overrun the museum like a great surge of filthy water, leaving behind a tide of litter. Potts was absolutely miserable and made no attempt to conceal it, as he swept up an endless collection of candy wrappers and soda cups from around the refreshment stand, cigarette butts and balled-up tissues from the wooden floorboards, and even, mysteriously, a man's toupee.

But mostly newspapers.

In fact, the crowd left behind identical copies of

the *same* newspaper—the early-morning edition of the *Daily Screamer*, the newspaper that had drawn them all to Dumfrey's museum in the first place, that had transfixed them with its headline:

THE CURSE OF THE SHRUNKEN HEAD: WOMAN PLUMMETS TO DEATH!

by Bill Evans

That was how the children received news of the old woman's death, not five hours after she had been sitting, fanning herself happily, nostrils quivering, in the front row at the nightly performance.

5

"Here's the latest," Thomas said, pushing a newspaper across the kitchen table to Pippa. "Want to read it?"

"Not really," she said. It was midnight, three days after the shrunken head had been delivered to the museum and two days after the old woman had fainted in the auditorium and subsequently taken a high dive off her balcony. Each day, sometimes *several* times a day, a new headline appeared in a larger and larger font on the cover of the *Daily Screamer*, all of them penned by the same Bill Evans whose pocket contents Pippa had correctly read.

MUSEUM OF HORRORS, they screamed, and *ANCIENT*

AMAZONIAN CHIEF ENACTS REVENGE FROM BEYOND THE GRAVE.

"Go on," Thomas said. "I'm the one who had to go fishing for the newspaper in Dumfrey's office. I thought Cornelius would pluck my eyes out."

Pippa sighed and cleared her throat. "'New York contains many secret places and many deadly secrets,'" Pippa read, "'but none perhaps so deadly as those concealed within the halls of Dumfrey's Dime Museum. . . .'"

"Good opening," said Thomas.

"Skip to the part where the old lady bites it," Max said. Pippa shot her a withering glance and continued reading.

"'The shrunken head of Ticuna-Piranha, a fabled Amazon chieftain, now sits among the exhibits at one of New York's most undervalued museums. A hideous specimen, it is said that merely a single glance into the depths of Ticuna-Piranha's eyes will curse the witness to a terrible fate—misfortune, illness, even premature death. This was proven true on Sunday morning, when Alice Weathersby, age eighty-two, plummeted to her death from her twelfth-floor balcony only hours after the head was unveiled. . . .'

"'WHO WILL BE NEXT?'"

Pippa folded the newspaper, sighed, and picked up a crumb muffin. "It's all a little mordant, don't you think?" she said, taking a large bite.

"What's *mordant* mean?" Max said without turning around. She was frying some eggs on the stove. Now she expertly flipped them.

"I think she means *morbid*."

Pippa turned. Sam had just appeared in the doorway. His hair was, as always, a dark curtain in front of his face. He came in and took a seat at the table.

"What's morbid mean?" Max asked, sliding her eggs onto a plate.

Pippa ignored her. "Someone *died*. And we're all celebrating."

"We're not celebrating," Thomas said. "We aren't the ones rushing the doors every day, are we? We just live here." He leaned over to pluck a bit of muffin from Pippa's plate. "Did you know the probability of dying by a fall from an apartment balcony is one in four hundred and fifty thousand?"

"Mr. Dumfrey's celebrating," Pippa said, ignoring his last comment. She was annoyed that she couldn't quite verbalize what she felt: there was something wrong about it. Earlier, she had seen the crowds swarming the display case that held the shrunken head, nearly toppling one another to get a better look, and she'd felt an instinctive revulsion, like when she saw alley cats fighting over a bit of rotten meat. There were many strange and gruesome things in the museum—the mummified big toe of an Egyptian pharaoh, the supposed eyeball of an actual Cyclops floating in a jar of formaldehyde, a baseball-size rock said to be the world's largest kidney stone—but she thought the shrunken head, and all the clamor about it, was the worst.

"Well, it's better than it was before, ain't it, when hardly no one came at all?" Max said, breaking up the yolk of her egg with a spoon.

Pippa decided her question was so hopelessly ungrammatical she couldn't possibly correct all her errors. So she just sniffed. "I'm not sure it *is* better," she said.

"Do you think there's something to it?" Max said. She had just stuffed her mouth with eggs, so it sounded more like *do oo fink eres umefing to if*, which was at least more grammatical than her last comment. "The curse," she clarified, swallowing. "The old hag died, didn't she? Maybe it's true. Maybe the head *is* bad luck."

"If it is true," Sam said suddenly, "the curse will fall on us next."

There was a second of silence. A shiver ran down

Pippa's back, as it sometimes did when she came across something unexpectedly cold or metallic or dangerous in someone's pocket, like a knife or a revolver. She remembered what she had overheard Mr. Dumfrey say to Miss Fitch backstage, and Miss Fitch's response: *Let's hope they're safe.* She hadn't told the others yet—the shrunken head, and the death of Mrs. Weathersby, had driven the words straight out of her mind—but now she wondered whether she ought to. She nearly opened her mouth to repeat the conversation.

Then Thomas laughed.

"Seems like good luck to me," he said.

Max finished her eggs and then—much to Pippa's disgust—took the plate and licked it. "I'm pooped," she said. "I'm going to bed."

But just then Pippa heard a noise from outside the kitchen: footsteps, descending from the first floor. "Shhh," she said, at the same moment Sam said, "There's someone coming."

All of them froze. Pippa's breath turned to ice in her throat. Please, she thought, please let it not be Mrs. Cobble. Or even worse, Miss Fitch. They were not supposed to be up, and they were certainly not supposed to be in the kitchen. But the footsteps kept going.

Thomas started to move toward the door.

"No, Thomas. Not yet," Pippa whispered. But he had already cracked the door and peered into the hall.

"It's all right," he said, withdrawing his head. "It was just Potts, and he's gone."

The four of them—Pippa, Thomas, Sam, and Max—snuck upstairs together, with Thomas scouting by shimmying through the vents that connected the floors, then returning to report the coast was clear. By the time they arrived in the attic, they were near breathless with laughter and only just managed to restrain themselves. But then Sam bumped into Danny's bed and the dwarf sat up with a roar, flailing his arms, shouting murder, and they dissolved into laughter again.

It was only two or three minutes from the kitchen to the attic—and yet it was the first time, Pippa thought, as she slipped into the clean white sheets of her cot, that she had ever felt as if she had real friends.

But just before she fell asleep she felt that sudden thrill of alarm that she hadn't been able to express or explain, and she remembered what Sam said: *The curse will fall on us next.*

Thomas was awakened on Tuesday morning by a blood-curdling scream. He sat up, his heart rocketing into his throat. It was not yet light outside; the sky was a mottled gray, like an old man's complexion. All around the crowded attic space, the residents of Dumfrey's Dime Museum came awake, yanked into consciousness by that terrible scream.

"What is it?" Lights clicked on in various corners of the attic.

"Did you hear that?"

"Of course I heard that, you dolt. I may be a dwarf, but I'm not deaf."

"You're not a dwarf, either, so just stop pretending."

"Sounded like someone had his head cut off," Quinn and Caroline said at the same time. Then, again simultaneously: "Jinx." And: "Stop copying me!"

Sam's words of the night before came back to Thomas in a rush: *The curse will fall on us next.* Without bothering to get changed from his pajamas, he kicked aside the vent in the floor and squeezed himself into it, just as Sam sat up, blinking and rubbing his eyes, saying, "What's all the noise?"

Thomas didn't answer. He shimmied down the vent, using his back and feet for leverage, going as fast as he could. The scream sounded again, so loud it sent a tremor through the vent, making his teeth vibrate. He had traveled the museum's walls, pipes, ducts, and vents for almost his whole life, and knew every twist and drip and screw and knob. He knew the way voices and whispers carried through the walls, could map the entirety of the museum in his mind, and now he knew instinctively that the scream had come from the ground floor.

He tumbled out in a far corner of the Hall of Worldwide Wonders and landed beside the display case that held an aboriginal boomerang, a Bolivian bow and arrow, and a bamboo blowgun from Borneo. Quickly righting himself, he sprinted toward the source of the noise. Now the scream had transformed into a kind of anguished sobbing.

As he rounded the corner he saw Dumfrey, collapsed, partially propped up in the wide lap of Mrs. Cobble, who was vigorously fanning his face.

"There, there," she was saying. "It'll be all right."

"It won't be all right!" Mr. Dumfrey wailed. "Gone! Gone! It's gone! We're ruined!"

Spotting Thomas, Mrs. Cobble said, "What are you doing, Thomas? Go and get some water for Mr. Dumfrey."

Thomas started to obey, but Mr. Dumfrey's thunderous shout stopped him. "No!" He struggled to sit up. "Ring the police! Tell them they must come immediately! *Tell them my head has been stolen!*"

For the first time, Thomas noticed the glass case that housed the shrunken head had been shattered. And in the place where the head should have been was simply an empty, smudged wooden shelf.

Thomas's heart went from his throat to the bottom of his stomach in less than a second.

"Go ahead, Thomas," Mrs. Cobble said, pushing her frizzled hair back from her forehead with the inside of a wrist. "You can use the phone in the office."

Thomas was almost at the vent when he heard

Dumfrey hollering after him.

"Forget the water!" he yelled. "Bring the whiskey!"

By the time the police arrived, all the residents of the museum had heard about the theft and assembled in the lobby. Betty had not yet had time to comb her beard, which extended in a wild tangle halfway to her waist. Monsieur Cabillaud was still wearing his nightcap, which Miss Fitch had sewed for him from a child's stocking. And Goldini had accidentally grabbed the wrong hat from his nightstand, so a rabbit was now sniffing around his boots.

Two policemen had responded to the call. Standing next to each other, they looked very much like the number ten. The first was tall and extremely thin. His skin seemed far too plentiful for his skeleton and pooled under his eyes and chin. The second man was short and as round and stretched and shiny as an inflated balloon. His name tag identified him as Sergeant Schroeder.

As Dumfrey stepped forward and began vigorously shaking his hand, Sergeant Schroeder looked Mr. Dumfrey up and down carefully. The more he saw, the harder he frowned. By the time he had taken in Mr. Dumfrey's curled genie slippers, made of red felt and embroidered with elephants, he was scowling.

"All right, then," he said, extricating his hand from Mr. Dumfrey's grip. "What seems to be the trouble?"

The tall one, Officer Gilhooley, produced a notepad and stood with his pencil poised over the paper.

"We've been pilfered—pilloried—pillaged!" Mr. Dumfrey said, with a dramatic flourish of his handkerchief.

"What's pillars got to do with it?" Officer Gilhooley said, and scratched his head with his pencil.

"He means, sir, that it was stolen," Pippa spoke up. Mr. Dumfrey looked at her gratefully, while Max rolled her eyes, no doubt at Pippa's use of the word *sir*.

"Yes, yes, exactly," Mr. Dumfrey said eagerly. "A theft. A most disgusting, deviant, deranged—"

"And what was—er—stolen?" Sergeant Schroeder asked hastily, cutting Mr. Dumfrey off before he could go on another rant.

Suddenly overcome, Mr. Dumfrey blotted his eyes. "My head!" he wailed. "My precious, perfect, irreplaceable head!"

This time both police officers stared at him openmouthed.

"He means, sir—" Pippa began.

Max interrupted her. "It was a shriveled, ugly thing.

Like an apple stuck in pickle juice. It was just there."
She pointed to the empty case, which was visible from
the lobby.

"I see." The two officers exchanged a look. Sergeant
Schroeder hooked both his thumbs into his belt. "And
was this—er—this head very valuable?"

"Valuable?" Mr. Dumfrey burst out. "My dear
sirs—the head was *invaluable*. Mind you, we have many
wonderful things in the museum. Many," he quickly
emphasized. "There is the mermaid from the Pacific
Ocean . . . and the sarcophagus of a pharaoh . . . and
the wings of an authentic fairy captured only last year
in an English garden. Perhaps you'd like a tour . . . ?
Our fees are very reasonable." Behind Mr. Dumfrey,
Miss Fitch coughed. "But no, of course not. This is no
time for a tour. You're on duty! My point is, gentlemen, simply that the shrunken head was the *crown jewel*
of our exhibit."

Thomas thought it was a pretty good speech, even if
Dumfrey was laying it on thick. But Officer Gilhooley
just stared at Mr. Dumfrey blankly. "So . . . ," he said.
"Let me get this straight. Is it valuable or invaluable?"

Dumfrey drew himself up and puffed out his chest
like a pigeon. "Its value is inestimable."

This time, Sergeant Schroeder spoke. He jabbed a

sausagelike finger at Dumfrey's chest. "So you can't estimate how valuable it is?"

Dumfrey turned red. "It's incredibly valuable! Stupendously valuable! Stupidly valuable! Its value cannot be described!"

Suddenly, Dumfrey collapsed, as though the words, leaving him, had left in their place a huge hole. He staggered backward, and Smalls stepped forward to support him.

Sergeant Schroeder spread his hands. "Let's just say one thousand dollars. Fair?" Dumfrey nodded weakly, and Officer Gilhooley made a scribble on his notepad. "Any idea, Mr. Dumbfin, how the perpetuator got it?"

"I locked the front doors myself at nine last night," Mr. Dumfrey said with as much dignity as he could, considering one of Smalls's massive arms, big as a gorilla's, was still wrapped around his belly. "I was alerted this morning by Mr. Potts, the janitor, that they were *unlocked*."

Sergeant Schroeder signaled to Officer Gilhooley, who walked to the front doors and squatted so he was eye level with the door handles.

"No sign of a forced entry," Officer Gilhooley said at last, straightening up.

Sergeant Schroeder sighed. "And who was the last

man to see the—ahem—*head* in its rightful place?"

There was a shuffling from the back, and Potts pushed his way forward. As usual, he wore a dirty cap pulled low over his eyes, and his jaw moved back and forth, back and forth, as though he were chewing on something invisible.

"That'd be me, sir," he said in his gruff voice.

"And who are you?" Sergeant Schroeder asked.

"Potts is the name," he said. "I'm the janitor here. Did my final sweep of the place at ten o'clock, just like normal, afore I gone to bed in the basement. Weren't nothing unusual then."

"And you heard nothing in the middle of the night?" Sergeant Schroeder pressed. "No sounds of breaking glass? No footsteps?"

It might have been Thomas's imagination, but he thought that Potts smirked. "I always take a little night-cap afore bed, sir, if you catch my drift. If a dozen angels came down and danced around like chorus girls, I wouldn't have heard nothing."

Thomas's eyes met Pippa's across the crowd, and then Sam's. Max was frowning. He knew what all of them were thinking: Potts had been awake, and much later than 9:00 p.m. In fact, he'd been out of bed. So why wouldn't he say so now?

There was a short silence. Sergeant Schroeder coughed and nodded to Officer Gilhooley, who discreetly replaced the notepad in his pocket.

"Here's the thing, Mr. Dumbfort," he began.

Mr. Dumfrey had recovered sufficiently to correct him. "Dumfrey."

"Dumfrey. Right. 'Course." Sergeant Schroeder exchanged a small smile with Officer Gilhooley, as though they were sharing a private joke. "I'm sure this, er, *head* means a lot to you."

"Not just to me," Dumfrey said. "To the world! To civilization at large! To the public! The great, the hungry—"

Sergeant Schroeder raised a fleshy hand, cutting him off. "*Be that as it may*," he said with great emphasis, "you gotta be realistic. We had three homicides on my beat this week alone. Yesterday, a fisherman turned up a body wearing a pair of cement slippers. We got five muggings, a home break-in, twenty-two incidents of pickpocketing, four lost cats, twelve barroom brawls, and *ninety-one* incidents of aggression toward the law. Not to mention someone breaking into Mario's Deli on Forty-Eighth Street and stealing a whole crate of Genoa salami. The city's full of sneaks and crooks and thieves and scammers. Do you catch my drift, Mr. Dumpty?"

This time, Mr. Dumfrey didn't bother to correct him. "I'm not sure I do," he said coldly.

Sergeant Schroeder's eyes glittered like small dirt-colored marbles in the pink flesh of his face. "All right, I'll say it plainer. The police, Mr. Dumpling, have much more important things to do than to look for your head."

And with a curt nod, he spun around on one of his polished heels and began trotting toward the door. Officer Gilhooley loped after him obediently, pausing just as he was passing through the door.

"Sorry for your loss," he said in practically a whisper.

"Gilhooley!" Sergeant Schroeder's voice bellowed from outside. And quickly, with a small start of surprise, Officer Gilhooley shut the door.

No one said a word. Even the museum, usually so full of drips and creaks and groans, seemed to be holding its breath. Thomas felt that the silence was more awful than anything. It was as though they were all standing in a tomb.

It was Mr. Dumfrey who spoke first. "Ruined," he said. "We're ruined."

"I'm sure it'll be all right, Mr. D.," Sam said quietly, and others immediately piped up with their support.

"Ugly thing," croaked Andrew, with an emphatic rap of his cane.

Phoebe nodded vigorously, her many chins nodding with her. "Hideous!"

"Gave me the chills," admitted Hugo. Danny reached up to pat the elephant man's hand sympathetically.

"We'll do fine without it!" Caroline said.

Quinn stepped quickly in front of her. "We'll be *perfect*," she amended, batting her white eyelashes and smirking at her sister.

"Always have before," said Goldini.

"Cheer up, Mr. Dumfrey," Betty said sweetly.

"It's no use!" Mr. Dumfrey raised his hand and the room abruptly fell into quiet once again. He removed his glasses and swiped moisture from under his eyes. When he replaced his glasses, Thomas thought he had never looked more serious. "I wasn't planning to deliver the news this way. I was hoping never to deliver the news at all. But there is no avoiding it."

Mr. Dumfrey's voice wavered. "You might as well know. The museum is broke. The head was our last chance at paying our debts and keeping the doors open. Now, I fear, we are sunk."

7

Max wasted no time after Dumfrey's announcement.

The museum was a sinking ship. And she, Max, was a rat.

"*What* are you doing?"

Max spun around, clutching her rucksack, and saw Pippa standing in their little makeshift room, hands on her hips, glaring. Despite the fact that Pippa was, in Max's opinion, a miserable little squeak, she had a glare that was frightening.

It was her eyes, and the fact that she could see through things—*into* things. When she glared, Max felt like a hole was being burned straight through her forehead.

At first, Max had thought it was only a trick—that Pippa was half a fraud, like Goldini and the almost-dwarf. But she knew better now.

"What's it look like I'm doing?" she mumbled, turning around and continuing to stuff her belongings in her rucksack. Now the burning hole was in the back of her neck and was far more tolerable. "You heard what he said. We're sunk. Finished. Kaput. Done for."

Pippa ripped the rucksack out of Max's hands with surprising force.

"Hey . . . ," Max started to protest, but Pippa grabbed her arm so tightly she was startled into silence.

"We're *not* sunk," she said fiercely. She practically dragged Max out of the attic and into the hallway, then up a steep flight of dusty stairs that led, Max knew, to the unused loft.

Max tried to shake off Pippa's grip and couldn't. "Let go of me."

"Stop your moaning," Pippa said. At the top of the stairs, she opened the door and pushed Max roughly inside.

The loft was a small room, hardly bigger than a bathroom, and packed nearly from top to bottom with crates, bundles of moth-eaten clothing, and bits of dusty equipment. Thomas was sitting high up on a teetering stack of wooden boxes, his head practically banging against the single skylight, which let in a small quantity of sickly white light. Sam had cleared a space for himself on the floor and looked like an elephant pretending to belong in a dollhouse.

"All right." Pippa had entered behind Max; she closed the door and leaned against it. "Now that we're all here, we can begin."

"Begin what?" Max said crossly, rubbing her arm where Pippa had been gripping it.

Pippa rolled her eyes. "To plan, of course," she said. "If we're going to find that stupid head and save the museum, we'll need to have a plan."

"If we're going to do *what*?" Max squawked.

Pippa narrowed her eyes. "Is there something wrong with your ears?"

"Is there something wrong with your brain?" Max fired back.

"Pippa," Sam broke in quietly, "you heard what the cops said. The city's crawling with thieves. It could have been anyone."

"There are forty thousand unsolved thefts in New York City every year," Thomas pointed out. Max really wished he would stop spouting off about probabilities and statistics and boring numbers that made her head spin. The problem was all the reading he did. A nasty habit.

"It wasn't just anyone," Pippa insisted. "It was someone who knew about the head and knew its value." She ticked off the list on her fingers. "It was someone who knew how to get in without forcing the lock—so someone with a key or *someone who was already inside.*"

"Mr. Dumfrey might have forgotten to lock up last night," Thomas said.

Pippa shook her head. "He's too careful for that." She inhaled deeply. "I'll tell you what I think," she said. Her eyes were glittering, as they did when she was onstage. *"I think Potts did it."*

"Potts?" Sam wrinkled his nose. When he did, a smattering of freckles wrinkled, too.

"He hasn't got the brains," Thomas said scornfully.

Pippa shook her head. "What was he doing up past midnight?"

"Maybe he was hungry," Thomas said.

Pippa looked as if she wanted to strangle him. "He would have come into the kitchen. Besides, why did he lie about sleeping through the night? Why didn't he tell the cops he was awake?"

"Maybe he just didn't think it was important," Thomas argued.

"Then answer me this." Pippa crossed her arms. "How come he had *one hundred* dollars in his pocket this morning, huh? Where'd he get it?"

To this, Thomas had no answer. Everyone at the museum was paid a wage, even the children, although Mr. Dumfrey kept the majority of their wages in a strongbox for when they were older. But no one at the museum, not even Mr. Dumfrey, was paid more than ten dollars a week.

"Even if he did take it," Max jumped in, "I still don't see what that's got to do with us."

"Oh? And I guess you don't care if the museum shuts down and all of us end up on the street?" Pippa said icily.

"I been on the street before," Max said, lifting her chin.

"And you're so eager to go back?" Pippa said.

Max hesitated. As much as she pretended to be hard, the truth was that she found living on the street practically unbearable. There was the stink and the noise, the clots of flies in summer, the driving rains in fall, and the icy grip of winter, like a small death. There was running from police and hiding in churches and getting chased out of stores. There was hunger, a foul taste in the mouth, an aching that filled you from nose to toes.

She had spent most of her life on the streets of New York City—performing knife tricks for coins, pickpocketing when she had to—and another three in Chicago before that, and in all that time she had thought of practically nothing but a roof and a fire when she needed one and a safe place to sleep where she had no fear of getting poked, moved, or chased off.

The museum was that, and more. In her short time there, she knew she had already started to love it: the soft whistles and creaks of the building, the constant jabbering of the other performers, the glass-enclosed exhibits, the hallways smelling of vinegar and perfume. The sunlight filtering through the window, wrapping everything in a golden haze. And then there was the way Mr. Dumfrey had looked at her— as though he'd been expecting her, almost. No one had ever expected her anywhere or cared whether she showed up.

"I thought not," Pippa said, when Max didn't speak. "Look. Mr. Dumfrey took a chance on us. On all of us. Plenty of other people wouldn't have. We're freaks, remember? Thomas has a spine like a rubber band. I can read minds. Well, almost," she clarified quickly. "And Sam—poor Sam. He can't even go a day without breaking something. And you . . ." She turned to Max, frowning. "Well, who *knows* what's wrong with you. You're violent."

"I am not—"

"My point is," Pippa said, cutting her off, "we have no one else." She turned to the others. "Well?"

For a second, there was silence.

"Go on, Pippa," Sam said. "Tell us what you're thinking."

Thomas should have known that when Pippa said she had a plan, what she meant was that she had a plan for *him*—which is why he now found himself squeezed into a shoebox-size space between an air duct and a nest of rusted iron pipes.

It was hot, airless, and cramped; he was fighting a sneeze that had begun as a tickle in his nose but now seemed to have him by the throat. Carefully, he extended one hand through the network of pipes and found purchase on an old iron knob. Holding his breath, flattening his lungs, trying to picture himself as a pancake, he pulled himself through a narrow gap between pipes, and at last found himself pressed against the iron grille, roughly level with the floor, looking out over the forbidden, the absolutely off-limits, chambers of Potts.

The performers all lived together in the attic, their respective sleeping spaces separated by a complex network of old junk that had drifted there over the years, like an upward-falling snow. Plaster statues, old desks, folding screens, and upturned mattresses—all were arranged for privacy in a labyrinthine formation bewildering to anyone who was a stranger to the museum.

Only Mrs. Cobble, Miss Fitch, Potts, and Dumfrey had their own quarters. Mrs. Cobble slept on the first floor, in a room accessible from the Special Exhibits Hall and directly above the kitchen, from which she claimed to be able to keep track of the larder even while asleep (a claim disproved by frequent midnight raids on the kitchen). Miss Fitch slept in the props and costume department on the second floor, in a bed allegedly once owned by a famous murderess and still sporting a bloodstain on its wood frame. Mr. Dumfrey maintained his bedroom behind his office on the third floor.

And Potts—the miserable, evil-smelling, bad-tempered Potts—had chosen to make his home in the basement. No one ever dared to disturb him down here, and Potts even kept his door locked, as if to double-guarantee against snoops and intruders.

Carefully Thomas threaded his fingers through the grate and pushed until he felt it give. With a small pop, the grate released. He set it aside on the floor while he wriggled through the narrow opening, head and shoulders first, emerging from the wall like a worm emerging from damp ground.

He was in. Thomas straightened up. All was silent, except for a quiet dripping sound. At last, Thomas's heartbeat slowed, and the sneeze that had been crawling through his nasal passages had gone back to wherever unsneezed sneezes go.

It was dark in the room and smelled like old tobacco and rotten milk. Thomas fumbled for a light switch on the wall. A single wire-encased bulb flickered to life in the ceiling, illuminating a narrow, windowless space, walls bubbling with moisture, and a rusted old sink in the corner, which Thomas identified as the source of the dripping. The room was heaped with clothes and junk, littered with old mugs in which suspicious liquid was developing thin films of mold, filled with all sorts of broken, useless, ugly things—a mirror so cracked it split Thomas's reflection into a hundred tiny Thomases; a stool with only a single leg, overturned; a razor coated with cream and hair.

"Now what?" Thomas said to himself in a whisper. Pippa had sworn Potts would be out of the museum for hours, but still Thomas felt the hairs on his neck standing up, as if someone were watching him, concealed in a corner. To calm down, he did calculations in his head. The perimeter of Potts's room was 56 feet, and the area 192 feet. The density of the laundry piled at the foot of his bed was roughly 24 socks per square trouser. . . .

Look for proof, Pippa had told him—but what kind of proof, she couldn't say. It was extremely improbable that Potts had the shrunken head just stuffed into his bureau with his socks, especially since the money in his pocket suggested he had already sold it. But maybe there was evidence the head had been here and then moved—or maybe the payment was merely a portion of the money, like an advance, and Potts was concealing the head among his things before he deemed it safe to move.

Thomas picked carefully through the dirty laundry strewn across the mattress, moved aside furniture, checked every corner and cubbyhole. He found several pairs of dice, one of them weighted, and a stack of well-worn playing cards.

Every surface was littered with matchbooks from various restaurants, most of them with names like the Rusty Nail and Pig & Whistle. He found a piece of paper bearing a handwritten Brooklyn address that he initially thought might be important, until he saw that it was labeled Anderson's Delights. He assumed it was another restaurant.

Other than that, nothing. Not a thing to suggest that Potts had been involved in the theft. No incriminating messages, no guilty confessions.

Thomas was just shutting the bottom drawer of the bureau when he heard heavy footsteps in the hall. He froze. The feet stopped just outside the door.

Potts.

A key turned in the lock.

There was no time to make it back to the grate and into the safety of the wall. Thomas looked around frantically for a hiding place—and then just as the door began to scrape open, hurled himself into the bottom drawer of the misshapen bureau, managing through a series of wiggles and shoves to get it closed. He squeezed himself into a ball, choking on the smell of old socks. Knees to eyeballs, feet to butt, bending, folding, an origami figure of a boy.

Flat as a pancake. Small as a shoe.

He heard Potts enter—smelled him, too, the stink of tobacco and unwashed denim that preceded Potts everywhere like a forward-drifting cloud. Thomas's heart was hammering so loudly, he was sure Potts would hear it. He wished he could flatten his heart, too, and stop it from pounding like a drum.

Potts crossed directly toward him—without hesitation. Thomas's mouth went dry as dust.

The bureau rattled; wood scraped on wood, as Potts began rummaging through the drawers.

"Where'd I put the blasted thing?" Potts muttered. He closed the first drawer. Moved onto the second. Sweat pooled on Thomas's forehead. His legs and knees were already aching. Any second now . . .

Then Potts gave a grunt of satisfaction. Whatever he was looking for, he had found it.

Thomas was safe.

Potts began to cross back toward the door, and Thomas allowed himself to relax, just slightly. Then there was the bang of metal and Potts cursed.

"What in the . . . ?"

Thomas's stomach dropped out through his feet. The grille. He had forgotten to replace it. Now Potts would know that Thomas had been in his room.

Sure enough, Potts had stopped moving. The silence

was still, electric, agonizing. It seemed to last forever. Then Thomas heard a sharp sniffing. Potts was trying to smell him out, the way a dog would.

"Come out, come out, wherever you are," Potts sing-songed. "Come out, you little worm. I know you're in here."

Thomas couldn't have moved if he wanted to. He was terrified into utter stillness. Go away, he thought. Please just go away.

Potts began shoving aside furniture. Thomas's whole body went white-hot with fear when Potts drew close to the bureau. Potts shoved the bureau away from the wall with a cry of "Aha!" But he didn't think of opening the bottom drawer, where Thomas hid in thick and filthy-smelling darkness, sweating against the splinters.

And then it happened.

The sneeze—the sneeze Thomas had repressed and swallowed until it returned to wherever unsneezed sneezes go—came roaring back. It blew up his throat and exploded into his nasal passages. It reverberated through his whole body. There was no stopping it. It was a storm, a force—and when Thomas sneezed, the whole bureau sneezed, too, and shot out its bottom drawer like a giant wooden nose expelling snot.

And even as the echoes of the sneeze were still

hanging in the air, as Thomas was wiping his nose with the back of his hand, shaken, exhausted from the force of that superhuman sneeze—even then, the looming shadow of Potts spread over him, and the stink of tobacco grew stronger.

"There's the little worm," Potts said, showing off all his rotten teeth. And he bent over and plucked Thomas up with one meaty hand.

"I'm very disappointed, Thomas," Dumfrey said, shaking his head so that the skin underneath his chin wobbled—as though it, too, were disappointed. "Very disappointed indeed."

"Caught in the act!" Potts bellowed. "Snuffling and sniffling in my underthings, the little weasel. He oughta be paddled raw as an almond!"

"That's enough, Potts." Dumfrey fixed him with a hard stare. His blue eyes glinted like ice. "You've made your grievances known. Now please leave us."

Potts grumbled something that sounded like "muffin" but was probably far more unpleasant, and gave Thomas a final glare before stomping out of Dumfrey's office.

As soon as the door closed behind him, Dumfrey's

voice softened. "What on earth were you doing?"

Thomas opened his mouth to reply, but just then the door flew open and Pippa hurled into the room, breathless.

"It was my fault, sir," she said. "I told him to do it."

Thomas stared at Pippa. He was shocked—grateful, too. He'd never thought Pippa would take the blame for anything.

"Is that true, Thomas?" Mr. Dumfrey asked quietly.

Before Thomas could reply, the door once again banged open, this time with such force that an oil portrait of a young Dumfrey—looking almost exactly like an old Dumfrey, except with more hair and fewer chins—tumbled off the wall with a clatter.

"Don't listen to Pippa." Sam was standing in the doorway, wide-eyed. "It was my idea." He noticed the toppled painting and winced. "*Sorry*, Mr. Dumfrey."

Dumfrey frowned and settled back in his chair. "Explain."

"I—I—well . . . ," Sam stuttered.

Pippa balled up her fists and then released them. "It's a long story. . . ."

Thomas jumped in. "It's about the head, sir."

"The head?" Dumfrey's eyes seemed to triple in size behind his glasses.

Now Thomas felt himself falter. Dumfrey's gaze was

like that: it turned your knees to noodles. "It's just that we thought . . ."

"It seemed possible . . . ," Pippa chimed in.

"It seemed *probable*," Thomas corrected.

"That Potts might have . . . ," Pippa said.

"Or *must* have . . . ," Thomas amended.

"Stolen it," Sam finished.

"Eighty-two and a half percent of all store burglaries are committed by an employee," Thomas blurted out. "I read it."

There was a long moment of silence, punctuated only by a loud, disapproving squawk from Cornelius. Dumfrey removed his glasses. With one end of his purple tie, he began polishing them. "Anderson was right," he murmured. "That head has brought nothing but trouble."

Thomas felt a small tingle of alarm race up his back. Anderson . . . he had heard that name before. . . .

No. He had *seen* it—on a piece of paper in Potts's room.

"Anderson, sir?" he prompted, trying not to sound too curious. Pippa shot him a puzzled glance.

Dumfrey barely looked at him. "Arthur Anderson. Anderson's Delights. Ever heard of it? No? He's the one who sold me the blasted head in the first place. A good friend of mine, even though he's an awful cheat. Once tried to pass off a yellow-painted penny as a recovered Spanish gold coin. Shameless! He warned me that the head was bad luck. I thought he was just saying that so I would sell it back to him . . . but he was right; he was right."

Thomas felt like exploding from excitement. "Sorry, Mr. D., it was all a big mistake," he said quickly, plastering on a smile. He grabbed Pippa's arm and started hauling her backward toward the door. Sam took the hint and followed them. "Won't happen again, we promise you."

Mr. Dumfrey started, as though only just remembering the children were there. "Wait!" he called out. "We must discuss a suitable punish—"

But before he could say *ment*, Thomas had hauled Pippa into the hall and Sam had slammed the door closed. From inside, there was another crash, as yet another painting tumbled off the wall.

"Sorry, Mr. D.!" Sam called out, and then hurried after Pippa and Thomas.

"You're *pinching* me," Pippa said, as Thomas dragged her forward. "What's the matter with you, anyway? You're acting like a bug crawled up your—"

"*You were right*," he whispered, cutting her off. "Potts did it."

"What are you talking about?" Pippa said.

"Potts went to see Anderson. At least, I think he did. He had the address of Anderson's store written on a piece of paper in his room—133 Seventh Street, in Brooklyn." Thomas glanced from left to right and, seeing no one, continued speaking in a rush: "It isn't a coincidence. It can't be."

Pippa was frowning, clearly deep in thought. "So . . . you think Potts is working for Anderson?"

Thomas shrugged. "You heard what Dumfrey said, didn't you? Anderson tried to get the head *back*, but Dumfrey wouldn't sell it to him. So maybe Anderson decided to take matters into his own hands. Maybe he paid Potts to pinch it for him."

"But Dumfrey said Mr. Anderson was a friend . . . ," Sam said doubtfully.

"Wouldn't be the first time Mr. D. was wrong about something," Thomas said. "Remember when he bought those two tiger cubs for the museum and tried to train them?"

"The magicians' poor rabbits . . . ," Sam murmured, shuddering a little.

"The trainer's poor *hand*," Thomas said.

Pippa roused herself. "All right, then. We have to talk to Mr. Anderson right away. We have to find out what he knows."

Thomas felt a spark of excitement in his stomach. For the first time ever, he felt like he and Pippa were on the same team. Sam, too. For the first time ever, he felt like they were doing something *important*—not just performing the same tricks over and over, like trained monkeys. And he had always, always, wanted to do something important.

What was the point of being different if you couldn't be special?

"To Brooklyn, then?" he said.

Pippa nodded solemnly. "To Brooklyn."

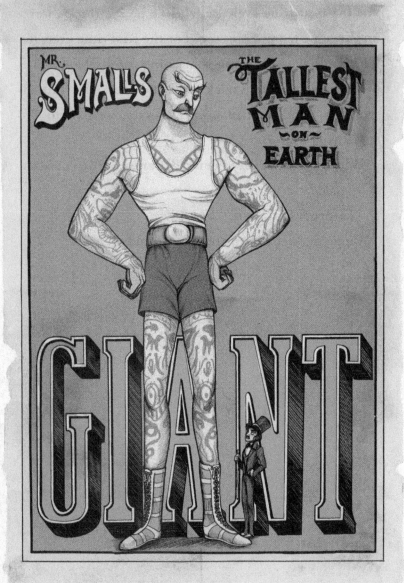

10

¿Anderson's Delights was situated in a long, low brick building at the end of a narrow street slicked with oil and foul-smelling puddles, next to the sludge of the Gowanus Canal, which wound through this section of Brooklyn like an enormous, green-scaled snake. At the end of the street, a homeless man wearing a battered felt cap, a pair of aviator's goggles, and pants shredded halfway to his knees was rummaging through a trash bin, humming.

Pippa was glad that both Max and Sam had agreed to come. There was safety in numbers. And even though Pippa couldn't stand Max, and tried her best to ignore her frequent complaints—("Smells like a fart over here!

What's the big plan, anyway? You think if Anderson did steal the head he's just gonna go ahead and cop to it?")—she could see the sharp metal knives, sheathed in leather, glinting in the pockets of Max's coat, and she was grateful for them. Especially as night was falling, and from the dark mouths of various doorways, men were watching them with sunken eyes.

The door to Anderson's Delights was locked. Sam reached up and knocked carefully. Paint flaked off at his touch, and a crack appeared in the wood. He winced.

"Sorry," he said.

"It's not your fault," Pippa lied.

They waited. Thomas shifted anxiously from foot to foot, tugging his hair, until it was standing straight up from his scalp. He never could stand still. Silence: no sound of footsteps, no murmur of voices. With each passing second, the light was draining from the sky. Pippa knew that meant curfew at the museum was rapidly approaching.

"Well," Max said. "That's that. No one's home. Too bad and try again tomorrow."

"Wait," Sam said softly. "The light's on upstairs. Look."

He was right: above them, on the third floor, a light

was glowing softly in the window. And it was flickering slightly, as though someone upstairs was passing in front of a lamp, walking back and forth in agitation.

By silent agreement, Pippa, Max, and Sam all turned to look at Thomas. Thomas sighed.

"All right, all right," he grumbled. "I'm going." In an instant, he was shimmying up a drainpipe—quickly, practically silent, except for the occasional squeak of his shoes or rattle of the metal pipe. Soon he became a small black shadow against the deepening twilight. And then, in less than a minute, he had reached the upstairs windows.

"What do you see?" Pippa called out softly.

"Nothing," he called down. "Curtains are drawn. Give me a second."

Like a spider, he flung himself from the drainpipe onto the narrow window ledge. Pippa gasped and unconsciously cried out as he teetered there for a second, windmilling his arms. But Thomas didn't fall. He found his balance; dropped into a crouch; and, after fiddling with the latch, slid open the window and eased himself inside.

They waited in anxious silence for one, two, three seconds. Pippa expected at any second to hear an explosion of shouting, but there was nothing. Then

Thomas's head reappeared at the window.

"Come quickly!" he shouted. "Upstairs! Now! Hurry!"

Sam didn't even hesitate. He drove a fist into the front door; with a tremendous *boom* it collapsed inward. Sam stepped aside and gestured politely for Max and Pippa to go before him.

"Thank you," Pippa said, and passed into the shop.

The hall was carpeted and smelled like mildew and cat urine. To their right was a dusty glass door that obviously led to the shop; on it the words *Anderson's Delights* had once been painted, but after several decades, only the letters *And on Deli* remained. A large sign that said CLOSED hung on the knob.

Directly down the hall was a narrow wooden staircase. Pippa raced toward it, and Max practically elbowed her out of the way.

"Move it," she said.

Just as they had reached the second floor, Thomas appeared on the third-floor landing.

"Hurry!" he shouted again. His eyes were practically bulging out of his head. A door was open behind him, and Pippa caught a glimpse of dark green wallpaper and a ceiling crisscrossed with rough wooden beams.

"We're coming—as—fast—as—we—can!" Pippa panted.

Max reached the third floor first. Pippa and Sam were right on her heels.

"This way." Thomas's face was stark white, as though someone had drained him of all his blood.

Together they piled through the open doorway, which led to Mr. Anderson's private chambers. There was a fire burning cheerfully in the grate, and several lamps were illuminated. The room reminded him immediately of the museum. Every surface was cluttered with objects: a stuffed rearing king cobra, its fangs bared and hood extended; a carved African mask; a rusted saxophone. A mug of tea sat on a large mahogany desk, and a book was lying open on a squashy armchair.

And there was a body hanging from the rafters.

Pippa screamed. Sam shouted. And Max threw her knife. Quick as a flash, the blade whizzed through the air and severed the rope, slicing the body down from where it dangled.

The children ran to him at once. His face was the bruised purple of a storm cloud. A rope was knotted tightly around his fleshy neck. He was wearing an old pinstripe suit and a pair of patched leather shoes, and they knew at once they were staring down at the face of Mr. Anderson.

Sam kneeled beside him. Pippa hugged herself. She

was suddenly freezing. For a minute, no one said a word.

"Is he . . . ?" Max asked finally.

Sam looked up at her. His dark eyes were hollows in his face. "Dead," he confirmed.

11

Max had claimed earlier that she'd known a lot of dead people. That was true. But she'd never seen one. It was not at all how she'd imagined it would be, not at all how people spoke about saying good-bye to their dead grandmothers or described attending the funeral of a beloved neighbor. "She looked so peaceful!" they would say, dabbing their dry eyes with a handkerchief. Or: "He looked just like he was sleeping."

Mr. Anderson didn't look peaceful, and he certainly didn't look like he was sleeping. And Max did not feel curious, or even superior, as she had imagined she might, standing above a dead person when she was still alive.

She just felt sad and a little sick.

It wasn't until Sam put a hand lightly on her shoulder that Max realized she'd been frozen there, staring, for who knows how long. Pippa was watching the street from the window; Thomas was gone.

"Are you all right?" Sam asked.

"Fine," Max said quickly. She winced and shrugged him off, both because she had let her guard drop and because Sam's touch, even when he was doing his best to be careful, was a little like the gentle pressure of a thousand-pound boulder.

"They're coming," Pippa said, turning from the window, and Max registered shouts and noises from the street. She wanted to ask what had happened to Thomas—where he had gone—but her brain felt like it was encased in sludge. She wanted to turn away from the body but she couldn't.

There was the pounding of footsteps on the staircase. Thomas once again burst into the room, followed by two grim-faced detectives and a beat cop Thomas must have found patrolling the street. The detectives wore identical belted trench coats and fedoras pulled low over their eyes. The only difference between them, as far as Max could tell, was in their chins: one man was clean-shaven, with a chin so pointy it looked like it could cut vegetables; the other had a chin as blunt as a shovel and covered in stubble. They even smelled the same: like cheap aftershave; tobacco; and, faintly, just faintly, like sour milk.

"Here," Thomas said, panting a little. "I mean, there." He pointed to the body of Mr. Anderson.

Max stepped aside to let the police detectives pass. The beat cop hung back, looking vaguely nauseous, tugging at his uniform. "Well," he said, with a nervous cough. "Seems like it's pretty cut-and-dry. I'll leave you to it. Too many cooks in the kitchen, and all that. No point in muddling the soup, as it were." He turned around and practically bolted out of the room. The detectives didn't even seem to notice. They were both circling the body in a way that reminded Max unpleasantly of sharks.

"He's—he's really dead, then?" Pippa said, as though she'd been hoping all along that Mr. Anderson might suddenly sit up.

The detective with the stubble straightened up from where he'd gone into a crouch. "He'll never be deader," he said, and spit matter-of-factly into a large vase on Mr. Anderson's desk.

The other cop flipped open his leather badge case and closed it so rapidly Max saw only the glint of metal.

Underneath the brim of his hat, small black eyes glittered. "Name's Hardaway," he said. "Assistant Chief Inspector Hardaway." He jerked his head toward the other man. "This here's Lieutenant Webb."

Lieutenant Webb grunted.

"Let's take things nice and slow," Hardaway said, pulling out a notebook from the pocket of his trench coat. "First up: you want to explain to me how four kids ended up with one dead body on a nowhere street in Brooklyn?"

There was a moment of silence. Max could hear the ticking of a grandfather clock and it was as loud as an accusation. The back of her neck was sweating. She looked around the room, trying to seize on something—anything—that might serve as an excuse.

"Well, you see . . . ," Thomas said, scratching his neck.

"It's very complicated . . . ," Pippa said, as Sam said, "It's very simple."

"Locket!" Max burst out. Her eyes had just landed on a tarnished silver locket coiled on the blotting paper on top of Mr. Anderson's desk. Everyone turned to look at her in surprise. "My, um . . . locket," she said, forcing herself not to fidget. She could lie to a cop. She could lie to a nun, if she had to. "Mr. Anderson said he could sell it for me. He—he told me it was worth twenty dollars." She was getting into the story and wishing she really *had* given Mr. Anderson a locket to sell for twenty dollars. "But then I had a kind of, um, change of heart! Because it was my granny's. Poor granny." She sniffled experimentally. The policemen looked sympathetic, and she sniffled again. Pippa was scowling, but Max ignored her. "She got run over by a streetcar. Just flattened like a pancake, and all her brains splattered like a bunch of jelly on the—"

Lieutenant Webb spit once again into the vase on Mr. Anderson's desk.

"He gets the idea, Max," Pippa said, through gritted teeth.

"Oh, right. Yeah." Max was annoyed that Pippa had cut her off in the middle of her dramatic monologue, right when she was getting to the good part about her fake grandmother's eyeballs rolling into the gutter. "So anyway, like I said, we came out to talk to Mr. Anderson about letting me have it back. The locket, I mean."

Hardaway stared at her and she forced herself to stand still. Then his eyes ticked slowly around the rest of the group. "Who turned the front door to a pile of splinters?"

"That was me, sir." Sam spoke up quietly. "We were worried when he didn't answer the door. The light was on, and he was expecting us. We thought something might have happened. So I may have, um, knocked down the door."

"With what? A battering ram?" Hardaway said. Fortunately, before Sam was required to answer, Lieutenant Webb—who had begun circling the small room, sifting through the wastepaper basket, and sniffing the cigar ends in the ashtray—now spoke up.

"Chief," he grunted, extracting a folded white sheet of stationery from underneath the corner of the blotter. "I got something. Looks like a note from Anderson."

Hardaway took the note from Lieutenant Webb and scanned it quickly. Then he folded it, slipped it into his pocket, and jerked his head toward the door. "All right," he said to the kids. "Go on. Get out of here. Straight home and no stopping."

"You sure, Chief?" said Lieutenant Webb. "The captain won't like it."

Hardaway's face flushed—at least, his chin flushed, which was the only part of his face Max could see very clearly. "I don't give a rat's tail what the captain likes," he said. "I've got a fiver on the game and a pint with my name on it." He turned back to the kids. "You heard me. Hit the road before I decide to change my mind and haul you all down to the station."

"But what about—" Pippa started to say.

"Thanks a lot!" Thomas jumped in, before Pippa could say any more. He looped an arm through Pippa's and practically dragged her toward the door, even as she struggled against him. "We'll, um, find our own way out."

But before they could move into the hall there were footsteps on the stairs once again, and suddenly a young man with a shock of orange-red hair sticking straight up from his head, like a tall flame growing from his scalp, burst into the room.

When he saw Mr. Anderson, he let out a strangled cry and took two stumbling steps toward the body. Before the police could seize him, he stopped and recoiled, shrinking back against the wall as though noticing the other people in the room for the first time.

"Who are you?" he cried. His eyes were wide and his voice was as shrill as the whistle from a teapot. "What's going on? What happened to my uncle?"

"Your uncle?" Hardaway repeated sharply.

"Uncle Arthur," the boy said, and then let out a sound that was somewhere between a sob and a sniffle. "Is he . . . ? Is he really . . . ?" Although he was probably no older than eighteen, his shoulders were slumped as though he was carrying an invisible rock on his back. He was wearing the most hideous outfit Max had ever seen: vivid green trousers and scuffed brown shoes paired with an orange-checked shirt that clashed horrendously with his hair. If his clothing could speak, Max knew it would be screaming.

The cops exchanged a quick glance. "Why don't you have a seat," Hardaway said, jerking his head toward a chair. It was more of an order than a question. "Take a deep breath. Tell us all about it."

Mr. Anderson's nephew ignored him. He pulled out a lime-green handkerchief and began worrying it between thin fingers. "I should never have left him alone!" he moaned. "Oh, Uncle. Uncle!"

"Pull yourself together," Hardaway said sternly, "Mr. . . . ?"

"Reginald," the boy said, still twisting the handkerchief and staring at the body of his uncle. "Reginald Anderson."

Hardaway nodded. "Start at the beginning, why don't you, and don't stop until you hit the end. Were you and your uncle close?"

Reginald nodded miserably. "Been working at the store since I was just a kid," he said. "My uncle took me in after my mom and dad died. Spanish flu laid 'em both flat the same winter. Uncle Arthur was like a father to me." His voice began to tremble again and his eyes filled suddenly with tears. "It's all my fault! I should never have gone to visit Betsy! I should never have left him alone!"

"Betsy?" Hardaway said.

"Betsy Williams, sir." Now Reginald's face slowly turned pink, as though someone had dipped him like an Easter egg into dye. "She lives in Boston. We're friendly-like, me and Betsy. I guess you could say we're engaged to be engaged. Well, we will be engaged to be engaged, if her dad ever comes around to—"

"Understood." Hardaway gave an impatient wave of his hand. "Get on with your story."

Reginald stared pleadingly at both detectives in turn. "Uncle Arthur's been in a bit of a funk. Business was bad and he was worried about money. But I never thought—not in a million years did I imagine— I would never have gone if—" He wailed again.

Lieutenant Webb coughed.

"So your uncle was in a bad way," Hardaway said.

Reginald frowned. "Like I said, he'd been in a funk," he said. "You see, he'd recently sold off an item to a friend. And he was convinced he'd made a bad deal and he should have asked for triple the price." Max caught Sam's eye. He gave an almost imperceptible nod as Thomas's hand tightened on Pippa's arm. Reginald was surely talking about the shrunken head. "So that had got him peeved, especially since we had a hard winter and not too many people buying."

"It seems to me like it all hangs together nicely," Hardaway said. "No pun intended," he added.

"But I don't understand," Reginald whimpered. "How did this happen? When did you find him?" His eyes swept across the room and landed on Max, Sam, Pippa, and Thomas—still huddled near the door—for the first time. He frowned and balled the handkerchief in a fist. "Who are you?" he demanded. "What are you doing here?"

"We're nobody," Thomas answered promptly. "And we're leaving."

No one spoke again until they were all safely onto the street. After the close, warm atmosphere of the room upstairs, with its smells of old cigar butts and cheap aftershave and mildew, the air was as delicious as a fizzy bottle of soda. Max didn't even mind the faint fishy smells coming off the Gowanus Canal. The homeless man she had spotted earlier was still there, and still lurking by the trash bins—almost as if he was waiting for them. But he didn't look up as they passed.

Suddenly, Pippa whirled around to face her. "Hand it over," she said, sticking out her palm.

Max's face went hot. "What are you talking about?"

"Don't play dumb, Max." Pippa shoved her palm practically in Max's nose. "Give it over or I'll search you myself. I can see it, remember."

Thomas and Sam were watching curiously. Muttering a curse, Max reached into her pocket and extracted the silver locket from Mr. Anderson's desk. Pippa snatched it from her, glaring so hard Max was amazed her eyeballs didn't rocket out of her face. Pippa marched back into the shop. Moments later she returned.

"Unbelievable," she said, as she breezed past Max.

"Hey." Max nearly had to jog to catch up with her. "If it wasn't for me, we'd probably be in jail right now. The locket was mine, anyway. My grandma gave it to me, remember?"

"You made that up," Pippa said.

"Good thing I did, too! The rest of you were just standing there with your mouths open." A rat scurried in front of them and Max dodged it neatly. "Besides, what does Anderson care? He roped himself, didn't he?"

"He didn't," Thomas said quietly.

Max turned to him, frowning. "What do you mean? The cops said—"

"The cops are wrong," Thomas said. "Look. I'll show you."

They stopped walking. The wind had risen and made a paper bag turn circles across the street. A single streetlamp twenty yards away cast a pale white circle on the cobblestone. In it, Max could see a stray cat, skinny as a stick, playing with a chicken bone. It was very quiet, and she suddenly longed to be back at the museum, with its comforting murmur of sounds and the rattling of the pipes and the burble of water boiling in the kettle and the smells of furniture polish and chamomile tea: the whole warm, chaotic, lovely mess of it.

Thomas unstrapped his belt. He was so thin that without it, his pants sagged down over his hipbones. He held up the belt to his neck. "If I were going to hang myself—"

"Don't joke, Tom," Pippa said, shivering. "It's awful."

Thomas ignored her. "Watch what happens if I string myself up." He cinched the belt tightly and mimed attaching one end to the ceiling. The belt slid to his jaw, extending upward on a diagonal and striking just below his ears, like an inverted *V*. He undid the belt.

"I still don't get it," Max said, crossing her arms. She wanted to get out of the street, out of the emptiness and the dark. But she would never say so.

"The mark on Mr. Anderson's neck," Sam said slowly. "It was all wrong."

"Exactly!" Thomas said. This time, he slid the belt against his neck and pretended that someone was pulling it tightly from behind. "Now watch this. Let's say I didn't string myself up. Let's say, instead, *someone strangled me*. Someone approximately my height."

In a flash, Max understood. The bruise on Mr. Anderson's neck went the wrong way. It went straight across his neck, instead of up toward his ears.

Pippa inhaled sharply. "It was murder," she said, in a whisper.

12

Murder. The word hung between them like one of Max's knives, sharp-toothed and frightening. Every time Pippa closed her eyes, she saw Mr. Anderson's face, purple as a bruise, and the terrible mark around his neck.

First that old woman had plummeted from her balcony. Then the head was stolen. And now, a murder. What did it mean?

The subway ride from Brooklyn seemed to take ages. Sam appeared to be sleeping, although Pippa was sure he wasn't. Max picked her nails with a blade and did her best to look unconcerned. Thomas produced a book from his back pocket. It had a bright red cover and was called *Statistics for Everybody*, and Pippa was sure he hadn't taken it with him from the museum.

"Where did you get that?" Pippa asked suspiciously.

Thomas blushed. Suddenly, Pippa understood.

"Oh no," she said. "Not you, too."

"It was just sitting on a shelf," Thomas said sheepishly. "Besides, it's not like Mr. Anderson will miss it."

"You're unbelievable," Pippa said, while Max grinned and gave Thomas the thumbs-up.

By the time they arrived at the museum, Pippa was practically numb from exhaustion. The windows, usually bright with lamps, were dark. The front door was locked, so Thomas knocked. It wasn't Potts who came to admit them but Betty, carrying an old gas lantern from the museum's collection of Victorian household items and wearing a nightgown shaped like a tent, her hair pinned into various rollers, her beard carefully braided for the evening.

"Why's it so quiet?" Thomas asked. "Where's Potts?"

"Keep your voice down," she whispered. "Mr. Dumfrey has a terrible headache. Potts nipped out to the pharmacy."

"Is he sick?" Pippa asked, feeling a pulse of anxiety.

Betty bustled ahead of them, her slippers slapping against the wood floor. In the circle of light from her lantern, the exhibits were lit up grotesquely on either side of them: shadows skated like bats over the walls and ceiling; glass reflected distorted faces and leering smiles.

"He's doing the books," she said. "Mr. Cabillaud insisted. And you know how numbers upset Mr. Dumfrey. He worked himself into an absolute tizzy." No sooner had she finished speaking than the children heard the shrill cry of the telephone.

Betty sighed. "*Now* what?" she muttered, shaking her head. Her long beard waggled.

They climbed the stairs, following the jerky progression of Betty's lamp. As they neared Mr. Dumfrey's third-floor chambers, a door slammed. Monsieur Cabillaud appeared on the landing, carrying an enormous leather ledger, his expression even more pinched than usual.

"What's the matter, Henri?" Betty asked.

"I have been dismissed for ze evening," he said stiffly. "Monsieur Dumfrey has had enough. When it comes to ze mathematics, he is worse even than Sam!"

Sam blushed. "I try," he mumbled. Math was his worst subject.

"There, there, Henri," Betty said, and patted Monsieur Cabillaud's shoulder consolingly.

from one of his books—*Robinson Crusoe* was the popular favorite, although he was always pressing for *War and Peace*. Sometimes Smalls recited one of his poems in progress, although he'd become so insulted after Goldini yawned in the middle of his sonnets that for weeks he'd been refusing to share anything more.

Danny might play a few notes on his violin, which was so old and warped no one but he could coax any notes from it, but which sang under his stubby fingers like a brand-new instrument. On special occasions, he even broke out his cherished bagpipe, which was normally stored in a beautiful velvet-lined walnut case underneath his bed. Then Phoebe—who was surprisingly light on her feet, despite being the fattest lady in New York—would demonstrate how to do the two-step and every so often, on rare, magical nights, would convince Mr. Dumfrey to dance with her.

But Mr. Dumfrey's news, and the danger that the museum might close, had soured the atmosphere, as though someone had farted and no one wanted to admit to it. Everyone pretended to act normal while, instead, doing the opposite. Hugo had a book open on his lap but didn't once turn the page. Betty didn't remember her rollers until the sharp stench of burned hair reminded her, and Danny plucked a single string of his violin mournfully, over and over, so it sounded as though the instrument was crying. Even Quinn and Caroline did not have enough energy to argue with each other.

Pippa couldn't believe that only two days ago, Mr. Dumfrey had nearly danced a jig when he descended midmorning and—seeing the visitors lined up outside the museum doors—crowed that they would all be rich.

Life without the museum would be a form of imprisonment: dull and hard and lonely. The museum was everything to her, as familiar as breathing, as close and comforting as the dented space in her mattress that fitted her body exactly. She had no memories of life before the museum, except for strange, shadowy images of a vast dark hallway and nightmare figures that sometimes came to her, stretching their skinny fingers between the bars of their cages.

She finally drifted to sleep when the moon had already started descending toward the horizon, and woke with the sun shining aggressively. She was alone. Confused, she got up and shoved her feet in the lambskin slippers Mr. Dumfrey had given all the children for Christmas last year, then padded to the stairwell. Why hadn't Mrs. Cobble woken everyone for breakfast, as she usually did? Why hadn't Potts come stomping through the attic, grunting, "Grub's on. Hurry up or miss out"?

Her stomach knotted up. Something terrible must have happened.

She practically flew down the stairs, slippers slapping loudly against the wood. She could hear voices, and she followed them down the hall, down the steep flight of stairs that led to the cellar, and burst into the kitchen.

Several dozen faces looked up at her in surprise. Caroline and Quinn were enjoying a rare moment of peace, seated side by side and dressed identically, sharing a single cup of coffee. Smalls was holding a vast dusty volume called *Collected Romantic Poetry*, his place marked with a massive finger. Sam, Thomas, and Max were sitting at the table, along with various other residents of the museum, many of them still in their pajamas, blinking sleep from their eyes or patting down hair that seemed to have been electrified overnight. Potts was glowering at Thomas from his usual spot in the corner.

Dumfrey was missing.

"Where's Mr. Dumfrey?" Pippa asked breathlessly, almost fearing to hear the answer.

"Went out to get the paper," Thomas said, yawning.

"Where's Mrs. Cobble?" Pippa asked, noticing that she, too, was missing.

"Up and left," Potts spat out.

"Traitor!" Miss Fitch shook her head. The children could always tell what kind of mood Miss Fitch was in by the severity of her part. Today her hair looked as if it had been raked and pulled with unusual ferocity. "Treacherous, two-faced traitor. As soon as Mr. Dumfrey suggested a reduction in wages . . ."

"She took her spoons and sailed out the door," Danny finished for her, waddling out from behind the table. He was wearing Mrs. Cobble's old pink apron, which reached all the way to his toes.

He began whisking eggs so vigorously, half of them ended up on the floor. "It's a damn shame. . . ."

"Language, Daniel!" Miss Fitch said.

"But it is. After all Mr. Dumfrey did for her. Did for all of us! I'd like to kick her in the shins. I'll do it, too, if I ever see that snaggletoothed hound again."

"We'll just have to make do without her, Danny," Betty said soothingly, reaching over and removing the eggs from him before he could whisk them into nonexistence.

In Mrs. Cobble's absence, everyone pitched in to

help get breakfast on the table. And though Quinn complained the eggs were too runny and Caroline complained they were too hard and Goldini burned the toast while attempting to make it vanish and reappear and Betty lost several beard hairs in the porridge, by the time they sat down to eat, Pippa was so hungry she thought it was the best breakfast she'd ever had.

She was trying to prevent Max from licking her bowl, when the door opened and Mr. Dumfrey appeared on the stairs, a newspaper tucked under one arm.

He seemed to have aged a decade overnight. His face was the gray of wet paper pulp. He wasn't smiling.

"Pippa," he said in a tone so sharp it made her chest constrict with fear. "Thomas. Samuel. Max. My office. Now."

The kitchen went silent. Pippa stood up from the table, conscious of the loud grating of the bench against the floor. Max, Sam, and Thomas stood, too. Together, they followed Mr. Dumfrey as he stomped up the performers' staircase ahead of them. Pippa felt as if she were on her way to the guillotine.

"What's got his panties in a pinch?" Max whispered.

"Shut up, Max," Pippa said. She had never seen Mr. Dumfrey so upset.

When they reached Mr. Dumfrey's office, Mr. Dumfrey ushered them inside without a word, closing the door firmly behind them.

"Sit." He gestured toward the motley collection of stools and crates he had pulled up to the desk. Pippa took a faded silk stool; Thomas folded himself up onto a milk crate; Sam eased himself down into an armchair, wincing when it creaked; and Max remained standing, scowling, arms crossed. In his corner cage, Cornelius was hopping up and down excitedly, occasionally letting out a throaty cry of "Cocoa!"

Mr. Dumfrey sank down into the armchair behind his desk. For a second, he said nothing, staring at each of the children in turn. Behind the lenses of his glasses, his small blue eyes glittered, and Pippa had the sense that he was staring deep into her mind and finding it seriously wanting. She lowered her eyes.

"Would you care to explain what this is about?" he said at last, and threw the paper with a flourish onto the desk. A small red bottle labeled *Sasquatch Blood* rolled onto the ground.

Thomas and Sam exchanged a glance. Thomas leaned forward.

"It's the *Daily Screamer*," he said cautiously.

"I'm aware," Mr. Dumfrey said drily. He removed

his glasses and began polishing them. "Thomas, perhaps you'll do us the honor of reading the first page out loud."

Thomas frowned and looked to the others for help. Pippa shrugged.

"Today, Thomas," Mr. Dumfrey said, returning his glasses to his nose.

Thomas cleared his throat. "'Disgraced Scientist Makes Daring Prison Break—'"

"Not that one," Mr. Dumfrey practically barked. "The *other* headline, please."

"'Horror Head Claims Another Victim,'" he read. "'By Bill Evans.'" He looked up uncertainly. Mr. Dumfrey gestured for him to continue.

Thomas shook out the paper and went on reading:

"'The Horrifying Head recently procured by Mr. Dumfrey's Dime Museum, and subsequently stolen in the middle of the night, has claimed another life. Mr. Arthur Anderson of Anderson's Delights was found on Tuesday evening at eight p.m. hanging from the ceiling in his apartment on Seventh Street in Brooklyn, and pronounced dead at the scene.'

"'Mr. Anderson was the seller of the head, and had allegedly been attempting to negotiate for its return.'

"'"Sold it off to the museum for hardly anything," said

Reginald Anderson, Mr. Anderson's distraught nephew.'

"'The head has not been long in New York City but already has left a blood-spattered trail in its wake. Two people who had recently been in the presence of the head have died violent deaths in less than a week. Coincidence? Or curse?'"

Thomas broke off and glanced up at Dumfrey, who had leaned back in his chair and closed his eyes.

"Please continue," he said, without opening his eyes. "We're almost at my favorite part."

Thomas swallowed back a sigh and continued: "'Further adding to the mystery of Mr. Anderson's death was the presence at the scene of four children subsequently identified as being part of the collection of "entertainers" who call Dumfrey's Dime Museum home—'"

Thomas nearly choked. Pippa inhaled sharply, and Sam groaned.

Dumfrey opened his eyes. "Continue," he growled.

Thomas licked his lips.

"'These four children, if they can rightly so be called, gained admittance into Mr. Anderson's apartments under false pretenses, escaped detection by the police under the same, and were only subsequently identified by yours truly based on descriptions provided by officers on the scene.'"

Max said a bad word, and everyone shushed her.

"'"I thought they were just some neighborhood kids," said Assistant Chief Inspector Carl Hardaway. "They looked normal to me."'

"'But normal is precisely what these children are not, as this journalist knows firsthand. Thomas Able, Philippa (Pippa) Devue, Sam Fort, and Mackenzie (last name unknown) have achieved notoriety due to their freakish, some would say unnatural, abilities. A body as limber as an elastic band; the ability to read minds, or at the very least, pockets; a preternatural strength; a ferocious and deadly skill with knives: these are some of the strengths of this group of freaks, of human abominations.'"

Max said another bad word. This time, no one shushed her.

Thomas turned the page. His hands were shaking so badly, the paper rattled loudly.

"'Should they be allowed to roam the streets unaccompanied? Is it advisable? Is it safe?'

"'What were they doing at the scene of Mr. Anderson's death, and is it related to the theft of the shrunken head, which some claim was a stunt orchestrated by Mr. Dumfrey himself? For more, turn to our editorial on page—'"

"That's enough," Mr. Dumfrey said, and Thomas stopped reading. For a moment there was complete silence. No one wanted to speak first, and Pippa couldn't bring herself to meet Mr. Dumfrey's eyes. "We return to the original question," he said softly. "Who wants to explain to me what this is about?"

"It's all lies," Max burst out. "Saying we're freaks and abdominals—"

"Abominations."

"—saying you pulled some kind of stunt. He should be cut open and turned into jerky."

"I'm sure Mr. Evans, like all journalists of his kind, has taken some liberties," Mr. Dumfrey said. "But he was right about one very important thing. Behind my back, without asking my permission, at a time when I believed you to be in the attic, you sneaked out and paid a visit to Mr. Anderson, my dear—and now dead—friend. So I want to know: Why?"

Sam coughed. "It was about the head, sir."

Dumfrey blinked.

Thomas came to Sam's aid. "We thought that Potts might have struck a deal with Mr. Anderson—"

"I've told you to leave Potts alone," Mr. Dumfrey said sharply, banging his fist on the desk. Pippa jumped, and another little bottle (*Strand of Marie Antoinette's Hair* read the label) rolled onto the carpet. Then Dumfrey sighed and sagged back in his chair. When he spoke again, his voice was much quieter.

"I know I'm not your father," he said softly, turning his eyes to each of them in turn. "Nonetheless, I consider you all my children. You too, Max," he added, since she seemed about to protest. "My children, and my responsibility to protect. There are dangers out there. Evils you're too young to understand—" Mr. Dumfrey broke off. He continued more calmly, "I can't imagine what you hoped to accomplish by invading Mr. Anderson's home, but I think we can agree that the mission was a failure. From now on, I expect you to keep out of this business entirely."

"But what about—" Thomas started to say.

"Entirely," Mr. Dumfrey repeated sternly. "Do I make myself clear?"

Thomas nodded slowly. Pippa felt heavy with guilt but also frustration. If the museum really *was* in danger of closing, she couldn't just stand there and watch it fail. They needed that head.

And Mr. Evans's article was right about something else—two people connected to the head had died in the span of a week.

Mr. Dumfrey pushed back from his desk. As though

reading her mind, he said, "Let the police do their job. If the head can be found, they'll find it."

"But they're not even looking," Sam protested.

"Then I guess the case is closed," Mr. Dumfrey said firmly, and Pippa knew that the conversation was over.

13

Midmorning, Thomas was sitting in the Odd-itorium, rereading *The Probability of Everything*, having already finished *Statistics for Everybody*, which he had found disappointing. Suddenly, he heard a loud commotion from the entrance hall.

"You've got some nerve showing up here." Miss Fitch's voice was shrill as a fire bell. "After all those lies you wrote up in the paper. I don't know how you sleep at night. I ought to snip your fingers off—"

Rounding the corner, Thomas saw that Miss Fitch had Bill Evans cornered and was waving a heavy pair of sewing scissors threateningly in his direction.

"It's all right, Miss Fitch," Mr. Dumfrey said. He, too,

had been attracted by the noise. Miss Fitch gave a final, injured snip of her scissors, then turned and stalked off, muttering under her breath about the shame of it.

Mr. Evans eased off the wall and adjusted his tie. "Charming woman," he said with a nervous laugh. "Is she always that friendly?"

"What do you want?" Thomas blurted out, before he could stop himself. He thought Mr. Dumfrey might scold him for being rude, but instead he saw a smile pass briefly across Dumfrey's face.

Mr. Evans addressed his words to Dumfrey. "You're not mad about what I wrote, are you?" He took off his hat and spread his hands in a gesture of appeal. "You know how it is, Mr. D. Gotta spice things up, give stories a bit of a twist if you want to sell papers. And, boy, are we selling them." He grinned. "They're going like hotcakes. People love a good horror story, and this business of the head's got everyone riled up."

Mr. Dumfrey stared at him with no expression. Mr. Evans's smile faltered, and he coughed.

"Look at it this way," he said, trying a new tack. "You need a little bit of publicity, now that the head's up and vanished." Thomas had to admit that Mr. Evans had a point. "Think of it: *The Four Orphan Freaks of Dumfrey's Dime Museum.* It's got a nice ring to it, doesn't it? That'll bring in the crowds. I thought maybe I could do a little roundup of the kids, a few interviews, maybe a photograph—"

"Absolutely not," Mr. Dumfrey said stiffly.

"Maybe it's not such a bad idea," Thomas interjected. "He's right. We could use the publicity."

Mr. Dumfrey shot Thomas a withering glance, and Thomas wished he hadn't spoken. Mr. Dumfrey returned his gaze to Bill Evans, drawing himself up to his full five feet five inches. "Now listen here, Evans. You don't have to tell me about publicity. I practically invented it. But I won't have you implicating Thomas or Sam or any of them. I won't have you hurling imprecations or insinuating allegations or—or—"

"Dragging us into it," Thomas suggested.

"Exactly," Mr. Dumfrey said.

Mr. Evans smiled. "All due respect, Mr. D., they're already implicated." His two front teeth were large and somewhat protruding, which gave him the look of a tall, skinny, eager rabbit. "Murder's no common potato, Mr. Dumfrey, and they're neck-deep in it."

"Murder?" Mr. Dumfrey repeated.

Bill Evans had started to make for the door. Now he turned around and said with false casualness, "Oh, yeah. The medical examiner's report came back. Mr.

Anderson didn't do himself in after all. He was strung up by someone who wanted to make it look that way." Evans's eyes slid over to Thomas and Thomas quickly looked away. His heart was beating fast in his chest.

He had been right.

"You can read all about it in the afternoon papers," Mr. Evans said, jamming his hat on his head. "Afternoon to you both. If you change your mind about the interviews, Mr. D., you know where to find me."

Then he was gone.

"So what now?" Pippa said.

They were all gathered after dinner in the loft. Sam had cleared a small central space in the cluttered room, and Pippa had poached some unused props and old exhibits from the storage cellar, including a large Navajo blanket, several woven pillows sent to Mr. Dumfrey by a maharaja, a three-legged stool once owned by George Washington, and a walnut table inlaid with ivory. Now they were all sitting, drinking Ovaltine from earthenware mugs. Steam from their cups intermingled above their heads.

"What do you mean?" Max took a long slurp of hot chocolate. "You heard what Dumfrey said. It ain't our business."

"Isn't."

"Same thing."

"No, it isn't."

"Ain't."

"But we have to do *something*," Thomas insisted, jumping in. "Mr. Anderson wanted the head back. And then he was killed."

"Maybe there *is* a curse," said Max.

"You can't really believe that," Thomas said, and Max shrugged.

"Does it matter? We're no closer to finding the head than we ever were," Sam pointed out.

There was a minute of heavy silence. Thomas's stomach made a noise like a dog's whimper. It had been a slow day, as Mr. Dumfrey had predicted. The murder of Mr. Anderson and continued talk of Mrs. Weathersby's death had eclipsed the short mention of Mr. Dumfrey and the museum from which the head had been stolen. With the exception of a few local kids, who had pressed grubby palms against the front door and peered in through the glass, and one rich-looking man and his snub-nosed daughter, who had come after lunch and imperiously demanded to see the "freaks," then inquired whether they might be rented out for a birthday party, there had been no customers at all.

The entertainers had passed the hours performing various chores and tiptoeing around Mr. Dumfrey, who remained locked in his study doing the books with Monsieur Cabillaud, as though he were a pressure cooker in danger of explosion. But in the absence of Mrs. Cobble, no one had remembered to go to the markets. And so dinner had been canned tuna and day-old bread and mustard.

Thomas took a long sip of his Ovaltine, hoping it would help ease the cramping in his stomach. "I still think Potts knows something," he said.

Pippa nodded. Her dark bangs practically concealed her eyes. "He knew Mr. Anderson. Or at least they'd met. So why doesn't he say so?"

Max shrugged. "Might not be anything to it. Maybe he pawned some stuff. Or did business for Mr. Dumfrey."

"Maybe," Thomas said, unconvinced. He had the vague, prickling sense that they were missing something—and that something very bad would happen as a result. "But then why—?"

"Shhh," Sam said sharply. "Someone's coming."

A stair creaked; there was a shuffling, a rustling of skirts, and a murmured word. Thomas held his breath. Max had frozen with her mug halfway to her lips. Pippa leaned close to the door, listening.

More footsteps. Then a voice, low, urgent, on the other side of the door at the top of the stairs.

"Were you careful?"

Sam's eyebrows shot nearly through his hairline. Thomas and Pippa exchanged a glance, and Max barely managed to swallow her hot chocolate without choking on it. They knew that voice. It was Phoebe.

"Very."

And that one: Hugo.

"Do you think—do you think anyone knows?"

"No. They might suspect. But they can't possibly know. We took every precaution."

"But if Dumfrey finds out . . ."

"Dumfrey won't find out."

Thomas was holding his breath, and he could feel his lungs like two water-filled balloons in his chest. As far as he knew, Phoebe and Hugo never even spoke to each other, unless it was to inquire about who was performing first or where the talcum powder had got to.

It was quiet for a moment—so quiet, he could hear a scuffling sound he couldn't quite identify. A mouse poked its head out from between two crates just next to Pippa. Pippa's eyes were tightly closed. Thomas knew she must be trying to think her way out through the door, into the minds of Hugo and Phoebe. Encouraged, the mouse advanced forward, sniffing experimentally at her bare calves.

Thomas opened his mouth to warn her, or try and frighten it off, but then Phoebe spoke again and he clamped it shut.

"And you're sure—you're sure the money will be enough?" She sounded breathless.

Even through the door, Thomas could hear the smile in Hugo's voice. "My dear," he said, "we will not have to worry about money for a long, long time."

At that moment several things happened. The mouse, having reached Pippa's big toe and decided it looked (or smelled) sufficiently like a wedge of cheese, bit down; Pippa's eyes flew open and she gasped, and kicked, and sent the mouse directly into the pot of cooling hot chocolate perched on the three-legged stool, where it landed with a small splash.

"What's that?" Phoebe cried from outside the door. "Did you hear that?"

"Who's there?" Hugo called out. Then, in a low voice: "We'll talk more tomorrow. Good night, Phoebe."

The stairs creaked again, and Hugo and Phoebe's footsteps receded. The mouse, now covered in chocolate, sat up contentedly and began grooming itself.

"I guess I won't have a refill," Max said, making a face.

With painstaking care, Sam lifted the mouse carefully from the pot by its tail and placed it on the ground after giving it a shake. The mouse squeaked in protest and scampered off, shooting Sam an injured look.

Pippa exhaled a long breath. "That was close," she said.

"All that talk about money and Dumfrey . . ." Sam looked up at Thomas. "Do you think they had something to do with this mess?"

"I don't know." Thomas shook his head. He had that feeling in his chest again: something bad was coming. "But I think we have to find out."

14

Thoughts of Phoebe and Hugo were soon to be driven straight out of Thomas's head.

He was outside even before the sun broke free of the horizon, when the air was still the dark purple of the velvet curtains in the Odditorium, when New York was at its quietest. From a high window across the street, a bunch of green-eyed tabbies—just a few of the dozens owned by Miss Groenovelt, the neighborhood cat lady—peered down at him in silence.

He went west on Forty-Third Street, past Cupid's Dance Hall, where the gutters were filled with lipstick-coated cigarette butts, stamped there by women who had stopped dancing only a few hours earlier; past Majestic

Hardware, its vast display of tools glinting dully like metal teeth behind the dust-coated windows; past Sol's candy store on the corner of Forty-Third and Ninth, shutters still rolled down tightly against the morning, its candy-striped awning rustling lightly in the wind. Garry, the night porter at the Hotel St. James, saluted solemnly, in the military fashion, as Thomas passed.

Beyond Ninth Avenue, the neighborhood got dingier, the buildings sadder, with the scrawny, desperate look of beggars. Thomas kept his head down, barely registering the Salvation Army soup kitchen, which in a few hours would be crowded with people jostling for a bowl of soup and some bread, or the old Union Carriage Factory, now closed, its windows boarded up, its doors glued shut with caulk.

His mind was turning over everything that had happened, from the death of the old woman to the theft of the head and Mr. Anderson's staged suicide, discovered so soon by the police to be murder.

That bugged him. It was a smart idea to make Mr. Anderson look like he'd killed himself because of worries about money. But it had been executed stupidly, carelessly. So the killer wasn't as clever as he thought he was. Or maybe—the idea struck Thomas so hard that it stopped him in his tracks—maybe two people were responsible. Two people who plotted together, had worked together to steal the head, then planted Anderson's card on Mr. Potts.

Two people . . . like Hugo and Phoebe?

He had this last, unsettling thought just as he reached the Hudson River. The gray surface of the water was stiff with small white peaks drawn up by the wind, like a large surface of whipped cream. Across the river, he saw the lights of New Jersey come on one by one. Thomas let the wind chase out thoughts of Hugo and Phoebe and worries about the museum, and instead watched the seagulls wheeling in the air.

In moments like this—quiet moments—Thomas sometimes let himself think about his real parents: who they must have been and whether they were still alive. Sometimes he felt only a curious detachment when he thought of them; other times, a fierce, dull anger, like a rock burning at the bottom of his stomach; and occasionally, a kind of longing he had no name for, like the tug he felt hearing the last notes of a song he loved.

The sun had finally broken loose of the buildings behind him, and orange light spread across the sky like a broken egg yolk flowing over a plate. Thomas realized he was hungry, and decided to go home to see what Mrs. Cobble was cooking, before he remembered that

Mrs. Cobble had quit.

He found a dime in the pocket of his stiff canvas jacket and decided to stop to buy eggs on his way back to the museum. The sun warmed his face and the knot in his stomach began to loosen. Maybe his premonition the night before, his sense that something terrible was coming, was wrong.

Maybe everything would be okay after all.

Sol was rolling up the metal shutters, revealing display cases filled with glistening rainbow-colored jawbreakers, thick slabs of taffy in every imaginable color, coiled ropes of licorice, and fudge wrapped in waxed paper. Thomas stopped to talk to him in the hopes of scoring a few free Peanut Chews, and so didn't notice the dusty gold Buick sedan rolling slowly down the street, and the men within it, their battered hats pulled low over their eyes, their collars turned up as though against a hard wind.

By the time Thomas reached the museum, the Buick was parked directly in front of the entrance. It was too early for visitors. The museum wouldn't open for another few hours. Thomas took the steps two at a time and pushed open the door, which was unlocked.

Then he froze.

There was a strange and unpleasant smell in the

air. It smelled like cheap aftershave and tobacco and faintly, just faintly, like sour milk.

Thomas's heart dove into his shoes. He knew that smell.

Monsieur Cabillaud was sitting behind the ticket desk, nose to page with one of the vast, overflowing ledgers in which Mr. Dumfrey kept track of the accounts due and overdue, and surrounded on all sides by towering stacks of papers.

"Where's Mr. Dumfrey?" Thomas asked.

Monsieur Cabillaud looked up, blinking blearily above the frame of his glasses. His eyes were red, as though he had been at it all night, and his tiny head was as shiny as polished wood. The bow tie he always wore was tilting dangerously to the left.

"Dumfrey," Thomas prompted.

"Zat is zee very same thing ze police have wanted to know," Monsieur Cabillaud said, frowning. "Do I look like Monsieur Dumfrey's *garde d'enfant*? Go upstairs, I tell zem, and look for him yourself. *Sacre bleu!* It is enough work to try and keep a roof above our noses. . . ."

Thomas didn't bother to inform Monsieur Cabillaud that the correct expression was *keep a roof above our heads*. His heart, already in his shoes, had flattened through the soles of his feet when Cabillaud had mentioned the word *police*.

He skidded through the entrance hall, under the familiar, weathered banner advertising *Pinheads! Bearded Ladies! Alligator Men! Dwarves! NOVEL AND ASTOUNDING EXHIBITIONS! MORE THAN ONE THOUSAND CURIOSITIES!* and sprinted down the central hallway, past the Hall of Worldwide Wonders, and to the performers' staircase. He passed Miss Fitch on the second floor. Her face was as tight and pinched as the puckered end of a lemon.

"Have you seen Mr. Potts?" she demanded, but Thomas didn't even bother replying.

"Thomas Able!" she cried as he shoved past her.

"Sorry," he panted out, even though he wasn't.

Just before he reached the third floor, he stopped and drew back. Mr. Dumfrey's door was closed, and Thomas could just make out the murmur of voices. Pacing the small landing was Lieutenant Webb, chewing on the end of an unlit cigar and occasionally spitting bits of tobacco onto the floor. Even inside, he wore his belted trench coat and hat, but Thomas could make out his eyes, glittering and hard, and the jutting angles of his forehead, like the skull of the Cro-Magnon Dumfrey had on display in the Hall of Worldwide Wonders.

Thomas's foot squeaked on the stair. Webb pivoted

in his direction and Thomas retreated quickly, around the bend in the staircase and out of sight.

He needed to hear what Hardaway—Thomas assumed it was Hardaway in the room with Dumfrey—was saying.

He returned to the second floor and moved into the Hall of Wax. Just between the life-size figure of Benjamin Franklin signing the Declaration of Independence and the model of Adam and Eve confronting the serpent (an old garden hose painted to resemble a boa constrictor) was a large air vent. Thomas dislodged its grate easily, as he had many times before, and crawled headfirst into the walls.

Thomas inched forward on his stomach, until he reached the air duct that fed directly into Mr. Dumfrey's chambers. Using his hands and feet for purchase, he shimmied up the narrow metal tube, feeling, as always, a little bit like a chunk of food that was going the wrong way through someone's throat. He could hear the rumble of voices through the metal and knew he was getting close.

The air duct flattened out again, and he eased forward, pressing his nose against a small metal grate that was situated directly above Mr. Dumfrey's overflowing desk. Lying on his stomach, nose squashed against the grate, he could see the shiny dome of Mr. Dumfrey's head and the wisps of hair combed across it; he could see, too, the battered top of Assistant Chief Inspector Hardaway's hat, which passed in and out of view, as Hardaway paced back and forth.

"It looks bad for you, Dumfrey," he was saying. "First your little group of freaks is sniffing around—"

"They're not freaks," Mr. Dumfrey said sharply. "They're extraordinary. And they weren't sniffing around. I sent them to Mr. Anderson's to conduct some business for me."

Thomas felt a surge of guilt. Mr. Dumfrey was covering for him—for all of them.

"Business," Hardaway repeated disdainfully, as though it were a dirty word. Thomas saw Hardaway lean forward over Dumfrey's desk. "What kind of business, Dumfrey? Were they cleaning up some of your mess? Finishing what you started? Pocketing the evidence?"

"Evidence?" Mr. Dumfrey jerked backward. "What— How dare you— What are you insinuating?"

Hardaway reached into the pocket of his trench coat. A second later, he slammed a leather-bound appointment book on Mr. Dumfrey's desk.

"Mr. Anderson died on Tuesday, April twenty-third, between five and seven o'clock. The medical examiner can tell us these things, Dumfrey. It looks as though he wasn't alone. He was expecting a visitor. See for yourself."

Hardaway opened the book and flipped forward a few pages.

"'Four thirty p.m., Tuesday, April twenty-third. *Appointment with D.*' What do you have to say about that?"

"I have nothing to say," Mr. Dumfrey said. "I haven't seen Mr. Anderson in several weeks. An initial means nothing."

"I can't say as I agree with you, Mr. *D.*," Hardaway said, putting a faint and unpleasant emphasis on the letter. "And the commissioner don't agree with you neither."

"Then he is mistaken," Mr. Dumfrey said. "You both are. I can't imagine it's the first time."

"Now listen up," Hardaway said, practically growling. "I don't know what kind of game you think you're playing, in this—this—this . . ." Hardaway gestured helplessly around him, obviously at a loss for words.

"House of Wonders?" Mr. Dumfrey suggested. "Museum of Marvels?"

"This freak show!" Hardaway exploded. "This flophouse! This dump of depravity!"

"Dump of depravity," Dumfrey murmured. "I like that."

Hardaway jabbed a finger at Mr. Dumfrey's chest. "I know what you types are like. You circus types. Weirdos, losers, and—and unnaturals! If it was up to me, you'd all be put in a cage—especially these so-called children. Little monsters, each and every one of them!"

Thomas realized he was shaking. There was a sick taste in his mouth. Of course he had always known he was different. In his darkest moments, he had even wondered whether that was why his parents had abandoned him.

But mostly he had never thought of different as a *bad* thing. He had thought of it as being special—like rolling snake eyes with a pair of dice, or finding four maraschino cherries in a dish of fruit cocktail.

But in that instant, he had a whole other vision. It was as though Hardaway's words had lifted a veil, and he saw Hugo and Phoebe and Danny and the rest of them as Hardaway saw them: Disgusting. Deformed. Abnormal.

What did that make him? What did that make Max, Pippa, and Sam? They were the freakiest of all the freaks.

Anger rose in his throat, choking him.

Hardaway was still talking. "I pay my taxes, Dumfrey. I work for the state. I got a wife and kids. I'm *normal*."

"Get to your point," Mr. Dumfrey said, his voice quivering with anger.

"My point," Hardaway said, "is I don't like freaks, and I don't like *you*."

Mr. Dumfrey stood up. "Are you accusing me of anything?"

There was a short pause. Hardaway said grudgingly, "No. Not yet."

"Then I suggest you leave. Immediately." Dumfrey moved around his desk and out of Thomas's view. Thomas heard the door creak open.

Hardaway rammed his hat even more firmly on his head. "I'm warning you, Dumfrey. If I get one whiff of something foul—one *sprinkle* of funny business from you or any of your collection of freaks—"

"They. Are. Not. Freaks. They are *marvels*."

"I'll haul you into the clink faster than you can say—"

But Thomas never heard Hardaway finish his sentence.

Because at that moment an ear-shattering scream came drilling through the walls, and Thomas, in his shock, tried to turn; and the grate gave way beneath him, and he went tumbling in a shower of dust directly onto Mr. Dumfrey's desk.

"Hello, Thomas," Mr. Dumfrey said, with barely a glance in his direction.

"Hello, Mr. Dumfrey," Thomas said, sitting up with a little groan.

Hardaway had already vaulted into the hall. Dumfrey sprinted after him, his robe flapping behind him like two scarlet wings, and Thomas followed.

The screaming continued. It was like an ice pick aimed directly between the ears. As they rounded the second-floor landing, Thomas saw Sam emerge from the Hall of Wax, white-faced.

"What *is* that?" he said. When he reached out to grab the banister, a chunk of wood splintered off in his hand.

"Nice one," Thomas said, as he raced down the stairs.

Doors slammed; footsteps pounded from all sides; a confusion of voices rose up together.

"What's going on?"

"What is it? What's happened?"

"Mercy! The old cow won't stop!"

As though sucked downward by gravitational force, the residents of the museum spiraled down the performers' staircase and made their way to the basement, where the screams continued, punctuated by brief gasping sobs and cries of "Help! Somebody! Oh, it's awful!" By now, Thomas recognized Miss Fitch's voice.

The hall outside Potts's room was narrow and packed with people. Hugo was standing just outside Potts's closed door, as though uncertain whether to go in. Inside the room, Miss Fitch continued to sob.

"Let me through." Hardaway was elbowing his way through the crowd. "Police. Coming through."

Everyone had gone quiet, with the exception of Miss Fitch, who was still blubbering and screeching behind the door. Thomas felt an awful sense of dread. He caught Sam's eye and Sam shook his head. He, too, looked afraid. Thomas pressed forward, following Mr. Dumfrey, who was trying to push his way past Hardaway.

"This is *my* museum," he was saying, and "You have no right."

Hardaway reached the door first and shoved it open.

Thomas felt like the world had turned a somersault around him.

Miss Fitch was standing in the middle of the room, her cheeks coated with black tracks of mascara, her lipstick smudged nearly to her chin.

"I just came in to see why he hadn't emptied the bins like usual," she said, with another sob. She brought a

15

"Almonds," Hardaway said, leaning down toward Potts's ghastly white face and sniffing like a hound dog. "Smell that? Almonds. Unmistakable."

Webb grunted. "You think he had some kinda allergy?"

Hardaway shot his partner a scathing look. "I think he had a *cyanide* allergy. That smell is a sign of cyanide poisoning. I'd bet my badge on it."

Cyanide. The word was like a cold sliver of rain down Sam's spine. It spread through the assembled crowd, hissing from lip to lip. And slowly, everyone turned to face Mr. Dumfrey.

Mr. Dumfrey, who kept an old tin of cyanide from the famous Morrison murder trial of 1843 on one of the shelves above his desk.

"Why is everyone looking at me?" Mr. Dumfrey's frown slowly transformed to a look of horror. "Surely you don't think . . . For God's sake . . . I had nothing to do with this!"

There was another awkward pause. Then Hugo broke the silence.

"We know you didn't, Mr. D.," he said, patting Mr. Dumfrey on the shoulder. Relief and guilt commingled in Sam's chest—he had, for just one second, been wondering . . . But of course Mr. Dumfrey could not have killed Potts. Why would he?

The other performers murmured their agreement.

A very unpleasant light was shining in Hardaway's eyes. "But you keep cyanide, don't you, Mr. Dumfrey? I saw it there myself."

"It was part of an old exhibit," he said, waving a hand. "'Pernicious Poisoners'—a nice little tableau— very popular."

Lieutenant Webb, who was still standing in the hallway, grunted. "Sounds like bunk to me."

Mr. Dumfrey whirled on him. "It isn't bunk, young man," he said, in an exasperated voice. "I'll have you know that the 'Malevolent Murders' section of the Hall of Wax attracts more visitors than—"

"Dumfrey!" Hardaway snapped, and Dumfrey quickly shut up. Hardaway took two steps toward Dumfrey, past a still-quivering Miss Fitch. His large jaw was working back and forth, and it reminded Sam of the fossilized jaw of the prehistoric ferret they kept in the Hall of Worldwide Wonders. "Get your things together You're coming with us."

"Are you arresting me?" For a second, Mr. Dumfrey looked truly afraid.

Hardaway smiled meanly. "Should I?"

"Of course not!" Mr. Dumfrey said. "I told you, I had nothing to do with poor Potts's death."

"Then you got nothing to worry about," Hardaway said. But he didn't sound as if he meant it. "Now step on it."

"Mr. Dumfrey!" Sam burst out. He wanted to say something—anything—to show Mr. Dumfrey they were all on his side. But the words had caught in his throat.

"Don't worry," Mr. Dumfrey assured him in a whisper. "It's just a matter of routine. Some questions and quibbles. I'll be back in no time. You'll see."

He placed a reassuring hand on Sam's shoulder, and then he was gone.

But hours passed, and Mr. Dumfrey did not return. Instead, more police officers arrived. The street was bathed in rotating red lights, and Sam watched from the windows as a crowd gathered outside the museum. He saw Billy the sidewalk apple peddler and Sol from the corner candy store and Sergio pushing his pretzel cart—all of them whispering and pointing and shaking their heads. He could only imagine what they were saying.

Two men lifted Potts onto a wheeled stretcher and covered his face with a white sheet. They carried him outside and loaded the body into a waiting van, and when the front door opened, Sam heard the roar of conversation from the crowd gathered outside.

"Poisoned . . ."

"Police took Mr. Dumfrey . . ."

"There was always something off about him . . ."

"About *all* of them . . ."

He turned away from the windows, letting the curtains swing closed, feeling sick. He turned around and saw Pippa standing right behind him.

"Mr. Dumfrey will be okay, Sam," she said. Sometimes it did really seem as though she could read minds, even though he knew that her gift was fuzzy, undirected, and usually only allowed her to see matchbooks and penknives in pockets and loose paper clips at the bottom of briefcases. In this instance, however, he knew she was probably just as worried about Mr. Dumfrey as he was.

"You'd have to be dumber than a dung beetle to think Mr. Dumfrey could kill anyone," she continued.

Sam did not say that he wouldn't be surprised if Hardaway and Webb *were* dumber than dung beetles. He just said, "Who did kill him, then?"

"You heard what Mr. Dumfrey said. It's not our business anymore." She sucked a strand of dark hair into her mouth, as she did when she was anxious or upset. Funny that they had spent so many years living here, side by side, but had only recently started to become close.

Started to become friends.

"Mr. Dumfrey needs our help, Pip. You were the one who said so."

"Mr. Dumfrey can take care of himself," she said, but she didn't sound totally convinced.

No one bothered to open the museum for the day. There seemed no point, with Dumfrey gone. Besides, they would only attract gawkers and gossips, people who wanted to point and sniff around and see the room where Potts had died. At 2:00 p.m., a policeman arrived and, in a high voice trembling with its own self-importance, instructed them that the museum would stay closed pending an investigation.

"Until when?" Monsieur Cabillaud cried.

"Until we say so," the policeman said. Before leaving, he posted a large sign on the double-fronted glass doors: CLOSED UNTIL FURTHER NOTICE BY ORDER OF THE POLICE.

There was nothing to do but wait. Thomas tried to distract them with a game of DeathTrap, but Sam had trouble understanding the rules and an argument broke out after Pippa accused Max of moving around the pieces when no one was looking.

Later on, as evening fell, Danny retrieved his violin, but after he launched into a mournful rendition of "My Love Was Sent to Hang for Murder," everyone begged him to stop. Phoebe made pancakes for dinner, and Miss Fitch was too distracted to lecture the children about sugar consumption. In fact, she even served them extra-large portions of whipped cream, which made Sam feel somehow worse.

"'The silence often of pure innocence persuades when speaking fails,'" Smalls said solemnly, laying one of his massive hands on Sam's head, as if Sam were still a child. "Shakespeare."

It might have made Sam feel better, if he understood what it meant.

At nine o'clock, Sam once again went to the window, and saw that although the crowd had mostly dispersed, there were still a half dozen people gathered in the street, including Bill Evans. Almost as soon as Sam had parted the curtains to peek out, a woman with a face so narrow it looked as though it had been compressed between two heavy metal plates, pointed at him and screeched "Look! It's one of them freaks! Right there, see? A face like the devil."

Sam stepped back from the window, his heart beating very fast.

At ten o'clock, when Mr. Dumfrey still hadn't returned, Monsieur Cabillaud wrapped his small head in a voluminous scarf, straightened his bow tie, and affixed a small gold pin to the front of his lapel, which he had allegedly earned for secret acts of bravery related to the Belgian government.

"I, Monsieur Cabillaud, will go and speak to your American police," he said grandly. "I will tell zem that zey have made a gravest error."

At ten thirty, Miss Fitch appeared in the attic, and in a shrill voice commanded everyone to go to bed. But no sooner had she left the room than Monsieur

Cabillaud burst into the room, his bow tie crooked, his scarf in disarray, his face drained of color.

"It is too late," he panted out, leaning against the doorway, sucking in deep breaths of air. "Zee police have arrested Mr. Dumfrey. Zey have arrested him for zee murder of Mr. Potts."

16

"**E**vans," Thomas announced the next morning, slapping a folded newspaper down on the foot of Pippa's bed.

"Good morning to you, too," she mumbled, sitting up. For a second, she thought that everything that had happened yesterday—Potts's death, the police, Mr. Dumfrey's arrest—must have been part of a horrible dream. She rubbed her eyes and the attic came into focus, as did the newspaper headline.

DERANGED PROFESSOR RATTIGAN STILL MISSING FROM PRISON.

"Who's Professor Rattigan?" she asked, wrinkling her nose.

"Oops." Thomas flipped the paper over, and Pippa saw an even larger headline, trumpeted practically across the whole page.

MURDER MUSEUM!

DEATH STRIKES AGAIN AT DUMFREY'S HOUSE OF HORRORS!

by Bill Evans

"What did that skunk write about us now?" Max, who was still in her pajamas, said.

"About what you'd expect. Dumfrey went crazy over the stolen head. Thought Potts might be to blame. So Dumfrey killed him. And we're all in on it." Thomas frowned and was quiet for several moments. "We have to go see him," he announced.

"Dumfrey?" Pippa asked.

Thomas shook his head. "Evans."

"Are you crazy?" Max burst out. "No way. He hates us."

"He doesn't hate us," Thomas said. "He's just trying to sell papers."

"Well, I hate *him*." Max crossed her arms.

"Listen." Thomas lowered his voice. "We've got to help Mr. Dumfrey. We all know there's no way he killed Potts, right? But somebody did. And Evans can help us. He's been sniffing around this story from the start. He has the *facts*."

Max made a harrumphing sound but said nothing. In the quiet, Pippa heard Sam snoring peacefully on the other side of the bookcase that divided the girls' sleeping area from the boys'. She wondered how he could sleep so well after everything that had happened.

"Mr. Dumfrey would do it for us," Thomas said, this time turning pleadingly to Pippa. His hair, she noticed, was sticking almost straight up from his head. "Mr. Dumfrey would do anything for us. He treats us like family. He *is* family."

"But . . ." Pippa shook her head. Thinking of Mr. Dumfrey in jail made her feel angry and hopeless and then angry again. Who would warm his slippers by the radiator for him? Who would make sure he remembered not to eat any chocolate before bedtime? Would he even get any chocolate? "How can we help him? What are we supposed to do? We're nobodies."

Thomas cracked a smile. "We're the freaks of Dumfrey's Dime Museum," he said. "That has to count for something."

Max stood up, scrubbing her eyes with a fist. "All right," she said. "But don't blame me if Evans ends up with a knife between his tongue and his tonsils."

Pippa forced a small smile back. "You in, Sam?" she asked, raising her voice.

He grunted something that sounded like "steel leap-ing" but she recognized as "still sleeping." Thomas grabbed a copy of *Statistics for Everybody* and chucked it over the bookcase. It landed with a thunk.

"Ow!" Sam exclaimed. A second later his head appeared over the bookshelf. "What was that for?" he asked.

"I'll take that as a yes," Pippa said. This time, she smiled for real.

Getting out of the museum proved more difficult than Pippa had expected. No sooner had she opened the front door than an explosion of voices began screeching—"There she is! That's one of 'em!"—and she was blinded by a series of flashes as dozens of cameras went off simultaneously. Sam leaned over and shoved the door closed so forcefully, it rattled on its frame.

"I think we'll take the back door today," he said lightly. But he wasn't smiling.

The back door opened up from the kitchen into a grungy courtyard set six feet below street level and filled with trash bins and glass seltzer bottles. It was, thankfully, empty of press and of onlookers. Forty-Fourth Street was also free and clear, except for a spiffily dressed man walking a pair of poodles and a blues singer busking for change at the corner. Hardly anyone but the milkman knew about the museum's back entrance, which was unmarked. Thomas led the way, then Max; Pippa followed her, and Sam took up the rear, hunching his chin to his chest and trying to make himself as inconspicuous as possible. Pippa hugged her thin jacket more closely around herself.

It was a pretty spring day, and the sun was perched high and round on a pillow of fluffy clouds, but the cold came from deep inside. Everything had changed overnight. They were trapped like specimens in their own museum, while people made up stories and lies about them. They might as well be pinned behind glass. And poor Mr. Dumfrey . . .

They walked two blocks east before cutting downtown, passing into an area thick with dazzling marquees and Broadway theaters, women in massive fur coats despite the weather, and newsies hawking papers on the corners; ticket booths and music halls and the smell of roasted peanuts. Here no one glanced at them at all, and Pippa began to feel a little better.

It was just before they reached the Times Square subway entrance when it happened. They were passing underneath a vast network of scaffolding. Dizzyingly high above them, Pippa could see men drilling and pacing the roofs, and the air was loud with the sound of jackhammers and shouting. Sam stopped to tie his shoelaces and Pippa paused a few feet in front of him, craning her neck, staring up at the buildings rising hugely toward the sky, like fingers pointing the way to something.

On the scaffolding forty feet above their heads, a dark shape teetered. At first Pippa thought a person had slipped or jumped; then her heart stopped and she saw that a vast concrete block was tumbling through the air toward Sam.

"Sam!" she screamed.

Sam looked up and covered his head just in time. The concrete block hit his fists and shattered on impact. Pippa ducked as a chunk of stone came flying in her direction.

Thomas and Max came dashing back toward them. Thomas hooked Sam under the arm and tried to lift him to his feet. "Are you all right?"

Sam gently detached himself from Thomas's grip. "I'm fine," he said. His face was white, and he looked dazed, but he stood up, shaking his head. He flexed his fingers, wincing. "What happened?" he said. "Where did it come from?"

Pippa shook her head. "It—it must have fallen," she

said. The sidewalk was covered now with concrete fragments. Businessmen hurried past them, shooting the children aggravated looks, as though they had been the cause of the mess. The block that had fallen must have been the size of a car tire.

Thomas looked up. The workers on the roof were still dark shadows against the sun. No one shouted down to them. No one seemed to notice that the block had fallen. "The angle is wrong," Thomas said.

"What?" Sam was dusting himself off. The shattered concrete had left a fine film of white powder all over his clothes.

"If it fell," Thomas said, "it would have hit there." He pointed to a spot closer by several feet to the building from where Sam had been kneeling.

"So what are you saying?" Pippa's voice sounded especially high-pitched, even to her ears.

"I'm saying"—Thomas turned to her—"it was pushed."

Sam laughed uneasily. "I could have been killed."

"*Would* have been, if you was normal," Max said.

"Were normal," Pippa corrected.

"Maybe that was the idea," Thomas said.

"Come on, Thomas." Sam crossed his arms. "Who'd do a thing like that?"

"I don't know." Thomas scanned the sky, as though

expecting more danger to come tumbling down out of the air. "Let's not stick around to find out."

Pippa turned and cast one last glance at the scaffolding and the dark silhouettes of workers on the roof. For a second, she thought she saw a man in a long coat watching them, standing motionless at the exact spot from which the concrete block had fallen. But then she blinked, and he was gone.

17

The offices of the *Daily Screamer* were all the way downtown, near the vast, majestic pillars of city hall and the ever-frenzied financial district, where men puffing big cigars shouted trading advice to one another as they walked, and even the shoeshine boys gave stock tips. Here, Manhattan narrowed to a point, and Pippa always had the sense that it was in these few blocks that all of the excitement of the city was concentrated, as though every other street was running as rapidly as possible to this bustling, beating heart of the world, which pumped out the paper money people died and killed for and dreamed about and craved.

And even though Pippa still noticed signs of the

Great Crash everywhere—businessmen wearing old shoes and patched-up suits artfully concealed with thread and shoe polish, and plenty of hobos shuffling around rattling tin cans—things had begun to move again.

The heart was beating still.

The building that housed the *Daily Screamer* was a disappointment. Only four stories tall, squeezed between two buildings nearly twice its size, and made of limestone stained dark, it was like a black tooth in the middle of a fine white smile. A grungy plaque above the door identified it as "Home to the Finest Newspaper in This City or Any Other."

"Ready?" Thomas asked, pausing outside the front door. Pippa nodded. Even from the street she could hear the ringing of telephones and clanking of machinery.

"Here goes nothing," Thomas said, and pushed open the door.

The first thing Pippa noticed was the smoke. The whole room was enveloped by it, so it looked as though a soft blue mist had descended inside, and, as a result, everything—the maze of desks jammed together in a mysterious zigzag formation; the stacks and piles and mountains of paper teetering on every available surface; the men and women hunched at their desks, clacking away on dozens of typewriters—looked a little bit blurry. The carpet was stained gray from years of footprints and cigarette ash, and even the people looked gray, as though they hadn't seen daylight in several months.

"Can I help you?" A woman at the nearest desk swiveled around to face them. Her blond hair, like everything else in the room, was a dingy color. She blinked at them from behind thick glasses.

"We're here to see Mr. Evans," Thomas said. "Bill Evans."

The woman frowned. "What business do you have with Mr. Evans?"

"What business is it to you what business we got with Mr. Evans?" Max broke in, eyes flashing.

"An interview!" Thomas said quickly, before Max could get them in trouble. "We're here because he wanted to interview us. For an important story."

The woman looked them up and down, as if she couldn't believe there was anything of importance about them.

Just as she opened her mouth, however, a voice boomed out, "Did I hear someone say *interview*?"

Mr. Evans himself came striding down a long, dim hallway like a magician stepping out from behind a curtain. He was smiling hugely, showing off his gums.

"Thomas!" he boomed. "And the great Samson Jr.!" Sam turned red up to the tips of his ears. "And little Mackenzie."

"Little—" Max spluttered. But Mr. Evans had already rounded on Pippa and was pumping her hand vigorously.

"And Pippa! Always a pleasure, always a pleasure. Tell me, Pip—what do I have in my pockets today?" Before she had a chance to answer (thirty-seven cents, two pieces of Wrigley's gum, and a new Zippo lighter) he burst into loud and raucous laughter, as though he had told a joke, and clapped her so hard on the shoulder, she stumbled a little.

"This way, kids, this way. Straight down the hall and first door on your left. Let's get comfortable. You want something to drink? Coffee? Water? Whiskey? I'm just joking. It's too early in the day for whiskey."

As he spoke, he herded them down the hall and into a small glass-enclosed office. The front door was stenciled with gold lettering that read BILL EVANS, HEAD REPORTER. Mr. Evans caught Pippa staring at it.

"Not bad, huh?" He rapped on the door with a knuckle. "Just got my own digs a few days ago. People can't get enough of this shrunken head stuff. It's bigger than the Rattigan story!"

It was the second time Pippa had heard the name Rattigan in a day. "Who's Rattigan?" she said.

Mr. Evans gave an exaggerated shiver. "Nasty man. Smart as a snake and batty as a belfry. But you didn't come to talk about Rattigan." He laughed again and closed the door, gesturing for them to sit down. "Go ahead and put your feet up. I'll crank up the recorder. Just a copy, you know, in case I miss anything while we're gabbing. Better safe than sorry!"

"We didn't come here to be interviewed," Thomas interjected.

Mr. Evans paused with one hand hovering above the Dictaphone. "I'm sorry, son," he said. "I don't follow you. You said you came for an interview."

"We did." Thomas swallowed visibly. "We came to interview *you*."

Mr. Evans leaned back in his chair, stroking his mustache. "I see," he said, and Pippa thought she saw a smile flicker across his face. Suddenly, he leaned forward again. "All right. How about we make a deal? You ask me a question, and I ask you a question. Tit for tat. Fair's fair, right?"

Pippa didn't really think it was fair—but what choice did they have? She met Thomas's gaze, and Thomas shrugged.

"All right," Thomas said cautiously. "But we go first."

Mr. Evans smiled again, big and toothy. "By all means. By all means. Fire away."

There was a moment's awkward pause. Pippa realized they hadn't exactly planned what they were going to say. Fortunately, Sam jumped in.

"Was it really cyanide that killed Potts?" Sam asked. Pippa shivered involuntarily. It was terrible to hear the question out loud. It made it seem so real. She hadn't exactly liked Mr. Potts—nobody had, really—but still. No one deserved to die like that. Poisoned.

"That it was, my boy. The ME—that's the medical examiner, you know, who works on the body—said it was a dose large enough to flatten an elephant." Mr. Evans extracted a small cigarette from the box on his desk and tried several times to light it with a match. Pippa was about to suggest he use the lighter in his pocket but stopped herself. She didn't want him to think she was showing off. "Probably killed him instantly, poor fellow." Mr. Evans exhaled a foul-smelling cloud in their general direction. Pippa coughed. Mr. Evans barely glanced at her. "Tissue, my girl?" he said.

"But when did—" Thomas started to say. Evans held up a finger.

"Not so fast. My turn. Fair's fair, remember." He stretched his long fingers and bent over his typewriter.

"First question," he said, as his fingers flew over the keys. "How long has Mr. Dumfrey been having money problems?"

"I—I don't know," Thomas stuttered.

"He doesn't tell *us*." Pippa jumped to his aid. "He doesn't like to worry us with that stuff."

"Mmm-hmmm." Mr. Evans continued typing for several long moments. Pippa wondered how he could have gotten so much material from their responses.

"Our turn again," Thomas said.

Before he could speak, Max broke in: "How come you wrote all those lies about us in the paper?"

"That's the business, my girl." Mr. Evans grinned. "My turn!"

"Wait," Pippa said, glaring at Max. "That wasn't a real question. It didn't count."

"Of course it did!" Mr. Evans said cheerfully, and jammed the cigarette in the corner of his mouth, once more hunching over the keys. "Now, let's see. Where were we? Oh, yes. When did you first become aware that Mr. Dumfrey hated Mr. Potts?"

"He didn't!" Thomas cried.

"Mr. Dumfrey doesn't hate anybody," Pippa said.

"Don't you see?" Sam said. "He couldn't have killed anyone."

"He wouldn't hurt a fly," Max put in.

"Any time we find a spider in the museum, he makes us release it outside," Thomas said.

"And he's an awful crybaby," Sam said.

"He loves Christmas," Pippa offered.

"And children," Thomas said.

Mr. Evans's fingers were flying over the keys so fast they were a blur behind the haze of cigarette smoke. "Excellent, excellent," he muttered.

"Is it our turn now?" Pippa ventured.

"It is," Mr. Evans said.

"What time did—" she started to ask, but Evans cut her off again.

"No fair! That's two questions in a row!" he said.

"Are you out of your mind?" Max said.

"That's three questions!" Evans trumpeted.

Pippa stared at him. "But—but—"

"A deal's a deal. Now I get three." He whipped the paper, already full, from the typewriter, and fed a new one under the roller. "Tell me this: Where do you go to school?"

"We don't," Pippa said. She hurriedly added, "Monsieur Cabillaud teaches us."

"The pinhead?" Mr. Evans said.

"That's a question!" Max protested.

"He's very smart," Thomas said defensively. "He did

great things for the French government."

"The Belgian government," Pippa corrected.

Thomas turned to her, confused. "Are you sure he isn't French?"

Mr. Evans was typing and puffing so furiously, Pippa was afraid he might combust. "Answer me this," he said. "If two trains leave from Grand Central Terminal at nine a.m., and one goes sixty miles per hour and the second one goes forty miles per hour and must stop for a new paint job in New Haven, how fast will the first train have to go to get to Boston on time?"

There was a brief pause. Thomas frowned. "That question makes no sense," he said.

"Aha!" Mr. Evans said triumphantly, and peeled yet another sheet of paper, densely covered with words, from the typewriter.

"It's our turn to ask a question," Sam said firmly. Pippa could tell he was holding himself very carefully, so he didn't accidentally break anything.

"Go ahead." Mr. Evans sat back in his chair and finally extinguished his cigarette. Still, the air was cloudy with smoke and Pippa felt like her lungs were encased in a wet, smelly blanket. "I'm all finished."

Pippa was desperate to ask what he had written, but she didn't want to waste another question.

"What time did Mr. Potts die?" Thomas asked.

"Wish I could tell you," Evans said. Now that he wasn't typing anymore, he seemed once again at ease. He leaned back in his chair and interlaced his fingers. "Doc Rosenkrantz—that's the ME at Bellevue—is a hard nut to crack. He keeps his lid screwed on tight, if you catch my drift. Funny. Most people like to see their names in print."

"Not us," Pippa said pointedly.

"You might change your minds," Evans said with a wink.

She scowled.

"Now listen, kiddos." Mr. Evans put both hands on his desk and began to stand. "I don't want to take up too much more of your time—"

"That's all right," Thomas said. "We have just a few more—"

"So I'll just see you out. Thanks for dropping by. Always a pleasure."

Before they could protest, Mr. Evans herded the children out into the hall and ushered them back toward the front door. Even as he was pressing them out the door, he was beaming and shaking their hands.

"Incredible, all of you. Don't mind what the papers say, it's all the biz, ha. I'm your biggest fan, really I am, don't forget, Bill Evans has your back. . . ."

The door slammed shut behind them. And suddenly they were standing in the blazing sunshine with the blue sky high above them, stretched like a wire between the buildings. Pippa took a deep breath of clean air.

"Well, that was a waste of time," Max said.

"No, it wasn't," Thomas said quietly.

Max rounded on him. "Are you crazy? He didn't tell us nothing."

"Anything," Pippa couldn't help but saying. Max glared at her.

"He did, too," Thomas said. "He told us the name of the doctor—the medical examiner—who looked at Potts. Dr. Rosenkrantz. He'll have the answers we need."

Pippa hated to say she agreed with Max. "But you heard what Mr. Evans said. He said Dr. Rosenkrantz— or whatever his name is—would never talk."

"So we'll have to *make* him talk," Thomas said, and he turned to Sam, and grinned.

18

"No way," Sam said, for about the seventeenth time in two minutes, as they descended into the vast black entrance of the Chambers Street subway station. "You must be out of your mind. I'll wind up in jail next to Dumfrey."

Thomas trotted beside him like a puppy hoping for a treat. "Okay, okay." He held up both hands. "No tough-guy stuff."

Sam stopped in the middle of the stairs, glaring, and an old woman, moving in the opposite direction, let out a volley of curses.

"Cross my heart and hope to die," Thomas said, making an *X* over his heart with a finger.

Sam sighed. "What's the plan, then?" he said.

They once again began making their way through the crowd, down the stairs, and into the tunnels. Sam was already tired. The interview with Bill Evans—the thought of seeing their names or, worse, their pictures, in the paper—had made his head hurt. His feet hurt, too. His shoes were too small—everything was always too small.

He just wouldn't stop growing. Sometimes, he lay in bed with his ankles sticking out over the footboard and his head banging up against the wall, and he tried to think very small thoughts: of being squeezed inside a walnut; of fitting, like Thomas, into a pipe in the wall; of being pressed underneath a gigantic thumb. He kept hoping that if he thought hard enough, it might help him shrink a little. But so far, nothing was working.

Dumfrey thought it was wonderful. "You're a strong man, Sam!" he always said with a hearty laugh. "The strongest boy in America. You'll look good with some size on you."

What Dumfrey didn't understand was that Sam didn't *care* about being a strong man. All he wanted was to be normal. He wanted to play with a puppy without worrying about knocking the air out of its little lungs. He wanted to be allowed to hold Cornelius in his hand, like Thomas did, and feed him bread crumbs. He didn't *want* to yank doors off their hinges accidentally. He didn't like the fact that he could not give Pippa a hug when she was upset because he risked crushing her ribs.

He remembered how the detectives had looked at him at Anderson's apartment, after the door had splintered to pieces at his touch. Like he was some kind of freak.

Well, he was.

"All you've got to do is get us in," Thomas said. His eyes were bright and it occurred to Sam that he was actually *enjoying* himself.

"In where?" Sam said suspiciously.

"The morgue," Thomas said, and ducked under the turnstiles without paying a token. Sam frowned and pushed two tokens into the coin slot.

"Like—like where they put the dead people?" Max stuttered.

"Sure," Thomas said, turning to her. "But you aren't scared of a few dead bodies, right, Max? You've seen plenty."

Sam heard the challenge in his voice. Max must have, too.

"Sure," she said, turning away from him.

"Even still," Sam leaped in, in a desperate attempt to

show that he, at least, was on Max's side, "we can't just walk in."

"We're not going to *walk* in," Thomas said. "*You*"—he placed a finger on Sam's chest—"are going to *break* in."

"Usually"—Sam panted—"when you say"—he huffed and strained—"you have a *plan*"—he adjusted his feet for purchase and heard the lock on the other side of the door whine in protest—"it has"—another hard shove and the door shuddered against his back—"more than one"—he turned around and pushed with both hands—"step," he finished, breathing hard, as the steel lock gave way.

The service door opened with a long *creeeeak.*

The morgue was in the basement of Bellevue Hospital, all the way on the east side, on First Avenue between Twenty-Sixth and Twenty-Ninth Streets. Pippa knew this because the previous year when one of Miss Groenovelt's spotted tabby cats had died, she insisted that it had been foul play and had carried the body there for an autopsy. She had come back sputtering in outrage after they explained that it was not the habit of New York City medical examiners to conduct postmortems on cats. Pippa had spent many afternoons sipping weak chamomile tea and comforting

Miss Groenovelt as she blubbered about poor Tabitha.

"Well?" Sam said, stalling. He hated hospitals, even more than he hated the thought of dead bodies. Hated the thought of illness and bedpans and, on the crazy ward, people strapped to their cots. "What now?"

Thomas answered him by slipping inside. Sam was glad that Thomas had at least taken the lead. He cast one last glance behind him. They'd snuck out just after dinner, and the sun was now setting beyond the spiky line of buildings, layering the sky with colors that looked as if they belonged in Sol's Candy Shoppe. For one wild second, Sam had the urge to run.

"Come on, Sam," Pippa whispered, gesturing to him to hurry up. He filed in after her, easing the door closed behind him.

Once they were inside, the sounds of car traffic from First Avenue, and the stink of fish from the East River, faded. They were standing at one end of a long, ugly hallway, poorly lit, that smelled simultaneously of lemon oil and unwashed sheets. From somewhere above them, Sam heard the squeak of shoes and the hum of machinery. He imagined, too, that he heard someone moaning.

To their right was a short flight of stairs leading upward, and signs pointing the way to registration and metabolic unit and psychiatric and accident and emergency: all words that made Sam feel like a thousand insects were crawling over his skin.

"This way." Thomas had unconsciously dropped his voice to a whisper. He gestured the group forward. At the far end of the hall—it seemed miles and miles away—was a small sign indicating the way to a second set of stairs.

They inched forward together. Although it was dinner hour and they were alone in the hall, Sam had the impression that eyes were everywhere, watching him. The hall was very cold and lined on either side with small rooms; he was afraid to look inside to see what they contained.

"This place gives me the creeps," Max muttered.

"Me, too," Sam said, and then wished he hadn't. He should have said, instead, that he wasn't scared at all.

When they were twenty feet from the stairs going down, a door suddenly opened in front of them, and a nurse's voice drifted out: "That's a good girl, Mrs. Marsh, be a sport. I'll be right back." Her elbow appeared; then her right foot.

They froze. Pippa gave a squeak of fear. Sam's stomach plunged all the way to his toes, and he wondered whether he would have to go to surgery if it were to get stuck there. The nurse was coming into the hall. She would find them and arrest them for trespassing, and they would be sent to jail.

Or even worse, to Bellevue.

At the last minute, the nurse clucked her tongue and said, "Now *don't* do that, Mrs. Marsh," and retreated back into the room. But Sam knew they had mere seconds before she reappeared.

Thomas was the first to recover. He sprang toward the first door he saw and threw it open. It was a broom closet, no wider than a coffin, and cluttered with cleaning supplies and buckets, old mops and stiff rags. Thomas practically shoved Pippa inside, and Sam crowded after her, uncomfortably aware of the fact that he was pressing against her back and that her hair was tickling his chest. Thomas folded himself up at their feet.

"Let me in!" Max whispered, jabbing Sam from behind with an elbow.

"There's no room!" Pippa squealed. "Sam, stop crushing me."

"Shhh," Thomas hissed.

"Sorry, I'm trying to—"

"I *said* you're crushing me."

"SHHH."

"Let. Me. In!"

Pippa pushed. Sam leaned back. And Max went stumbling backward into the hallway, just as Thomas reached up and closed the door.

Sam nearly went hurtling after her. He heard the creak of a door again, and the nurse's cooing voice.

"We can't just—" he started to say.

"SHHH," Thomas and Pippa said at once.

"—leave her," he finished in a whisper.

But even as he spoke, he heard the nurse's voice through the door.

"What are *you* doing down here, dearie?" the nurse said. "There's no visitors allowed in the contagious ward."

Sam knew how much Max would hate to be called dearie. He only hoped she would restrain herself from sticking a knife in the woman. Then she'd never get out of Bellevue.

Luckily, when Max spoke she sounded very unlike herself: young, and deeply apologetic. "Sorry. I—I got lost, I guess."

Sam felt a warm rush of admiration for her. She knew how to lie to get herself out of a bad spot. He would probably have gone straight to pudding.

"Oh, you poor thing!" the nurse said. "Let me guess.

You're here for your mommy, aren't you?"

"Yeah," Max said quickly. "I'm here for my, um, mommy." On this last word, Max rapidly turned a choking sound into a cough.

Pippa shifted so her shoulder was digging uncomfortably into Sam's chest. Sam tried to glare at her, but it was too dark. And Thomas was planted directly on his feet, which were starting to go numb.

"Let me take you upstairs, dear," the nurse said. "I'm sure we can find your mommy."

"That's okay—" Max started to say.

But the nurse cut her off. "It's no trouble at all, dearie. No trouble at all. Come on, this way. Take my hand, like a good girl."

It might have been Sam's imagination, but he thought he heard Max mutter something very quiet (and very rude) under her breath. But the nurse kept babbling over her—"There's a good girl, how frightening to be lost in this big place on your own"—and then Sam heard the squeak, squeak, squeak of the nurse's shoes against the tile floor. He could no longer feel his feet, and Pippa's shoulder made every breath painful.

At last, when the nurse's footsteps had receded, Thomas pushed open the door. Pippa practically shoved Sam out into the hall, gasping.

"You nearly turned me into a pancake," she said accusatorily.

He rubbed the cavity of his chest, where her shoulder had been digging a hole. "Well, you nearly turned me into a doughnut." He stamped his feet to try and get the feeling back.

"Come on," Thomas said. "There's no time for arguing." And he started again in the direction of the stairs.

"What about Max?" Sam said. The nurse would surely soon discover she wasn't a visitor.

"Max can take care of herself, Sam," Pippa said. "We'll meet up with her later."

"But—" Sam started to protest.

"Do you want to help Dumfrey, or not?" Thomas's eyes were bright like two hard stones. Sam squeezed up his fists. But Pippa was right. If anyone would be okay, it was Max.

That's why he liked her so much.

"Fine," he said, and let out a breath he didn't know he'd been holding. "Fine," he said again.

"This way," Thomas said.

They hurried in silence down the length of the hall, to the stairs leading into the basement, and the sign pointing the way to the morgue.

19

The morgue was dark, and colder than Pippa expected. From somewhere in the blackness came the sounds of dripping, as though a faucet had been left on. She took a step forward and Thomas yelped.

"You stepped on my heel," he said.

"Your heel ran into my toe," she whispered back.

"What's that smell?" Thomas said, a little louder.

Pippa inhaled. It smelled a little bit like tub water after someone had just finished bathing or like sweaty feet that had been scrubbed repeatedly with soap.

Suddenly, the electric lights came on with a buzz and a whirr. Sam had found a switch on the wall, and

Pippa exhaled a little. She had imagined there would be bodies everywhere. But they were in a large room, very bare, very clean. One wall was fitted with cabinets, each the size of a small refrigerator.

"All right. What now?" Sam said.

They looked instinctively to Thomas, but he shook his head. "I—I'm not sure."

Pippa took a few steps into the room, lifting her fingers and grazing the wall of large metal cabinets. Immediately, she felt a jolt. She had a sudden vision, like a lightning bolt through her brain: a body, frigid and motionless, and two white feet, bloated as rotten fish. She stumbled backward, holding her head.

"What?" Thomas rushed toward her and grabbed her elbow. "What's the matter?" It was only then that she realized she'd cried out.

"P—people," she stuttered, pointing to the wall: a jigsaw pattern of cabinets, all fitted together. Now that she was focusing, she could see beyond them—*inside* them. She saw bodies, each draped in a sheet, all cold and sad like slabs of beef on a butcher's counter. "It's full of people."

"Over here." Sam's voice echoed a little in the big, dim space. He had moved into the adjoining room. Pippa saw three steel-legged tables, each draped in clean white linen, under which she could see more bodies, silhouetted: the lines of the chest and knees and even, in one case, a foot protruding from the sheet. Her stomach turned over. One of them was a woman, and one of them a girl not much older than Pippa herself, with blond hair the color of new straw.

"I wonder if one of them is Potts . . . ?" Even though Sam spoke quietly, his voice was amplified by the emptiness of the room, so Pippa felt as though he were shouting.

"That one," she said, raising a shaking hand toward the middle of the three tables. Even without lifting the linen she could see. It was effortless, far easier than looking in someone's pockets—perhaps because she did not have the resistance of another person's mind to contend with.

Recently, she had noticed a shift, a change in the way that her mind's vision worked. It was becoming easier to slide behind locked drawers and into suitcases, to *feel* what was there so strongly that it became a picture in her brain.

Sam peeled back the sheet, holding it carefully between two fingers, as if death were a germ and he were in danger of catching it. Thomas sucked in a breath and took a step closer to the body. Potts's face was ghastly and pale. His chest was as white as milk, and dark stitching crisscrossed his chest and stomach, where the doctors must have opened him up. His hands, which Pippa had seen so often clutching a mop, holding an old rag, or jiggling a toilet handle, now lay flat and useless on the table.

Footsteps echoed from somewhere above them. Sam made a strangled noise.

"Someone's coming," Pippa said, feeling a sudden surge of terror.

"Look." Thomas seized a piece of paper lying next to Potts; it was covered in densely packed writing. "It's the report on his death."

The footsteps were coming down the stairs.

"Take it," Pippa said. "And let's get out of here."

"We can't just steal it," Thomas said. His eyes were clicking rapidly along the page, left to right, like the Underwood typewriter in Anderson's office. "They'll know someone was here."

"And they'll know *we're* here if they catch us," Pippa said.

By now, they could hear voices. A man was saying: "Should be illegal, bodies turning up at all hours. Nine to five, I say, and let the rest of 'em wait."

A second, higher voice, squeaked, "Absolutely, sir. Very true, sir."

The first voice snapped, "Don't be an idiot! Of

course we can't expect dead people to maintain regular hours! Inconsiderate, every one of them. For God's sakes hold up the feet."

They were coming down the stairs. Sam flipped the sheet back over Potts's head. Thomas stuffed the report into his pocket. Pippa looked around wildly for a second exit, but there was none. They were trapped.

"We have to hide," Thomas whispered. And before Pippa could argue, he was drawing her into the first room, toward the large wall full of body-size cabinets.

"No." Pippa stopped short when she realized what Thomas expected of her. "No *way*."

"There's no other choice," he said.

Sam wrenched open a cabinet and, finding it empty, practically dove inside it.

"I won't," Pippa repeated. Thomas slid open the nearest cabinet, and the face of a dead man stared up at them. Pippa nearly screamed. He moved on to the next one. Also occupied, this time by a monstrously fat woman.

"A little help, Pip?" he whispered. He was sweating.

There was a scuffling sound on the stairs. One of the men exploded: "What did I tell you about his feet?"

Pippa's stomach was filled with lead. She knew that Thomas was right. They had no choice. "Over here," she whispered to Thomas. There was another empty cabinet, and she and Thomas squeezed in together. Pippa had to lie down on her back. It was very cold.

To keep them fresh, she thought, like vegetables, and felt the hysterical desire to laugh. She forced herself to breathe.

But as Thomas eased the cabinet closed, and they were swallowed in darkness, she couldn't help feeling as though they might never get out; they would get stuck here forever and die and end up just like the others.

Only a second later, the men stepped into the morgue. Their voices were very loud; they were less than three feet away.

"All right, what do you want to do with 'im?"

Pippa knew they must be bringing in another body. She prayed that the men would not think of placing him in a cabinet; she and Thomas would surely be discovered. Even though it was cold, her palms were sweating. She could hear Thomas breathing and, though she was comforted by his presence, wished she could tell him to shut up.

"Take him out for a date," the older man said, then gave an ugly laugh. "What do we usually do with 'em? Leave him out on the table, so the doc can start the slice and dice."

Footsteps squeaked on the floor as the men passed into the other room. She wished they would hurry. Pippa was desperate to get out of this terrible hole and wondered whether this was how Mr. Dumfrey felt, sitting in his jail cell. Thinking of Mr. Dumfrey steeled her nerves slightly. She was doing this for Mr. Dumfrey.

After what seemed like forever, the men's footsteps returned and then retreated up the stairs. Pippa tried to sit up, forgetting how small the space was, and banged her head.

"Ow," she said aloud in the darkness.

"Are you all right?" The cabinet slid open and Sam's face was revealed, blinking down at her and Thomas. Pippa squinted in the electric light, which seemed suddenly blinding.

"I'm all right," she said, sitting up, although she had a cracking headache. "Let's get out of here."

She had seen, she thought, enough dead people for one evening.

20

It wasn't until they reached the street that Thomas remembered Max—and then, only because Sam reminded him.

"We have to find her," Sam said. "We can't just abandon her."

Pippa looked as though she was inclined to disagree.

Thomas said, "She might have found her way out. She might be halfway back to the museum by now." He was desperate to return to the museum and read the report on Potts's death, still tucked neatly into his pocket.

"But what if she isn't?" Sam persisted with unusual force. For the first time it occurred to Thomas that

Sam must like Max—must like her a lot.

"All right, let me think." Thomas's head was pounding. Going back into Bellevue was a terrible idea. Someone would soon discover they had stolen the report from Potts's body, assuming it had not been discovered already. They needed to get off the street, as far away from Bellevue as possible.

But Sam was already heading toward Twenty-Eighth Street and the entrance to Bellevue.

"Where are you going?" Thomas said, hurrying after him. With a groan of protest, Pippa followed.

"To find Max," Sam responded.

"You can't just charge in there," Thomas said. "What excuse will you give?"

There was a girl tottering up the street, her hair in pigtails and wearing makeup, as though she had just stepped off the stage. Thomas noticed, vaguely, that her face looked sort of like a pickle: miserable and sour.

"Sam, *wait*," Thomas said, and in the process accidentally jostled the girl on the street. "Sorry," he mumbled, barely looking at her.

"Sorry!" the girl exploded. "Sorry? Is that all you've got to say to me, you giant nitwit?"

Thomas stopped, startled by the girl's outburst. Sam and Pippa stopped with him.

"I'm . . . very sorry?" Thomas said cautiously. It occurred to him that the girl might be one of the patients from Bellevue.

"Are you *serious*?" It was the girl's voice—familiar, abrasive, like the hard strike of steel against stone—that struck Thomas as suddenly familiar. "You ought to be licking my boots right now—all of you—you ought to be down on your knees and kissing my toenails—"

"Max!" Thomas cried out, just as she jutted her face further into the streetlight, and the familiar point of her chin and hard little nose and white scar were revealed beneath the thick coat of makeup.

Sam's jaw was nearly on the ground. "Is it—is it really you?"

"Who else would it be, you twerp?" Max nearly screamed, and gave Sam a hard whap on his arm. Thomas was sure it couldn't have hurt him, but Sam flinched and drew back several inches. Pippa stifled a laugh.

"Left me to the wolves . . ." As she spoke, Max began scrubbing at her face with the sleeve of a coat. Up close, the makeup was even more hideous than Thomas had judged it from a distance. Thick mascara clumped her lashes, and bright circles of rouge bloomed on her cheeks like a rash. Her lipstick was a hideous red and smudged around her lips. No wonder Max looked so upset.

"Calm down, Max," Thomas said. "Tell us what happened."

Max paused long enough to glare at him. "How do you expect me to calm down when I just spent the past hour playing Little Miss Muffet with a bunch of loonies?" she demanded, and then resumed her furious scrubbing. She yanked her hair out of the pigtails and threw down the hair ribbons, hard, in the gutter. "I look like a class-A idiot!"

"I think you look kind of . . . pretty," Sam ventured, in a small voice. For a moment, Thomas thought she would hit him again.

"Come on," he said, before Pippa could dissolve into giggles and make everything worse. "Let's get out of here."

By Thirty-Third Street, where they got into the subway, Max had calmed down—although she still refused to look at Sam, whom she inexplicably blamed for the whole episode. By vigorously raking her fingers through her hair, she had restored it to its normal state of wildness.

She told them how she had been hauled upstairs by the nurse and presented at the registration desk.

"And before I know it, some *wacko* in a nightgown comes barreling over, practically throws herself at me, and starts calling me sweetie pie," Max said, outraged. The makeup had mostly come off, except for thick smudges of mascara, which gave her the look of a raccoon. "Well, what was I supposed to do? She painted me up like a clown and made me play cards. I only got out of there when she nodded off."

Except for a homeless man dressed in toeless boots, a long overcoat, and a pair of aviator's goggles, the children were alone on the subway car as it lurched through the tunnels. Thomas, seeking once again to make peace, at last extracted the medical report from his pocket, smoothed it down on one thigh, and began to read.

"What about . . . ?" Pippa nodded toward the homeless man, whose chin was nodding on his chest.

"It's all right," Thomas said. He couldn't wait any longer. He scanned the page and its densely packed writing.

"Well?" Max said irritably. "What's it say?"

"Give me a second," Thomas said, frowning. Some of the words were unknown to him; others were illegible. Under *Cause of Death*, the medical examiner had printed *poisoning by cyanide*. That they already knew.

"Here," he burst out, and read, "'Subject'—that's Potts—'died between the hours of midnight and two in the morning on Thursday, April twenty-fifth.'"

Pippa shivered. "How awful."

Thomas kept on reading. "'Judging from the contents of the subject's stomach—'"

"Eww!" Max and Pippa burst out together and then glared at each other. Thomas ignored them.

"'—and also from the time of death, the poison was likely administered with the subject's dinner at around eight p.m. on Wednesday. Stomach contents—'"

"Thomas!" Max and Pippa shrieked.

"'—show dinner of roast beef, pickled onions, and'"— Thomas grimaced—"prune juice."

"Roast beef?" Max frowned. "We had canned tuna and old bread that night."

Pippa shook her head. "Potts didn't eat at the museum on Wednesday night. I remember—Goldini broke a cup and no one could find the broom and I thought Miss Fitch would burst into flame. Potts came home later."

Thomas had reached the end of the report. He stared at it for a moment longer, as though the words would float off the page and reveal something further to him. The subway screeched and jerked to a halt, and Thomas suddenly realized the train had arrived at their stop. But as Thomas and the others pushed onto the platform, he had the strangest sensation that they were being watched. He turned around as the doors slid closed and the train began to chug forward. The homeless man was awake now, staring at him with an amused expression. Thomas felt a small shock, as though he'd accidentally touched a socket without drying his hands. He had the strangest feeling he'd seen the man before.

But then the train was gone, swallowed up by the black tunnel, and Thomas pushed the thought out of his mind. It was late. He was probably imagining things.

"Thomas?" Sam, Max, and Pippa were already halfway down the platform, waiting for him.

"Sorry," he said, and hurried to catch up.

"We were talking about Potts's dinner," Pippa prompted.

Sam shoved his hands in his pockets as they moved down the empty platform toward the stairs that led to the street. "I guess the question is, where on earth did he eat?"

It was nearly ten o'clock at night and far too late to continue their investigation. They headed directly back to the museum. A fog had rolled in from the river and snuck between the buildings like some vast, yellow-furred animal. Even after Thomas had slipped beneath his thick woolen blanket in the attic and Sam was snoring peacefully next to him, he couldn't get warm—as though the fog had followed him up into the room and was tickling the soles of his feet.

His mind was turning restlessly. Potts had been murdered—why? Had he perhaps gone to see Mr. Anderson? But for what purpose? Thomas rolled over, pounding a lump from his pillow with a fist. Mr. Anderson couldn't help, either; he, too, had been killed. All after the disappearance of that stupid head . . .

Thomas remembered the gasp from the ancient lady—Mrs. Weathersby—in the front row the day the head had been revealed. She, too, was dead. What was the connection? Could the head really be cursed?

He dismissed the idea immediately. He had read every single book in the museum's library, many of them multiple times. He knew all about ghosts and witches, spell casting and ancient curses from the battered books Phoebe the Fat Lady brought home.

But he was very practical. He had been orphaned at a young age. He knew in all probability his real parents were dead. Or maybe they weren't. Maybe they just hadn't wanted him, because he was different, because he could make his joints bend backward and his heels touch his head.

He wasn't troubled by this idea—at least, he was not troubled by it very much. That was real life. He knew that people were afraid, and they disliked difference, and they sometimes acted cowardly.

He knew, too, that in real life, curses did not kill people. People killed people.

But *why*?

He got up. He would never sleep this way—not until he warmed up. He decided to go down to the kitchen and search for some milk in the icebox. Mrs. Cobble had sometimes heated it on the stove for him, with a little cinnamon and honey, to help him sleep.

It was very dark, and moonlight filtering through the high windows cast enormous shadows everywhere. He moved silently down the stairs, and had almost reached the ground floor when he heard muffled sounds of weeping. He froze, then inched forward, around the bend, holding his breath.

It was Phoebe.

She was crouched in the middle of the Hall of Wax, her bulging back and shoulders touched with silvery light. Her long hair was loose and she was cradling her head in her hands. Hugo was crouching next to her. He kept one hand several inches from her back, as though he wanted to touch her but was afraid that, for all her bulk, she would shatter.

"Shhh," he was saying. "It'll be all right."

"It won't be all right," she whispered fiercely, snapping up her head to glare at him. "How can you say that?" She let out another low moan, an animal sound, and covered her face again. "Poor Mr. Dumfrey! After everything he did for us . . . and now he's in jail! I'll never live it down. I won't."

"Bee," Hugo said—a nickname Thomas had never heard. "Bee, please. We're only doing what we must. To be happy. We deserve to be happy, don't we?"

Phoebe only responded by sobbing harder.

Thomas drew back and retreated up the stairs, abandoning his plan for warm milk. He would never be able to sleep tonight, anyway, even if he were bathed in a tub of it.

There was no longer any doubt. Phoebe and Hugo were involved, somehow, in some way, in this mess.

It was up to him to prove it.

21

Breakfast was getting worse and worse. When Max made it downstairs the following morning, she found Thomas, Pippa, and Sam sharing a plate of hard cheese and saltine crackers.

Sam slid over as soon as he saw her to make room for her on the bench. Ignoring him completely—she was still angry at him, mostly because he had told her she looked pretty with her hair tugged and pulled like a poodle's—she elbowed in next to Pippa.

Thomas was bent over a newspaper and every so often he groaned.

"What's the matter?" Max asked, popping a saltine in her mouth.

"What do you think's the matter?" Pippa said, and, whipping the newspaper out of Thomas's hands, slammed it down in front of Max.

Max was not a strong reader, but she recognized the name of the paper, *The Daily Screamer*, and could just spell out the headline that dominated the front page.

VILLAINS OR VICTIMS?

DUMFREY'S HORROR-HOUSE—A DANGER FOR OUR YOUTH

"So what's it all about?" Max said, shoving the paper back, so she wouldn't have to read the whole article herself. She didn't actually know *how* to read—at least, nothing more than a few street signs—though Monsieur Cabillaud was threatening to teach her.

"It's about us," Thomas said. He read: "'Dressed in foul-smelling rags, the children of Mr. Dumfrey's Dime Museum have been so systematically abused, they do not appear to know how pathetic they appear. . . .'"

"Pathetic?" Max screeched. "Smelly?" True, she did not often wash her hair. And true, she liked to wear her lucky jacket on a daily basis, the one with several pockets for her knives. But she was positive she didn't smell.

"'Isolated from children their own age, forced into the most despicable tasks, like cleaning the museum of spiders'—I never said he forced us to, did I? Just that he liked them released outside—"

"Go on, Thomas," Pippa said.

Thomas continued, "'and denied a basic education'"—Thomas frowned and lowered his voice, since Monsieur Cabillaud was sitting nearby—"'the children confuse major European countries and are unable to complete the most basic arithmetic'—he's twisted everything around, you see?—'and defend Mr. Dumfrey as if he were a father and not the man who has kept them in captivity all these years.'"

Max slammed a fist against the table, causing the cheese to levitate temporarily off its crackers. "I'll have him skinned!" she said. Then: "What's *captivity* mean?"

"It means," Pippa said, with a superior-sounding sniff, "that Mr. Dumfrey's been keeping us prisoner."

"That's bunk," Max said. "Mr. Dumfrey saved us." She watched Danny drift into the kitchen, his worried face barely level with the table; and Smalls, gripping a coffee mug, which in his enormous hand looked like a doll's teacup; and Monsieur Cabillaud with his scarf carelessly arranged around his tiny head. They belonged here, all of them. It was probably the first place they had ever belonged in their whole lives.

She, Max, belonged here, too.

"Listen." Thomas dropped his voice to a whisper.

"Something happened last night." Gesturing for them all to lean in, he explained what he had seen and overheard the night before. Then, leaning back, he said, "I have a plan."

"Big surprise," Max grumbled.

He acted as though he hadn't heard her. "We're going to have to split up. Max and I will follow Hugo and Phoebe. Sam and Pippa can try and figure out where Potts was on Wednesday night and who he was with."

"I think Max should come with me," Sam said immediately. "In case we need to, um, interrogate someone. Or intimidate someone. Or both."

Max rolled her eyes, even though secretly, she was pleased that Sam thought she was intimidating.

"Fine," Thomas said smoothly. "Pip and I'll follow Hugo and Phoebe, then. We'll meet back here later. Everyone got it?"

Pippa sighed. "Got it."

Sam smiled. "Got it."

"Got it." Max popped a saltine into her mouth and pocketed another for the road.

There were over two dozen bars, pubs, restaurants, and luncheonettes in the area immediately surrounding the museum, ranging from the decent to the disreputable to the disgusting, and it turned out Potts had, at some point or another, eaten, drunk, or gambled in nearly all of them.

Max had cooked up their cover story: they would pretend to be looking to track down their uncle and would give a description of Potts when asked what their uncle looked like. This required that they pose as brother and sister, an idea Sam initially resisted. But people would be more likely to talk, Max argued, if there was no question of murder, feeling proud of herself for thinking of it. Thomas wasn't the only brainy one in the group.

"I still don't see why we have to be related," Sam grumbled, after leaving Momma Maroon's Luncheonette, where the proprietor, an enormously fat woman with a face as red as an apple and thick eyeglasses, had said she could see the family resemblance perfectly.

Up and down the streets, into bars where the air was vibrating with smoke and foul smells, and restaurants where grubby-looking men were bent over thick bowls of soup and the floors were covered in peanut shells; hour after hour of the same response. *Yeah, sure. He sounds familiar. But haven't seen him in a few weeks at least. Sorry, kids. Better luck next time.*

"I'm starting to hate that word," Sam said on the

corner of Forty-Ninth Street, after their latest failure. "Luck."

Max kicked a trash can in frustration, and a stray cat leaped out from its depths and bared its teeth before slinking away. "This is crazy," she said. She had been excited to set out. But that was hours ago, and her saltine and cheese had long since been digested. She was hungry, and her feet hurt, and her jacket was making her hot. "He could have gone anywhere, with anyone, in the whole stupid city."

"We can't give up now," Sam said, but he sounded just as tired as she felt.

"What are we supposed to do?" Max said. "We've been at it for hours already." Max shoved her hands in her pockets. She was enraged and she didn't know why. She tried to direct her anger at Sam, but it didn't work. He looked tall and saggy and exhausted, like a piece of taffy that has been overstretched, and she could only feel bad for him.

Instead, she pushed her anger outward, onto the whole world, expanding it until it grew like a mist to cover everything around her. The world, Max felt, was an evil, rotten, pit of a place. Exhibit 1: She'd been dumped like a discarded banana peel by her own parents. Exhibit 2: She barely remembered the orphanage where she'd landed, but she did remember cages, like for animals, and people inside them, and darkness. Exhibit 3: Her foster mother took her in just to have someone to scrub her linens and wash out her toilet bowl, and Max had run away. Exhibits 4 through 87: She had lived on the streets and raised herself, learned to pickpocket and steal, memorized the best places to sleep so she wouldn't get chased off by the cops, made friends with the rats.

And the last, final proof: she had finally found a place where she was safe, and that, too, was in danger.

"All right," Sam said with a sigh, looking more like a sad stretched piece of taffy than ever. "Let's go home."

On the corner of Ninth Avenue and Forty-Fourth Street, Sam stopped to tie his shoes for at least the third time that day. Max waited for him impatiently, shifting her weight, both dreading what they would have to say to Pippa and Thomas and eager to get it over with.

They had paused in front of Paulie's—a restaurant so grubby that they had skipped over it entirely. Even Potts couldn't have been tempted to eat there. Through grease-streaked windowpanes, Max saw a dozen people huddled like refugees over their plates.

Down the street, Max noticed a woman wearing an enormous hat and a fur collar, despite the sunny April weather. She was distributing fliers and jabbering at a high volume to everyone who passed, although Max could not make out what she said. And on the opposite side of the street, coming from the direction of Eighth Avenue—

"Pippa!" she called out, waving. "Thomas!"

They looked just as tired and discouraged as she felt. Thomas had a dusting of white plaster in his hair, which made him look like an old man. Pippa's dress, normally stiff and starched and perfect, was splattered with mud and torn at the hem.

"What happened to *you*?" Max and Pippa asked, at the exact same time.

"I asked first," they said again, together.

"We lost them," Thomas said. "We followed them halfway across the city and back again, in and out of shops, then down to Fourteenth Street, and—poof! They disappeared."

"Disappeared where?" Max asked.

"If we knew that—" Thomas started to say. But by that point the woman with the fliers had advanced even farther down the street, and Max made out, finally, what she was saying.

"These poor, helpless children," she wailed as she shoved pamphlets in the hands of passersby.

"Extraordinary and underappreciated! Uneducated! Underfed! Overexploited and worked half to death, like plow mules. It's an outrage, and Mr. Dumfrey must be held accountable. . . ."

"Uh-oh," Max muttered. She felt like she was frozen and watching a steam engine bear down on her. But before she could squeak out a single word of warning, the woman's eyes pivoted in her direction—small, beady eyes set deep in a face as pink as a baby's scrubbed bottom.

"You!" she cried, her eyes gleaming as she took in Thomas and his dusty hair, Max's ragged coat, Sam with one shoe untied, and Pippa's torn and ragged dress. "How remarkable! How *extraordinary*! Which one of you is Sam? Aha—the little one is Thomas! And this must be Philippa, and Mackenzie."

"Max," Max said, but the woman ignored her.

"It's really an incredible coincidence," the woman said. "I've just been talking about all of you—you poor, poor things. Are you cold? Or too hot? Can I get you anything to eat?"

Max was hungry, actually, but she kept her mouth shut.

"Who *are* you?" Thomas said.

The woman laughed, a laugh as shrill as the whistle

from a steam pipe. "How silly. Of course. I haven't introduced myself. It's just as though I feel we know each other . . . My name is Andrea von Stikk." She paused, as if waiting for her words to take effect. "Of the Von Stikk Society for Children's Welfare? Of Von Stikk's Home for Extraordinary Children?" She looked at them expectantly, and, when no one said a word, shook her head and sighed. "Poor creatures. You really have been terribly undereducated. But all that will be sorted out quickly when we get you into our home. We have a wonderful school, of course, and programs for educating young boys and girls in over a dozen fields of work. . . ."

Max heard several words she disliked strongly: for example, *work* and *school*.

"Now, come along," the woman said, and spread her arms as though she intended to wrap them in a hug—another thing Max hated. "Let's find somewhere *decent* to sit and talk."

As she said the word *decent*, she cast a disapproving glance at Paulie's restaurant, and it gave Max an idea.

"Sorry," Max blurted. "We're in a rush. Important business."

"Business?" Andrea chirped primly, as if she'd never heard the word.

"Places to go, people to see, bodies to bury—you know, the usual. Anyways, nice to meet you, see you never, and thanks for the chat." As Max spoke, she took Pippa by the arm and hauled her into Paulie's. Thomas and Sam hurried after them.

"But wait!" Andrea shrieked. "You can't go in there! It simply isn't suitable for childr—"

The door swung shut behind them, blocking out the sound of her outraged voice. And, as Max had expected, she didn't follow them into Paulie's. She wouldn't dare.

"If she called me poor dear one more time . . . ," Pippa said, shaking her head and making a vaguely threatening gesture with her fist. Max felt a brief flicker of admiration for her. But it was quickly snuffed out. "Ew," Pippa said, looking around them. "What *is* this place?"

The air in Paulie's was thick with the smell of boiled cabbage, cigarette smoke, and rancid meat. Behind the counter, a mammoth man wearing a blood-caked apron was frying up bacon. A waiter with the guilty look of an escaped convict was hurrying among the rickety tables, which were covered not with tablecloths but old, grease-spotted newspapers. In one booth, a man with dirt-encrusted fingers was noisily slurping coffee as black as tar; at the counter, two toothless women were dealing cards. The other patrons of Paulie's looked as sad, scared, and pathetic as any Max had ever seen.

"What're you doing in here?" The man in the butcher's apron—Max assumed he was the owner—came bellying out from behind the counter. "We're not buying nothing, so you can take whatever you're sellin' and get going."

They needed to stall. Max wasn't ready to risk another run-in with Angela von Stuck-up, or whatever her name was.

"We're looking for our uncle," she said quickly. Pippa and Thomas gave her a confused look, but Sam picked up on the game right away.

"That's right," he chimed in. They had practiced their parts all day long. "He wanders off sometimes. Gets confused." Sam lowered his voice conspiratorially. "He's not all there in the head."

The man in the butcher's uniform smiled. Half his teeth were rotting. "Sounds like one of our customers, all right," he said, and then let out a booming laugh. Max was blasted by the smell of his breath and did her best not to flinch. "The name's Paulie," the man in the apron said. "This is my joint. I'm here all day, every day. I remember everybody who walks through those doors. What's he look like, this uncle of yours?"

"Dark hair," Sam said. "Tall—even taller than me. Wears a gray cap, pulled low, and has scars on his cheeks."

It was the same description they had given to twenty other restaurant and pub owners that morning. But this time, Paulie began nodding slowly, so his many chins wobbled like a turkey's neck.

"Yeah," Paulie said thoughtfully, wiping his hands across his apron. "Yeah. Sounds familiar. This would have been . . . Wednesday, right?"

Max swallowed back a little cry of excitement. Thomas and Pippa exchanged a glance. Wednesday was the night Potts had been poisoned.

"Exactly," Max said eagerly. "Wednesday."

Paulie stepped aside as the waiter skirted by them, holding a stack of dirty plates. "Yeah, he was here," Paulie said. "They sat right over there."

This time, Max couldn't conceal her excitement.

"*They?*" she asked. "He was here with somebody?"

"Sure was. Didn't get a good look at the other guy. He was wearing a hat. Your uncle seemed worked up about something, though."

The waiter was still hovering nearby. He had deposited the stack of plates and was now pretending to wash the counter, although Max felt sure that he had never washed a single surface in Paulie's in his life. He was eavesdropping. She gave Sam a nudge.

"And you don't remember anything about the—the other guy?" Thomas asked.

Paulie turned to him. "He your uncle, too?" He gave a mean smile. "Like I said, I didn't get a good look at the other guy. All's I know is your uncle was nervous."

Thomas nodded, frowning a little. Pippa had closed her eyes and her face was very pale. Max realized, with a little start, that she was trying to read. She was trying to think her way into the folds of Paulie's brain.

"Look," Sam spoke up suddenly. "We're going to be honest with you."

Max shot him a look. This was not part of the script they had agreed on.

"It's really important we find out who our, um, uncle was with on Wednesday," Sam said. "The truth is he was poisoned, and—"

Sam did not get any further. Because the waiter, with a short, anguished cry, vaulted over the counter, knocking over the entire stack of dirty dishes, and sprinted for the door.

22

S am was the first to move. He reached for the waiter but succeeded only in getting his apron, which promptly tore off in his hand.

The waiter ricocheted off a table, upsetting a bowl of soup and sending a chair crashing to the ground, where it promptly splintered. Everyone was shouting, and the women at the bar began to shriek.

The waiter made it to the door and tore off down Forty-Fourth Street.

The kids sprinted after him. Thomas was next out the door, and then Sam. Max followed them and Pippa came last, her breath high in her throat, her head pounding. Trying to read Paulie had left her exhausted and frustrated.

What good was being a mentalist if you couldn't read minds?

When Pippa emerged onto the street, the waiter was already crossing Ninth Avenue. Thomas was fifteen feet behind him and gaining fast. Pippa tore after them, forgetting entirely to look both ways for traffic and throwing herself into the street. Several horns blared; an ice-cream truck swerved to avoid her, and she passed practically underneath a horse pulling a coal wagon, provoking an outraged whinny and a string of curses from the driver.

Thomas was gaining on the waiter. Ten feet, then seven . . . Pippa watched with her heart in her mouth as Thomas swung himself up onto a parked car and then vaulted like a gymnast into the air. . . .

At the last second, the waiter swerved, and Thomas landed hard, directly where the waiter had been a second before. He tumbled, did a somersault, and scrambled to his feet. But by then, the waiter had regained an advantage.

"Stop him!" Sam cried. "Somebody stop him!"

Two young men in sailor uniforms were approaching from the opposite direction. Hearing Sam shout, they braced themselves, intending to block the waiter's progress. But he barreled through them at such speed that they tumbled backward, landing in a tangled heap on the sidewalk. Sam, bolting toward them, caught a foot on one of their knees and went sprawling down to the pavement, landing with a gigantic crack where the sidewalk split underneath his palms.

Ahead of Pippa, Max suddenly stopped and began rummaging in her pockets. Pippa just managed to swerve to avoid her.

"What are you doing?" she called over her shoulder. Max was crossing the street and didn't seem to hear. "Come on!"

The waiter was nearly at Eighth Avenue, close to a big corner magazine stand. Once he reached Broadway, he could easily lose himself in the crowd or duck into any one of the theaters. It was up to her. . . . But she couldn't run any faster . . . she was losing him.

Suddenly, there was a whistling in her ears, and she felt a hard breeze blow by her. Before she could register what had happened, the waiter was pinned against the side of a building, his shirt at his ears, struggling like a fish on a line. Pippa approached him at a trot.

Then she saw the knives—one on each side of his neck—keeping his shirt tacked to the wooden wall of the magazine stand.

Winded and panting, Sam and Thomas joined her. Max came last, darting out across the traffic from the other side of the street, where she must have planted herself to aim.

"Nice . . . going," Sam said, gulping for air.

"Nothing to it." Max shrugged.

"P-please." The waiter was wiggling and squirming, desperately trying to pull himself free of the knives that had him pinned to the wall like a bug on a display board. "P-please. Let me go. I didn't do nothing. I swear, I swear. I didn't mean nothing by it."

"Yeah?" Sam reached up and withdrew the knives. The waiter collapsed in a heap, moaning a little. "Then why'd you run?"

The waiter cowered, holding up both arms to shield himself as if worried that Sam might use the two knives to gouge out his eyes. His thin bottom lip was quivering. "You gotta believe me," he said, and Pippa thought he might start to cry. "I didn't mean nuthin' by it. I was just doing my job, see?"

"Didn't mean nothing by *what*?" Thomas said.

"The rats." Now the waiter did start to sniffle. He ran a hand under his nose and Pippa was disgusted to see that it left a trail like that of a slug. She could only pray he would wash before returning to work.

Thomas and Sam exchanged a bewildered look. "What rats?"

"It's part of my job, see?" the man continued. "When the rats start to get bad, I'm supposed to take the tin from the back and spread the poison around in the corners and the kitchen." The waiter choked back a sob. "The rats was so bad on Wednesday I put extra out. Sprinkled it even in the shelves and under the tables. But I musta—I guess I musta accidentally got some in your uncle's grub. See? But I swear—I swear!—I didn't mean to!"

The waiter began to wail so loudly, several people on the opposite side of the street turned to stare.

"Shhh." Max hushed him harshly. "Calm down, all right? No need to blubber like a baby." But this just made the man wail even louder.

"What kind of poison do you use on the rats?" Thomas asked patiently.

"Cy—cy—cy—" the waiter blubbered.

"Cyanide," Pippa breathed, and the waiter nodded. Thomas glanced meaningfully at the other three. Potts had been killed with cyanide. Could it have been an accident after all?

Thomas put a hand on the waiter's shoulder. "Listen," he said. "We're not blaming you. We know you were just doing your job. But the police have to know, too. You have to—"

"WHAT IN THE DEVIL'S NAME IS GOING ON HERE?"

The four children turned all at once. Paulie had just appeared behind them, red-faced and panting, carrying a wooden spoon the size of a shovel. In between short gasps of breath, he continued bellowing.

"CRIMINALS—TERRORIZING MY STAFF—FALSE INFORMATION—OUGHT TO BE—THROWN IN THE CLINKER—"

"Let us explain," Sam said, but Paulie paid him no attention. He rounded on the waiter, who was still cowering on the street and making himself as small as possible.

"And YOU!" Paulie roared, pointing his spoon at the waiter's head as though he meant to begin beating him with it. "IDIOT! COURAGE OF A COCKROACH! BRAINS OF A BEETLE!"

"I'm sorry!" the waiter cried out. "I got scared. It was the poison that did it, Mr. Paulie, sir. When I heard their uncle got bumped off on the day I put out the p-poison for the rats . . ."

Paulie had at last regained his breath. Now he turned back to the four children. Pippa had to draw back as the spoon came dangerously close to her nose.

"Oh, no you don't," he said, leaning in close with his

foul breath. "I see what you hooligans are playing at. Trying to pin this one on me and my restaurant. You'll have me ruined. Ruined!"

"We ain't trying to pin nothing on nobody," Max said.

"Or anything on anybody," Pippa corrected her.

"The fact is," Sam said, "the police have the wrong guy. They need to know—"

"They don't need to know a noodle! And they won't, either." Now Paulie spun back around to face the waiter, who had finally managed to stand up but shrank back as soon as Paulie's gaze fell on him. "If I hear you so much as made a peep in the direction of the cops, I'll have your head mounted on my wall for a hat rack. I'll have you chopped up and served as stew! You understand me?"

The waiter's eyes moved nervously back and forth. He pointed a finger at the children. "But—but—but they said—"

"I don't give a rat's tail what they said!" Paulie screamed so loudly, it looked as if all the veins in his neck would burst. On the corner, a woman and her poodle both gave an alarmed yelp. "I'll ask you again: DO YOU UNDERSTAND ME?"

The waiter hung his head, so a curtain of hair swung down over his face. "Yes, Mr. Paulie, sir. I do, Mr. Paulie, sir."

Paulie turned to the kids. "Now get out of here before I paddle you back into next Tuesday."

Max smiled, showing all her teeth. "I'd like to see you try."

"Come on, Max." Sam put a hand on her arm. "We're going," he said to Paulie.

Paulie's eyes followed them all the way down the street. Pippa could feel his stare like a beam of light boring into the skin on the back of her neck.

And suddenly, in one flash, she had him. She was traveling his gaze like a path, tunneling back through his eyes, parting the dark curtain of his mind. She was there, in, sifting through images . . .

She stopped short, crying out.

"What is it?" Thomas turned to her, alarmed.

Just as quickly, the images faded. She was shoved rudely out of Paulie's mind and found herself blinking, stunned, on Forty-Fourth Street. It was the very first time she'd read a mind and not just the contents of someone's purse or pocket. Her heart was beating very fast, and though the effort had exhausted her, she felt like bursting into song.

"I—I did it," she said in a whisper. "I read his mind. It was quick and I didn't get much, but I was in."

"Did you get anything?" Sam asked gently.

Pippa shut her eyes, thinking. "I saw Potts at the table," she said. "He was nervous."

"We already knew that," Max said. Pippa opened her eyes and frowned.

"What about the man he was with?" Thomas asked. "Think, Pip. Did you get anything on him?"

Pippa licked her lips and closed her eyes again. "I . . ." The image she'd seen in Paulie's mind was there, clear as anything, but it made no sense at all. All of the energy drained out of her at once. "I . . . I saw a fish."

"A fish?" Max practically screeched.

Pippa nodded miserably. Thomas sighed.

"That's all right, Pip," Sam said. "You did your best."

"It was a green fish," she offered.

"Probably because the whole thing stinks!" Max said. "I don't believe for a second Potts died because of some rat poison."

"I don't know," Thomas said quietly. "It's always possible . . ." But he sounded unconvinced.

"And what about Hugo and Phoebe?" Max was getting worked up. "I bet they're in this mess from their elbows to their eyebrows."

Pippa shook her head. She thought of the exhausting

morning they'd had. "All they did was shop," she said. "Until we lost them, at least. They stopped at the dress-maker's, the milliner's, and Woolworth's on Fifth Avenue. . . ."

"And where'd they get the cash for all that?" Max demanded, crossing her arms. It was a good question.

Thomas sighed and raked a hand through his hair, so it stood up practically on end.

"Tomorrow we'll try again," he said. "Sam and Max can follow Hugo and Phoebe. And Pip and I'll sniff around Paulie's again. Maybe you'll be able to get a bet-ter read this time," he finished, and Pippa blushed.

"Fine," she said, trying not to seem offended.

They walked back in silence to the museum, tired, despondent, and no closer to freeing Dumfrey. But Pippa comforted herself with the thought that tomor-row they would have another shot. If there was a clue to be found in Paulie's restaurant, she would find it.

But about this, she was wrong. Because that very same night, at exactly eleven, Paulie's restaurant burned to the ground.

23

The next day the *Daily Screamer* trumpeted: *THE CURSE STRIKES AGAIN*, in letters so big they practically exploded off the page. It appeared that Evans, too, had sniffed out the site of Potts's last meal.

Underneath the headline was a grainy picture of the blackened stretch of sidewalk on which Paulie's restaurant had stood only yesterday. All of the other front-page news—an article about Professor Rattigan's continued evasion of the police, rumors of conflict in Europe, and a piece about the kidnapping of a prominent politician's baby—was crammed into a space no larger than a dollar bill.

But it was no longer just the *Daily Screamer* that was

interested in the curse of the shrunken head. Every other paper in New York and beyond had picked up the scent.

Thomas read selections aloud in a strained voice. "'Mystery Crime Spree Sweeps Manhattan.'

"'House of Terrors: The Dark Side of Dumfrey's Dime Museum.'

"'Free Bird! Dumfrey released on lack of evidence, after a blaze only a few blocks from—'"

Thomas broke off. It took him a second to register what he'd just read.

"Wait a second," he said, pressing a finger to the paper, as though otherwise the words might leap off the page and scurry away. "It says here Mr. Dumfrey was *released*."

"Let me see," Pippa said, snatching the paper in a very un-Pippa-like way.

At that very second, the alley door banged open as though a battering ram had collided with it from the other side. Sam jumped, spilling tea all over Max. Max screeched.

And Thomas cried out, "Mr. Dumfrey!"

"The—very—same," Mr. Dumfrey huffed, as he attempted to squeeze through the door sideways. "More or less." His stomach was the last thing to make it through the doorway, with a pop like the sound of a tennis ball being released from a can. He patted his stomach and beamed. "My stay as a guest of New York City's finest has done me some good. I haven't fit through that door in years!"

Everyone crowded around him, speaking loudly, asking questions at once.

"We thought you'd been locked up," Danny said.

"How *did* you escape?" Goldini asked wonderingly, with just a hint of jealousy in his voice.

"I missed you terribly, Mr. Dumfrey!" Quinn cried, clinging to his arm.

Caroline, refusing to be outdone, grabbed his other arm. "I missed you more!"

"She did not."

"Did too."

"Did not."

"'O Captain! My Captain!'" Smalls was vigorously pumping Dumfrey's hand, his face lit up in a boyish grin. "'Our fearful trip is done.' Walt Whitman," he added in a whisper, seeing Thomas's puzzled expression.

"All in good time, my pets," Mr. Dumfrey said, holding up a hand. "All in good time." He sat down in the nearest chair with a little groan of satisfaction, and placed his feet up on the bench. "I don't suppose there's any breakfast . . . ?"

"There's sardines," Pippa said doubtfully. "And a little bit of toast."

"Delightful!" Mr. Dumfrey leaned back in his chair. Pippa scurried to get him a plate. His scarlet dressing gown was ripped in one place, and he had a banana peel in his pocket. Other than that, however, he looked no worse for the wear. "It's good to be home. Very good, indeed," he said.

"Mr. Dumfrey?" Miss Fitch coughed delicately.

"Yes?" He turned a beaming smile on her.

She gestured primly to the banana peel sticking out of his pocket.

"Ah, yes," he said. He plucked the peel from his pocket, sniffed it, and deposited it in the trash. "A woman tried to clobber me with a picnic basket. It's even better than I'd hoped," he said, his blue eyes shining. "Picnickers and busybodies, cameramen and curiosity seekers . . . it's wonderful, truly wonderful!"

"What are you talking about?" Thomas said. "*What's* wonderful?"

Mr. Dumfrey stared at him. "The crowd, my dear boy!" he said, as though it was obvious. "Haven't you seen them? Packed in the street like, like, like—" At that point, Pippa set a plate of sardines down in front of him. Dumfrey thumped the table with his fist. "Exactly. Like sardines. Thank you, Philippa."

"But they hate us," Sam said. "They think we're killers and freaks."

"They think you've been slaving us," Max said.

"*En*slaving us," Pippa corrected her.

Dumfrey waved a hand. "Who cares what they think, so long as they're interested? When the museum opens again—"

"But zat's just eet, sir!" Monsieur Cabillaud squeaked. "Zee museum must remain closed, by order of zee police."

"Not for much longer, *mon ami*," Mr. Dumfrey said. "The police are on the right scent. They know poor Potts was killed by accident."

"By accident?" Miss Fitch said.

"The criminal has confessed," Mr. Dumfrey said, munching contentedly. "Of course, he didn't mean to kill, poor devil. The man was only following orders. But who, in these days, uses cyanide to poison rats? Arsenic is far more humane."

Thomas exchanged a glance with the others. So the waiter had told his story to the police after all.

"But what about Paul—the restaurant," he corrected

himself quickly, afraid of appearing to know too much about it. "Why did it burn down?"

"The owner himself," Dumfrey said, licking a finger. "Insurance money! No doubt terrified that the place would be shut down by the board of health. The police have arrested him, too."

Thomas frowned. It was all stacking up neatly. But could Potts's death really have been an accident? Was it unrelated to Anderson's murder and the theft of the head?

The head—it always came back to the head.

Mr. Dumfrey was still talking. "Extraordinary. Truly extraordinary. 'We are but playthings to the gods.' Aristotle. Or perhaps Shakespeare. Or my old friend Harrison the Headless Wonder. He was quite philosophical. In any case, the police had no choice but to let me go, even if our good friend Hardaway was none too pleased about it. Still trying to pin Anderson's death on me, but he has absolutely no evidence. I'm very grateful to that waiter. It's not always easy to do the right thing. I wonder who managed to convince him?" And he gave Thomas a nearly imperceptible wink.

Thomas ducked his head, so Mr. Dumfrey wouldn't see him blush.

Mr. Dumfrey let out a satisfied burp, then thumped

his chest. "Delicious!" he exclaimed. "Nothing like sardines in the morning." Pippa opened her mouth as though to disagree, but at a gesture from Thomas, said nothing. Mr. Dumfrey checked his pocket watch and gave a little start. "Ten o'clock already! By the hand-cuffs of Houdini . . . Miss Fitch, fetch me my writing paper and my ink. I plan to send a letter to our friends at the New York City police. The museum must be reopened at once, of course. Monsieur Cabillaud, pre-pare the ticket booth and bring up the jelly apples for the refreshment stand. Smalls, draw the curtains in the Hall of Worldwide Wonders and for God's sake, make sure we have enough chairs this time! Danny, Betty—I want the exhibit halls to sparkle. The glass is so smudgy you can barely tell George Washington's hatchet from his wooden teeth! And, Goldini, get me Bill Evans on the horn. Offices of the *Daily Screamer.*"

"Bill Evans?" Thomas echoed. "What's he got to do with it?"

Mr. Dumfrey pushed back from the table. The other residents of the museum bustled around the kitchen and hurried up the stairs to fulfill Mr. Dumfrey's wishes.

"He's got everything to do with it," Mr. Dumfrey said serenely. "I must thank him, of course, for keeping the museum in the spotlight."

"He wrote lies about you in the paper!" Pippa burst out.

"He's saying you're a murderer, Mr. D.," Sam said solemnly.

"Exactly!" Mr. Dumfrey beamed. "It's wonderful for publicity. For once, I'll be one of the attractions. An escaped criminal? A murderer who has evaded the long arm of the law? That, my children, is worth fifty cents at least!" He roared with laughter. "Now move along, move along."

"You didn't give us anything to do," Pippa pointed out.

"Oh! How silly of me." Dumfrey patted various pockets and eventually withdrew an entire dollar bill. He placed it in Pippa's hand. "I thought you might take a day off. Go to the movies. Spoil your dinner with popcorn and Turkish taffy." He gave another nearly imperceptible wink. "I believe I am in your debt, after all."

Thomas exchanged a glance with the other three. So Mr. Dumfrey *did* know that they'd spoken to the waiter.

"Thanks, Mr. Dumfrey," Thomas said.

Mr. Dumfrey turned stern again. "I expect you back by afternoon," he said. "Tomorrow, it's business as usual."

24

The Viceroy Theater, on the corner of Eighth Avenue and Forty-Fourth Street, had seen better days. Only one of every four lights encircling the marquee was still working; the majority had burned out, been pecked apart by pigeons, or been shattered by vandals. The carpet in the lobby was threadbare, the chairs creaked awfully, and large water stains decorated the faded silk walls.

Still, it was one of Sam's favorite places. He loved the smell of buttered popcorn that clung to the upholstery, and the old movie posters displayed on the walls, in part to conceal the water stains.

Most of all he loved the darkness. Sitting in a movie

theater, he could be just anyone: a normal kid from a normal family, out to have a normal good time. For once, he was the one who got to watch and point and laugh.

Today the theater was showing a triple feature of *Daughter of Frankenstein*, *Castle of Frankenstein*, and *Frankenstein's Revenge*. They found four seats together in the middle of the theater. Sam, who had been deliberately delaying to see if Max would catch up, was annoyed when Thomas plopped down next to him. Now she was separated by two people. Pippa took the seat to the left of Thomas, and Max settled in beside her and rested her knees on the back of the seat of the person in front of her. When the woman—her curly blond hair piled high on her head like whipped cream on a sundae—turned around to cluck her tongue, Max only grinned, showing off all the popcorn kernels in her teeth.

"She doesn't mean to be an animal," Pippa said apologetically.

"Yeah I do," Max said.

Sam sighed and turned his attention to the screen. A small part of him had been hoping that Max might grab his hand during the scary bits, even though the rational part of his brain knew this was unlikely for two reasons: 1) Max didn't get afraid; and 2) if she did grab his hand, he'd probably crush all the bones in her fingers.

"I wish they'd just get on with the movie already," Thomas said, crunching loudly on some candy-coated almonds, as the screen flickered gray and white and a *click-click-click* filled the theater as the reel started to roll forward. Sam slouched further in his seat. They'd have a news report or two to get through first and the cartoons.

Thomas was speaking with his mouth full. "It's worse than reading the paper. The whole reason you go to the movies is to escape . . ."

His sentence ended in a gurgle.

HORROR HAPPENINGS! said the words flashing across the screen.

Sam sat up, feeling as though his seat had given him an electric shock. There, on the screen, was Bill Evans.

"Not this moron again," Max said loudly. Several people hushed her.

An enormous, black-and-white Bill Evans was sitting behind his desk at the *Daily Screamer*, a small brass plaque reading HEAD REPORTER prominently displayed in front of his typewriter, a cigarette clamped in his mouth.

"It's not just the murders and the unexplainable

deaths," he was saying, to an off-screen interviewer. "The whole place is full of secrets. Take those four kids—"

Sam was so hot he felt as if he were melting, from the tips of his ears inward. He sank down in his seat, even as Thomas piped up.

"Hey, he means—!"

"Shut up," Sam hissed. "Shut. Up."

Several people swiveled around to stare. Sam was glad it was dark. He was sure he was the color of a radish.

"Now look." Evans jabbed a finger on his desk to punctuate his words. "I got nothing against them personally. They never did me wrong. But the way they're sniffing around, always in the wrong place at the right time, is suspicious."

To Sam's infinite mortification, the newsreel now showed a photograph taken from the museum's recent promotional brochure. In it, Sam, Pippa, Max, and Thomas were dressed in costumes and posing on the Odditorium stage. Sam was holding an enormous block of concrete above his head. Thomas was in a back bend. Max was balancing a knife handle on the tip of one finger, and Pippa had both hands to her temples and was squinting in deep concentration.

"Something stinks at Dumfrey's Dime Museum,"
Bill Evans continued, "and I intend to get to the bottom of it."

Fortunately, the newsreel shifted to a different
subject at that moment: a segment about the escaped
scientist, Professor Rattigan, who had been convicted
to life in prison for unlawful experimentation on
human beings.

"He could be anyone! He could be anywhere!" the
announcer was saying onscreen, as images flashed
of Professor Rattigan's old underground laboratory,
filled with walls of cages that had once held people.
Sam's stomach turned. The sight of the cages made
pain shoot through his head. "*He could be sitting next to you
in the dark right now.*"

"I—I don't feel good," Sam whispered.

Thomas's eyes were still glued to the screen. "Movie
hasn't even started," he said, shoveling more of the
candied nuts into his mouth.

"I'm not staying," said Sam, getting to his feet.

"Hey, kid, you're blocking the screen," a man
grunted.

"Move it!"

"Sorry," Sam spoke to the dark blob of faces all
around him. Still blushing furiously, he ducked and

began fumbling toward the aisle. Thomas groaned and Pippa whispered, "What are you doing, Sam?"

He was squeezing past Max when his toe caught on one of her shoes. Suddenly, he was pitching forward in the dark. Instinctively, he reached out to steady himself, grabbing the back of someone's chair. There was a loud snap, as though a giant had just bitten off the world's largest green bean, and then the chair was no longer steady, and a woman was screaming, and Sam was falling again.

The theater lights came on at once, and the screen went dark.

"Murder!" A woman was lying on her back, feet kicking the air, in the theater seat Sam had accidentally ripped free of the floor. "Murder! Theft! Help!" Her pocketbook lay beside her. It had popped open, spilling its contents across the floor.

Everything was confusion. People rushed over to help the woman to her feet. Ten people were talking at once.

"He went for my throat!" she was saying, wild-eyed. "He was after my purse!"

Sam had just climbed to his feet, and was about to apologize, when a man wearing wire-framed glasses swiveled in his direction.

"Hey!" the man squawked, lifting a finger to point. "It's the kid from the news report! It's one of them freaks from the museum!"

Sam felt time slow. He could feel the thunderous space between each of his heartbeats. One by one, as in a nightmare, the people in the theater turned to look. Sam wanted to run, but he was rooted to the ground.

Even the man's voice seemed to have slowed, deepened, as though Sam were hearing him through a thick muffling layer of molasses. "It's all of them!" the man said, as his finger slowly swept across the row of seats to encompass them all: Max, scowling; an irritated Pippa; and Thomas looking, amazingly, as if he were enjoying himself.

A new eruption of sound: time sped up again, and Sam was crowded from all sides. People were grabbing his shirt, firing off questions so quickly he could understand none of them.

"That's our cue." Max was beside him all of a sudden. She grabbed hold of his hand and he was so shocked, he forgot to squeeze back. "Out of the way!" she called, shoving and pushing. "Coming through!" She piloted him firmly toward the exit, plowing through the knot of people who had gathered, using elbows when she had to.

He was almost disappointed when they reached the

street and the sunshine, and she released him. But at least there were no people pointing and yammering at him. At least he could breathe again.

"Wait for us!" Pippa burst out of the movie theater after them, and Thomas emerged a second later.

"What a waste," Thomas muttered. *"Frankenstein's Revenge* is supposed to be the scariest one."

"You could have stayed," Sam pointed out.

"By myself? No, thank you." Thomas shoved his hands deep in his pockets and looked away. A little muscle flexed in his jaw, as it did when he was working a really hard trick, trying to squeeze himself into a shoebox or Chinese vase.

Sam realized, then, that Thomas was angry. "You enjoy it, don't you?" He felt a little sick to say the words out loud. "You actually *like* being the center of attention."

Thomas shrugged. "So?"

"They're laughing at us, Thomas," Sam said. He was shaking. He was angry, too—so angry he could break something for real this time, deliberately. "They think we're freaks."

"So what?" Thomas finally looked at him. "Who cares what they think? It won't change anything. It won't change *us*."

Sam opened his mouth to respond but he was startled by a shriek. Pippa's face was the vivid red of a ripe tomato, and she was glaring at Max.

"I don't believe you," she spat out. "You didn't."

Max had her arms crossed tightly. "I don't know what—" she started to say, but Pippa lunged for her, and even as Thomas shouted, and Sam moved forward to separate them, Pippa had plunged her hands deep in the pocket of Max's jacket. A second later, she was holding a battered woman's wallet.

"You stole this," she said, practically spitting the words, as though they were full of poison.

"I didn't steal it," Max said. She licked her lips nervously. "I found it."

"Yeah, on the floor—when it fell out of that woman's pocketbook," Pippa said.

Max shrugged. "Finders, keepers."

"You're going to march right back inside and give it back to her," Pippa said, waving the wallet threateningly in Max's face.

Max swatted at her. "Get your hands out of my breathing space."

"Don't touch me," Pippa said, swatting back.

"You ain't my mother."

"Aren't! Aren't! You *aren't* my mother!"

"Well, you ain't, either."

Pippa made a low growling noise in her throat. Max's fists were balled at her side. Both girls moved at once, lightning quick.

"Pippa," Thomas cried out, at the same time that Sam said, "Max, don't."

Max had a fistful of Pippa's hair in her hand, and Pippa was twisting the skin on Max's cheek. Both girls were shouting, and Sam was shouting, too, though he hardly knew what he was saying. Thomas flung his arm around Pippa. He dragged her backward even as she struggled against him, clawing at his arm and demanding to be released. Sam hooked two fingers in the back of Max's shirt collar and rooted her in place.

"Let me go!" she shouted. "I'll poke her eyes out with toothpicks! I'll nail her noggin to the ground!"

"Max, *please*," Sam said. People were beginning to stare at them again. Down the street, a shoeshine boy had paused in his work, brush raised, mouth open. His client had lowered his newspaper to watch. On the opposite side of the street, a beat cop had paused and was peering in their direction, hand raised to his hat to shield his eyes from the glare.

"Look, everyone calm down, okay?" Sam kept his voice as quiet and steady as possible. He prayed for the cop to move on. The last thing they needed was more trouble.

"She started it," Pippa said. She was panting. "Let *go* of me," she said, wrenching away from Thomas.

Max snorted. "I didn't start nothing, *you* started it—"

"All right, all right," Sam jumped in, before things could get any worse. The cop finally moved on, casting one last glance in their direction. Some of the tightness loosened in Sam's chest. "Let's just head back to the museum, okay? We can talk everything out once we're—"

But Sam's voice was drowned out by a sudden commotion from down the block. A freckle-faced boy wearing a newsboy cap and carrying a stack of papers was shouting at the top of his lungs.

"Extra! Extra! Read all about it!" he hollered as people crowded him, snatching up newspapers, dropping coins in his hand. "The shrunken head strikes again! Reporter Bill Evans falls victim to the curse!"

25

"**B**ill Evans?" Pippa exclaimed. The girls' fight was all but forgotten, even though Pippa's scalp still ached and there was a vivid red bruise on Max's cheek where Pippa had pinched it. *"Dead?"*

Thomas, who had purchased a paper, glanced up for a moment. "No. He *could* have died, though."

"I wish he had," Max said.

"Listen to this," Thomas said, returning to his paper. "'Bill Evans, star reporter and the man responsible for breaking the case of the curse, was returning to his home on Ludlow Street last evening when he was nearly killed by an out-of-control driver. He was rushed to Mercy General Hospital . . .'"

"First that old woman at the museum, Mrs. Weathersby," Pippa said, ticking them off on her fingers. "Then Anderson. Then Potts. And now Evans." She shook her head.

"Maybe there really is a curse," Sam ventured.

"There's no curse," Thomas said, folding up the newspaper. "Let's go."

"Where to?" Sam said.

"Back to the museum," he said. "We need to talk to Dumfrey."

"But first . . ." Pippa slapped the wallet into Max's hand. Max, grumbling, disappeared into the theater and reemerged a minute later, hands shoved in her pockets.

"Happy now?" she mumbled.

"Delighted," Pippa said.

In two hours, the museum had undergone a remarkable transformation. The steps were swept clean of cigarette stubs and debris, and Andrew was busy washing the windows, sleeves rolled up to show off his scaly forearms. A vast crowd was still assembled in the street, including Miss Groenovelt, who was carrying one of her cats in her arms and had another two perched on her shoulders. Pippa even spotted two old men she was sure were the Sadowski brothers, a pair of legendary hermits she had never seen outside their apartment.

The children circled around the block and sneaked into the museum through the alley door. As soon as they entered the kitchen, Danny gave an outraged shout and pinned them against the wall with the handle of a mop.

"Oh no, you don't," he said, waving a finger at them threateningly. "Not after I just cleaned the floors. Your shoes are black as a pirate's teeth."

"My shoes are *not* dirty," Pippa said haughtily.

"Sorry, Danny," Thomas said, ducking under the broom handle and starting for the stairs. "Official business."

They left Danny spluttering and waving his mop.

The lobby floor was scrubbed clean of footprints and smudge marks. The advertising banner, which had begun to droop sadly to the floor—*Pinheads! Bearded Ladies! Alligator Men! Dwarves! NOVEL AND ASTOUNDING EXHIBITIONS! MORE THAN ONE THOUSAND CURIOSITIES!*—was now hoisted high and proud over the ticket desk. Miss Fitch bustled in and out of the various exhibit halls, directing the other performers.

"The polish goes on clockwise, Betty! Otherwise it's sure to look spotty. Quinn, where did Danny get to with that mop? Who moved Napoléon Bonaparte's riding boots? They go to the *left* of Pocahontas's moccasins. Hugo. Hugo!"

Hugo emerged, red-faced, from the Odditorium. "Yes, Miss Fitch?"

"Fetch me my sewing basket, please. Marie Antoinette's dress has developed an awful tear. I'll have to patch it."

"Have you seen Mr. Dumfrey, Miss Fitch?" Pippa asked.

"Holed up in his office," she said, without turning from the historical figures portion of the Hall of Wax. "Of course he *would* be, and leave us to do all the work. . . ." Suddenly, she spun around and scowled. "Where have you been? I've been looking for you for hours."

"Quick," Sam whispered, "before she puts us to work."

"There's so much to be done." Miss Fitch was counting tasks on her fingers. "The toilets need cleaning and the beds must be stripped and—"

"Thanks, Miss F.!" Max said loudly. They darted up the spiral stairs, ignoring Miss Fitch's cries of protest.

"Mr. Dumfrey—" Pippa burst through Mr. Dumfrey's office door first and then stopped abruptly, so that first Thomas, then Max, and finally Sam collided with her. She stumbled forward several feet. Max let out a sharp cry. "Watch it, you big oaf!" she said. "You nearly snapped my back in two." They saw Mr. Dumfrey standing by the window, partially concealed by a towering stack of ancient Cambodian burial urns.

"Pippa!" When Mr. Dumfrey spun around, his face was very white and there was a look in his eyes she had never seen before—as though he'd been staring at a ghost. "You scared me, children."

The radio was playing very loudly. "Rattigan was last sighted on the morning of April twenty-fourth," said the announcer, "wearing a felt hat pulled low and the rags of a beggar. . . ." Mr. Dumfrey switched it off with a trembling hand, and the resulting silence was even louder.

"Well," he said, coughing. "Well. Back so soon, are we? Didn't fancy a movie?"

No one bothered trying to explain what had happened. Instead, Thomas tossed the newspaper down on Mr. Dumfrey's desk. "Did you hear?" he said. "Bill Evans nearly got killed last night. They're saying it's the curse again."

Mr. Dumfrey barely glanced at the headline. "Oh, yes, yes," he said, with a dismissive wave of one hand.

"I heard it on the radio. Unfortunate. Terrible. Poor man. We should really send a card." And he turned back to the window and lapsed into silence.

"Are—are you okay, Mr. Dumfrey?" Pippa ventured. She had never in all her life known him to ignore the possibility of press, whether good or bad. And Bill Evans's near death was, she had no doubt, a great opportunity for a ton of bad press.

Mr. Dumfrey jumped. He cracked his head on the edge of one of his shelves, and an avalanche of papers began to sift down around him. "What? Me? Oh—I'm fine." A brass paperweight, supposedly from the desk of Abraham Lincoln, conked him on the head, and he winced. "I'm absolutely fine. Wonderful, in fact."

"O-o-o-kay," Thomas said, drawing out the syllables. He cleared his throat. "Listen, Mr. Dumfrey, we were thinking of going down to the hospital to drop in on Bill Evans."

"We were?" Max said. Thomas shot her a warning look.

Pippa jumped in, "We can bring him a card."

Mr. Dumfrey, who was trying to shuffle his papers into a pile, straightened up. "Oh," he said, jogging the stack of papers once in his arms. "*Oh.*" He moved woodenly toward the desk, set the papers down with a thump, and patted his tie. "Oh," he said, a third time.

"You're sure you're okay?" Pippa said again.

Mr. Dumfrey whipped off his glasses and began furiously polishing them with a corner of his scarlet robe. "I'm absolutely fine, Pippa. It's just . . . I don't think you should be out and about today. It'll be dark soon."

Pippa exchanged a bewildered look with the others. "It's only three o'clock," she pointed out.

"Is it?" Dumfrey slipped the glasses back on his nose upside down and then corrected their arrangement. "Well. Time flies, doesn't it? Or perhaps it doesn't. No matter. Miss Fitch needs you here. And the streets are full of criminals."

"You just sent us to the movies," Thomas said.

"Did I? Well, well." He managed a weak smile. "I suppose I'm just upset, you know, about everything that's happened. We're having a memorial for Potts tomorrow, at the museum, at noon on the dot. I expect you all to be wearing your best funeral faces. Miss Fitch can make you something appropriately bleak to wear." He sighed. "Poor Potts . . . he wasn't the brightest of the lot, or the nicest, either, or the best looking . . ."

"I think you might want to work on your speech," Thomas said.

Dumfrey jerked in his chair, as though he'd been electrocuted. He peered closely at Thomas. "My speech? Of course . . . my speech." He reached suddenly for a pen, once again dislodging the papers from the corner of his desk. "Excellent suggestion, my dear boy. I'll write a speech that'll have the hardest-hearted scoundrel weeping in the aisles. I'll write a speech that'll knock the socks off a nun!"

"What about Evans?" Pippa prompted.

"Oh! Evans." Mr. Dumfrey waved a hand. "Yes, yes. Go and see Evans, if you'd like. Give him my best." He licked the tip of his pen and paused, his hand hovering over a blank piece of paper. "Now let me see . . . Potts, Potts. What on earth will I say about Potts?"

They left him bent over his paper, frantically scribbling, and Pippa felt better, satisfied that everything was back to normal.

It didn't take them long to find Evans once they arrived at Mercy General. A bored receptionist, her face concealed behind a copy of the *Daily Screamer*, directed them upstairs without even glancing in their direction. They took a rickety elevator to the third floor and could hear him even before the doors had opened fully.

"So then I said to him . . . that may be a bear, but it's

the prettiest bear this dog has ever seen!"

A chorus of female laughter, like the twittering of birds, followed this pronouncement.

Thomas gestured the group forward. This floor was surprisingly empty. There were no nurses bustling in and out of rooms, pushing patients in wheelchairs, and calling to one another. Just several empty hallways branching out from an equally empty waiting room, where a radio was buzzing forlornly in the corner.

As soon as they traced the sound of Evans's voice, it was easy to see why. All the nurses—at least two dozen of them—were crammed into Evans's room. Every available surface of the room was occupied either by a woman or a flower arrangement, so the air smelled as thick as a perfume factory.

"You are too much!" one of the nurses was saying, as Thomas, Pippa, Max, and Sam gathered awkwardly in the doorway. Pippa coughed and two dozen heads swiveled in their direction.

"Pippa!" Evans cried, sitting up a little further in bed. He was wearing a short-sleeved undershirt and had his left arm in a large cast. There was a faint bruise on his left cheek.

"Thomas! Mackenzie! Sam! I don't believe it. You brought the whole gang. How wonderful."

"Awwww." A nurse with black hair and a powder-white face was smiling in a particularly stupid way. "You didn't tell us you had children, Bill. Shame on you."

"He isn't—" Pippa and Max started to say.

"We're not—" Thomas and Sam said at the same time.

But their protests were drowned out by Evans's booming laugh.

"I wish!" he said. "Sorry to say, darling, these extraordinary children are no relations of mine. But come in, come in. Not you, Sam—you might break something. I'm kidding!" He roared with laughter.

"Hey." Another nurse, this one with a wide, childish face and a wad of gum in her mouth, squinted at them. "Don't I know you kids from somewhere?"

"We were hoping to talk to you *alone*," Pippa said loudly, with an emphasis on the word *alone*, before Evans could cause a scene and introduce them as the freaks from Dumfrey's museum.

"Of course, of course. Anything for you." Mr. Evans turned apologetically to the crowd of nurses. "You heard the little lady. Mind giving us some breathing room, sweethearts?"

The nurses shuffled one by one out of the room, giggling and whispering, waving to Evans and promising to return soon. One or two of them shot Pippa a dirty look.

"Well, now," Evans said, as soon as they were alone. "What can I do you for?"

"We, um, just came by to see how you were feeling," Pippa said. It was embarrassing to see a grown man in nothing but an undershirt, tucked up in bed like a small child, and she had difficulty meeting Mr. Evans's eyes. Instead, she focused on a strange blurry birthmark she could see on his right forearm.

Mr. Evans caught her staring. "You've found my dirty little secret," he said, winking. Pippa, looking more closely, realized it wasn't a birthmark at all but an old tattoo, faded and green with age, of a large flat-nosed fish. "Got this when I was in the navy. Sailor first-class. USS *Saratoga*." He turned his arm so that the tattoo was concealed. "Good thing we sea dogs are made of tough salt. I'm telling you, my number almost came up yesterday."

"What happened?" Thomas asked. He pulled himself onto a countertop, between two large arrangements of pink and white carnations.

Evans touched a finger to his nose. "Aha. There's the rub. I knew you kids would come looking for the real story."

Pippa opened her mouth to protest, but Evans cut her off.

"It's all right," he said, settling back against his

pillows. "I'd do the same thing myself. Never could resist a good story. You know what they used to call me back in Atlanta? The Bloodhound." Evans chuckled and then immediately began to cough. He thumped his chest with a fist.

"Are you sure you're all right?" Sam said. He was still lurking in the doorway. Max, on the other hand, had her back to Mr. Evans. She was circling the room, smelling flowers, opening cabinets, and probably, Pippa thought, looking for something she could steal.

"I'm fine, I'm fine. Just a little banged up. I got lucky. When that car clipped me, I rolled over the hood and everything went dark as dungeons. I woke up here. If it had been going any faster . . . If I'd fallen differently . . ."

"The papers said you were walking home," Thomas said. "Is that true?"

Evans snorted. "True enough. Nearly made it, too. I was half a block away on Hester. I could have spit on my own front stoop. That's when it happened."

"Do you remember anything about the car?" Thomas asked.

Evans grinned at him. "Good question, Tommy. You'd make a crack reporter in no time. You aren't looking for a job, by any chance? I could use an assistant, now that I'm head honcho at the *Daily Screamer*. No? Well, your loss." The smile suddenly faded from his face, and his expression turned grim. "Sorry to say, I didn't notice squat about the car, except that it was headed directly for me."

Thomas lapsed into silence. There seemed nothing left to say. They were at a dead end.

Max spun around to face Mr. Evans. She had located a box of chocolates some visitor had brought for Evans and had stuffed two at once into her mouth. "Whaf abuf the drivumpf?" Everyone stared at her blankly, and she rolled her eyes and swallowed. "What about the driver?" she repeated. "You said you were on the windshield, didn't ya? So you must of got a look at his face."

Pippa couldn't help but be a little impressed. The feeling quickly passed, however, as Max popped three more chocolates into her mouth.

"It was dark," Mr. Evans said apologetically. "But I did notice his hair."

"What about it?" Thomas said.

"It was red. Carrot red. No—no. More like fire red."

Thomas stiffened. Pippa felt a small thrill of excitement, and Sam looked quickly to Max.

They knew someone with fire-red hair—had just met him recently: Mr. Anderson's nephew.

26

"**A**re you thinking what I'm thinking?" Max said, as soon as they had regained the street. She had a slight chocolate mustache above her lip.

"Oh! Have you learned to think?" Pippa said.

"Not now, Pippa," Sam said. He turned to Max. "I'm pretty sure we're all thinking the same thing."

"Anderson's nephew," they chorused together.

Thomas blew out a long breath. "Okay," he said. "So now we just have to track him down, and—and . . ."

"Ask whether he axed his uncle and poisoned Potts?" Max raised an eyebrow.

Sam thought of the boy's pale face and spattering of

freckles, the way he trembled and nearly keeled over when he saw his uncle on the ground. Could someone like that be a murderer?

He wasn't sure. In gangster movies, killers almost always wore black. Reginald Anderson had worn green trousers and an orange-checkered shirt. Still, he supposed in real life murderers were just as likely to have bad taste as nonmurderers. "I don't get it, though," he said. "He worked for his uncle. Why kill him?"

"Maybe he wanted the business for himself," Pippa said.

"Or maybe he made a deal with Potts." Thomas's face was scrunched, as it often was when he was thinking hard. "Maybe he wanted the head for himself. Maybe he was going to resell it."

"And his uncle found out and got mad," Sam said slowly, trying to follow Thomas's reasoning.

"So Reggie bumped him off!" Max put in.

"And then Potts had to go," Pippa added.

"Right." Thomas's eyes were shining. "It all fits."

"But even if he did do it," Pippa said, "he won't just confess."

Thomas looked at Sam. Then Max turned to look at him as well. Slowly, so did Pippa.

"What did Thomas say the other day?" Sam said,

wishing his voice wouldn't sound so squeaky. He cracked his knuckles. "We'll just have to make him talk."

"That's the spirit," Thomas said, and grinned.

The subway station at Lexington Avenue was packed with people: shoeshine boys carrying wooden boxes, families on their way to visit relatives in the distant suburb of Queens, beggars carting bags full of tin cans, and women stepping daintily around them—all of them jostling, muttering, and sweating in the dank air. Thomas worked his way through the thick knot of people, dodging elbows and ducking under briefcases, compressing himself in the negative space between couples, and Sam plunged after him, blushing and apologizing.

"Excuse me. So sorry. Didn't see you there. Mind your toes. Excuse me."

"Young man. Watch where you're stepping." An outraged woman wearing a large hat trimmed with ostrich plumes spun around to face him. The feathers on her hat whipped angrily in Sam's face.

"I—I—I—" he stammered to apologize. But the feathers were tickling his nose, and all that came out was a gigantic sneeze. "A*choo!*"

"Heathen!" she shrieked and turned around, once

again treating him to a mouthful of feathers.

"Do you see a train?" Pippa called to Thomas as she struggled to circumnavigate an enormously fat man standing guard over a pile of luggage. Thomas had reached the edge of the platform and was peering into the cavernous mouth of the subway tunnel.

"I see lights," he called back. "It shouldn't be l—"

He didn't finish his sentence. One second he was there on the platform, staring back at them. The next second he had vanished. It took Sam a moment to realize what had happened, and then the truth came to him on a sudden drumbeat of terror.

Thomas had fallen onto the tracks.

"Thomas!" Sam lunged forward but his long legs got tangled on the fat man's luggage. Someone yelled. The people on the platform ping-ponged off one another and then re-formed, tighter than ever, like a vast wave dispersing and then regathering force.

"Thomas!" Pippa shrieked. She, too, was fighting to the edge of the platform. And Max—where was Max?

Then Sam heard it—a growing rumble from inside the tunnel.

A train was coming.

He forgot about being polite. He shoved forward, ignoring the outraged yelps and muttered curses of the people waiting for the train. When he reached the platform edge, he saw that Max had dropped onto the tracks, and she was trying to coax a dazed Thomas to his feet. Her face was lit white, drawn and terrified, and she looked almost unreal; in that second Sam realized that she was bathed in light—they both were—lit up like a photographic still.

Sam felt as if he were moving through oatmeal. Light—light growing—two vast points of light as big as moons.

Like a huge mechanical monster, the train was blazing down on Max and Thomas.

"Max!"

Still holding on to Thomas, Max reached up her free hand. Sam wrapped his fingers around her wrist and pulled. She felt like nothing, like a feather. Her face contorted in pain and she let out a cry as she was yanked onto the platform just as the train hurtled into the station, brakes screeching, horn blaring.

"Are you crazy?" she shouted, rubbing her shoulder. "You nearly tore my arm off!"

"I saved your life!" he answered. He was shaking.

Suddenly, Max's face went white.

She had let go of Thomas.

Still on her knees, Pippa was frantically trying to

peer into the three-inch gap between train and platform. Tears were streaming down her face. "Thomas!"

All around them, people were shouting. At the very front of the train, a little door flew open and the driver burst out and came running toward them.

"Oh God, oh God! I tried to stop but—"

"Wait!" cried Pippa, pressing her ear to the gap. "QUIET!"

From underneath the train came the muffled sound of someone saying, "I'm okay. Would you mind getting this train off me?"

In another instant, the driver had jumped back in his compartment and slowly driven the train out of the station. As the crowd on the platform cheered, they saw Thomas squeezed between two rails, lying as flat as he could make himself, wide-eyed, clothes spotted with grease. Alive.

"It's a miracle," someone shouted, as Thomas climbed to his feet carefully, wincing with every other step.

Sam was moving before he knew it. He dropped to his knees and grabbed Thomas around the wrist, lifting him onto the platform and to safety. Pippa barreled into his arms, nearly knocking him back into the tracks again.

"It's all right, Pip. It's all right," Thomas said, patting Pippa awkwardly on the back.

"I thought—well, I thought—" Pippa's voice, muffled by Thomas's shoulder, broke.

"Let him breathe," Sam said, laughing. His whole body was full of an electric joy. He felt he could leap down into the tracks and stop an oncoming train, if he had to. He wondered why he had not thought to try it before.

"You idiot." Max whacked Thomas on the arm as Pippa pulled back, drying her face with her sleeve. "You nearly gave me a heart attack."

"You?" Thomas grinned, raising his eyebrows at Max. "You were scared?"

Instantly, she scowled. "Only a little."

Pippa reached and gave Max's hand a quick squeeze. "I was terrified," she said, and Max almost—*almost*—smiled. Then both girls took a quick step apart, as though remembering that they hated each other.

"Are you sure you're okay?" Sam asked, as Thomas shifted again and then immediately winced.

"I think I twisted an ankle," Thomas said, testing it.

"You could have done much worse than that." Pippa had regained her composure and was glaring at Thomas in her usual disapproving way. "What were you thinking? How could you slip onto the tracks?"

"Did you know," he said, ignoring Pippa's question, "that the probability of accidentally slipping onto a subway track on any given day is one in one-and-a-half million?"

"What's that supposed to mean?" Max asked. Her voice was thin and high.

Thomas's face grew serious. "It means I didn't slip," Thomas said simply. "I was pushed."

27

They split up to do a sweep of the platform, even though Thomas doubted it would be of any use.

He'd felt a hand on his back and a shove, but he hadn't caught even a glimpse of his attacker. Besides, whoever it was might have easily slipped aboard the train and been halfway to Thirty-Third Street by now.

Still, they combed the crowd, looking for anything or anyone suspicious—someone who looked familiar or someone who stared too long or someone trying *not* to stare.

Max had reached the far side of the platform, where a broad staircase led up to the street level and people came flowing in from above, when she spotted him. He was standing at the shadowy end of the platform as far from possible as the other commuters, wearing a great coat with its collar pulled halfway up his head. The rest of his face, except for his eyes, was concealed by a big, wide-brimmed slouch hat.

Her heart stopped. A second train had just arrived and he shouldered his way onto a subway car. As the doors slid shut, he turned around to face her. Max ducked, fearing he would see her. When she looked again, the train was moving off into the black mouth of the tunnel.

"Rats," she said loudly, and a woman shook her head. Max moved at a jog down the platform, scooting between commuters, until she reached the others.

"What is it?" Thomas said, as she approached.

"Hugo." Saying the name made her feel sick. She liked the elephant man. Her first night at Dumfrey's, when everyone was busy ignoring her and Pippa was acting like Max was a piece of dried dog turd that had accidentally been dragged inside on someone's shoe, Hugo had smiled at her and placed one of his massive hands on her shoulders and said, "If there's anything you need, just ask." But facts were facts. "I saw him. He got on the train."

There was a moment of stunned silence. Max was

uncomfortably aware of the way Sam was staring at her, as though it was her fault. She jammed her hands in her pockets and glared at him, and finally he looked away.

"I can't believe it," Pippa said, in a whisper. "Hugo wouldn't . . . He couldn't . . ."

"I saw him," Max said stubbornly.

Sam sighed and raked a hand through his hair. It immediately flopped back over his forehead. "So what should we do?"

They turned instinctively to Thomas. "Nothing," he said, after a pause. "We stick with the original plan. We go and talk to Reggie. We'll deal with Hugo later."

They boarded the next subway but didn't speak again until they'd reached Brooklyn.

Max had a bad taste in her mouth, as if she'd accidentally swallowed a hunk of moldy cheese. She had the uncomfortable feeling they were farther than ever from the truth. Unconsciously, she squeezed the handle of the knife in her pocket—her oldest, smallest, and best knife. She wished the truth were like a target and she could stake it out, pin it down, as easily as she could put a blade through a bull's-eye.

She was getting the feeling, however, that the truth was more like a very wriggly fish. Every time she thought she was close to understanding, it slipped from her grasp.

It was after five o'clock when they finally emerged from the subway in Brooklyn, several blocks away from Anderson's Delights. But they were disappointed when they arrived. The door was locked. A single bit of police tape still fluttered forlornly from the bars of one ground-floor window. A sign hanging on the door said CLOSED.

"Rats," Max muttered, for the second time in an hour. "What now?"

Before anyone could answer, a voice called out from across the street.

"If you're looking for the Anderson boy, you won't find him in there."

They turned around and saw an old woman, clomping painstakingly down the street, a wooden cane in each hand. Her skin hung in loose folds around her face.

"Try Gary's on Nevins," said the old woman. "You'll have better luck in Gary's."

Gary's was a vast, dark bar, with lots of polished wood everywhere and walls stained from years of smoke to a color resembling the skin of an eggplant. As soon as they stepped inside, Max was assaulted by the smell of old leather shoes. The light was dim. At the bar, various people were slumped over their glasses, practically motionless, looking in the smokiness like large mountains seen from a distance.

"No kids allowed," growled the bartender, who was busy wiping a glass.

"We're just looking for a friend." Sam spoke up quickly. "Reginald Anderson . . . ?"

The bartender gave a harsh bark of laughter. "Yeah, kid. Me, too. If you see him, tell him I'm still waiting on the ten bucks he owes me. He hasn't shown his mug around here since I creamed him at the tables." And the bartender nodded, slightly, toward a group of men playing pool in the corner.

They were halfway to the door when a man with bleary red eyes and a face covered in stubble put a hand on Max's arm.

"Try Honest Louie's, on Third Avenue," he whispered, blasting Max with hot breath.

"Thanks," she said, wrenching her arm away from his.

They headed to Third Avenue. But there, too, they learned that Reggie Anderson owed money, and had not been seen for at least a week. The bartender directed them to try the Empire Diner, but there they found out that Anderson hadn't paid his last two tabs and had been banned from the restaurant. One of the waitresses, a big blond woman with candy-colored lips, said they might find him at Deluxe Lounge, on Denton Place.

"Let's hurry," Thomas said. The sun was a large round drop hovering just over the horizon, and the sky above them was a deep, electric blue. It was nearly seven o'clock. "Dumfrey'll skin us if we don't get back before dark."

The Deluxe Lounge was very small and very dirty. A bartender with the sad, drooping look of a wilted lettuce leaf was quietly mopping under one of three large oak tables that dominated the center of the room. A skinny black cat was perched on the bar, picking at a plate of sardine bones. Dusty bottles lined the shelves, and the air smelled like rubbing alcohol and old potatoes.

There were only four patrons, and every one of them turned to stare when Max and the others pushed through the door. Two of them had been throwing darts; one of them was bucktoothed and bleary-eyed. A man with a long, curly beard, which looked like an overgrown hedge tacked to his chin, paused with his hand raised. And the largest person Max had ever seen except for Smalls, with fists as big as pork chops and a face as broad and flat as a stone, stopped with a mug halfway to his lips.

"S-s-sorry," the old bartender stuttered. "No kids allowed."

"Let 'em stay." The man with the bushy beard lowered the dart he'd been about to throw. The bartender gave a nervous squeak and scurried through the swinging doors at the back of the bar.

The bearded man smiled. His teeth were yellow and very crooked. "Well? What do you want?"

The others had gone quiet. Sam was studying his shoes, Pippa was opening and closing her mouth like a fish. Even Thomas seemed nervous.

Max lifted her chin. "We're looking for Reginald Anderson," she said.

The bearded man snickered. "You are, are you? What do you want with that sorry scrap?"

"He's a friend of ours," she said, forcing herself to hold the man's stare.

All four men exchanged a look and chuckled unpleasantly.

"What's so funny?" Max said. She didn't like feeling as though she were on the outside of a joke that didn't include her.

"A friend of yours, huh?" The bearded man took several heavy steps forward, hitching his belt up over his stomach. "Then maybe you'll be so *kind*"—he emphasized the word by spitting into a polished brass spittoon in the corner—"as to take care of a few of your friend's debts."

"He owes me two dollars," grunted the huge man, cracking his knuckles. Each sound was like a thunderbolt.

"He owes me five," said the man with the bleary eyes.

"We don't got any money," Max said.

"Have," Pippa whispered. "We don't have any money."

"Well, that's too bad for you." The bearded man took another menacing step forward, so he was standing only a foot away from Max. He leaned forward. "Because any friend of Reggie Anderson sure ain't no friend of mine. Jerry, how about you show Reggie's friends the door."

Jerry was the man with the hands like pork chops and a chest as broad as a barrel. He stood up from the table. Max reached into her pockets, but before she could withdraw her knives, Sam stepped in front of her.

"All right, look," he said, his voice breaking slightly. "Everybody just calm down. We don't want to hurt you—"

The bearded man roared with laughter. "Did you hear that, fellas? This little pipsqueak's worried about hurting us." He shoved a sausagelike finger in the middle of Sam's chest. "You've got some nerve, boy."

Max tried to swing at him, but Sam held her back with one arm.

"You're the pipsqueak!" she cried.

"Max, stay out of this," Sam said.

"Yeah, Max." Pippa's mouth was a fine white line. "These idiots aren't worth it."

"You better watch your mouth, sweetheart," growled the bearded man.

"Don't threaten her," Thomas said, eyes flashing.

"Cute. All of you. Very cute." He spit again, and a glob of milk-white saliva just missed the toe of Sam's shoe. "This is the last time I'll ask you nicely," the bearded man said, once again turning his attention to Sam. His eyes shone like two dark stones. "Actually, you know what? Forget being nice. Jerry?"

Max's vision seemed to slow down and get clearer, as it always did when things began to happen very fast. She saw Jerry charge forward as the bearded man stepped out of the way. She saw Jerry's fist headed straight for Sam's nose; she saw the fat wet slugs of Jerry's lips pulled back in a grin over his broken teeth; she noticed his filthy cuffs and ragged fingernails.

Before Jerry's fist could connect with his face, Sam lifted an arm almost casually and smacked Jerry's hand away as if it were a fly buzzing around his face. Jerry spun nearly a half circle, roaring with pain.

"I warned you," Sam said apologetically.

"Come on, Jerry!" All the men were shouting now, waving their hands and stomping their feet. "Don't let the boy smack you around!"

Jerry came at Sam again, this time with both hands, his teeth bared like an animal's. Sam let out a long sigh.

He brought his fist through the air slowly, indifferently, as if he intended Jerry to inspect it for him.

Crack.

His fist connected with a noise like a thunderbolt. Even Max jumped. The bearded man abruptly stopped shouting. Only the bleary-eyed man was still laughing, and his friend elbowed him sharply so he gasped and fell silent.

Jerry took one step back. His eyes rolled up to the ceiling. And then, just like that, he slumped backward, crashing through one of the wooden tables, leaving it in splinters.

Sam was blushing so hard, Max was sure he'd pop all the blood vessels in his face. "I-I'm sorry," he stuttered.

"I tried to tell him."

The bearded man had a wild look in his eyes that reminded Max of old Elijah Timmons, the man who was always pacing the street in front of Mr. Dumfrey's museum holding a big sign predicting the end of the world. His hands were trembling, too, just like Elijah's did.

"What did you do?" He grabbed Sam by the shirt collar. "How? *How?*"

"I—I didn't mean to." Sam kept his hands behind his back, as though he was worried they would reach out and hurt someone of their own accord.

The bearded man released him and stood for a second, panting. Suddenly, his face took on a murderous look. Quick as anything, he reached for something in his pants pocket.

"Look out!" Pippa screamed. "He's got a—"

They never found out what he was reaching for. Max was already moving, faster than the speed of thought. In a flash, the knife was in her hand, and her hand was an extension of her knife. Air, space, angles, speed. She felt it, she knew, in her fingers and in the handle of her knife. For one second she *was* metal; she belonged to the knife and could sense the cold sharpness of its blade, aching to be released.

Then the bearded man was carried backward, half-way across the room. With a satisfying thud, the knife pinned his shirtsleeve to the precise center of the dart-board.

"Bull's-eye," Max said, and smiled.

28

They'd failed to find Reggie Anderson, or any information that might be useful in locating him. All they knew was that he played pool, darts, rummy, and poker, and was terrible at all of them. His debts gave him motive, Thomas knew, for the theft of the shrunken head. But he had a hard time picturing the boy in the mismatched clothing, who'd nearly fainted in front of the police, stringing up his own uncle and then poisoning Potts after dinner.

The sun was hovering low and lazy over the Manhattan skyline, fat as an orange. Thomas voted they return to the museum. At least there, they could confront Hugo—although Thomas had no idea what, exactly, they would say.

Back at the museum, however, they were again disappointed: both Hugo and Phoebe had vanished.

"Very strange," Danny said, as he plunked a large pot of watery stew on the table. In Mrs. Cobble's absence, he had taken over the duties of chef, after Goldini had spoiled a whole omelet while trying to make it levitate from the pan. "With not a word to nobody."

"Not a word to *anybody*," Pippa corrected, and then shrank backward when Danny glared at her, raising a bushy black eyebrow.

"I bet they jumped ship, just like Mrs. Cobble," said Andrew darkly as he sloshed a bit of stew in his bowl. Thomas sniffed experimentally and swallowed a sigh. It smelled a little like the inside of a shoe. "You wait and see. He'll be quoted in the papers tomorrow."

"Nonsense. All of his things are still here," Betty pointed out as she tucked her long beard neatly into the front of her dress so that it would not drag on the table.

"*Hers* aren't, though," Miss Fitch said. "One of her good dresses is missing. And a small suitcase she borrowed from Goldini. Gone!"

"I needed that suitcase," Goldini said morosely, as he passed a coin between his fingers, making it appear and reappear. "It had a beautiful false bottom. Darn it!" He cursed as the vanished coin failed to materialize again. "I'm sorry," he said, wiping his forehead. "I'm very upset. Mrs. Cobble . . . Potts . . . and now Hugo and Phoebe . . ."

Betty patted him on the shoulder. "Hugo and Phoebe will be back, Paul."

"I wouldn't bet on it," growled Andrew, and then picked up his soup and began to slurp.

"Must you eat like an animal?" Miss Fitch said.

"I'm the alligator boy, ain't I?"

"What on earth happened to that coin?" the magician muttered.

"It'll be the end of us," Danny said, as he hauled himself up onto a chair. "These are bad times. With Hugo and Phoebe gone—"

"Hello! What's for dinner? It smells absolutely delicious. I'm famished, I must say." Mr. Dumfrey had appeared in the doorway, beaming, apparently recovered from his bout of weirdness earlier.

Everyone fell silent. Danny looked to the ceiling as though suddenly fixated on the paint. Miss Fitch stared guiltily at Betty, and Betty looked pleadingly at the magician. The magician concentrated on searching his pockets for the missing coin.

Thomas dropped his gaze to his stew and began eating quickly, forking pieces of mystery meat quickly into his mouth until his cheeks were as full as a chipmunk's, so he would not be forced to speak. He knew no one wanted to break the news of Hugo and Phoebe's disappearance to Dumfrey.

"Now, now. Why so quiet?" Mr. Dumfrey helped himself to a generous serving of stew. "What were you talking about before I came in? I thought I heard Hugo's name."

There was another awkward pause, in which everyone pretended to be absorbed by the table legs, the walls, or the bottom of their soup bowls.

"That's just it, Mr. Dumfrey," Pippa spoke up at last. "It's Hugo. He's . . . gone."

"Phoebe, too," Miss Fitch said.

Thomas had expected Dumfrey to express anger, or at least surprise. Instead, he barely glanced up from his bowl. "Really?" he said, taking a large bite. "How curious."

There was a brief pause. Thomas exchanged a quick look with Pippa.

"Aren't you . . . worried?" Pippa asked cautiously.

Mr. Dumfrey swallowed. "Of course not! Why should I be worried? Hugo's a grown man. Phoebe, too—a *full-grown* woman. Fattest lady of all the fattest ladies I've ever seen, and quite a beauty!" He patted his mouth delicately with a napkin. "They'll be back."

"Fair-weather friends," Andrew muttered. "Turning tail at the first sign of trouble."

Mr. Dumfrey slammed his fist down suddenly on the table so that all the bowls of stew jumped. "Enough," he said. "I've known Hugo since he was a little eleph—a little boy. I won't hear a word against him. I won't hear a peep against Phoebe, either. Now I suggest we all concentrate on this delicious stew. Tomorrow's a big day."

Thomas ate the rest of his stew without tasting it—which was actually a good thing, considering how bad it was. Should he tell Mr. Dumfrey what had happened on the train platform? But Mr. Dumfrey would tell him it was a coincidence. And what if it *was* a coincidence? Was Hugo capable of stealing from Mr. Dumfrey? Or of killing? And what about Reggie Anderson? Where did he fit in with all this?

Thomas was so lost in thought that he didn't notice he'd come to the end of his bowl of stew until he bit down on something very hard.

"Ow," he said, spitting, as a hard vibration zipped from his jaw to his head.

"My coin!" the magician cried. "You found it!" And he snatched Thomas's spoon from his hand and tipped the missing coin into his pocket.

29

By the next morning, the Odditorium had been transformed for Potts's funeral. Enormous garlands of crepe-paper roses in tasteful black and white were draped throughout the room. A large podium, hastily constructed but covered in plush black velvet, dominated the stage, and beside it stood various enormous funeral wreaths: arrangements of lilies and orchids, baby's breath and chrysanthemums. It must, Thomas thought, have cost Mr. Dumfrey a fortune.

Memorial cards bearing an image of Potts scowling slightly less than usual were fanned across various surfaces, and Thomas noted that interspersed with them were pamphlets advertising the museum's exhibits.

Thomas couldn't repress a smile as he heard Mr. Dumfrey ushering people into their seats.

"A sad day, a very sad day for all of us. Of course the museum must stay closed today, out of respect for poor Potts. This is no time to gape and gawk at our world-famous display of Indian arrowheads, the largest collection in the world! The Aztec mummy exhibit must stay closed; it's an emotional time, and we can't have the ladies fainting. And of course it would be in very poor taste to open up our brand-new Basement of Horrors, considering the terrible end Potts came to, before he has even had a good Christian burial. What a sight . . . the way he frothed at the mouth . . . the way he screamed! We'll have a reenactment, of course. You can even lie down on the mattress where he died. But not until tomorrow. Today we grieve, and we remember. Ah, Mr. Evans, there you are!"

The museum was packed. Mr. Dumfrey's recent arrest, combined with the ongoing mystery of Potts's murder and the sensation of the shrunken head, made for a once-in-a-lifetime opportunity for publicity. Thomas was sure most of the people in the room didn't care at all about Potts; they only wanted to stare at Dumfrey and gawk at the extraordinary children who had been so often in the papers.

Which was why he, Sam, Pippa, and Max were hiding backstage.

"Dumfrey's talking to Evans," reported Max, who was picking popcorn kernels out of her teeth. She was peeking out at the audience from behind the heavy purple curtains and reporting on what she saw. "Now he's getting his picture taken. . . ."

"Oh, look. Freckles came!" Pippa was also spying on the audience as it assembled. Freckles was their nickname for the famous sculptor Siegfried Eckleberger, who had modeled most of the faces in the Hall of Wax and had, additionally, been like a grandfather to Pippa, Sam, and Thomas. "I wish he hadn't, though. I still haven't finished the book he lent me and I'm sure he'll ask me about it. Wait. Is that the *mayor*?" She nearly spat out her soda.

"No way. The mayor's fatter. Oh no. I don't believe it."

"What is it?" Thomas had been lying on his back, staring up at the ceiling and thinking. He kept feeling as though he was missing something. Now he sat up.

Max turned around. Her face was pale. "It's that bloodsucker, Andrea von Snoot."

"Von Stikk," Pippa corrected her.

"Whatever. The crazy lady from the Home for

Extraordinary Children, or whatever it's called. What do you want to bet she came just to give us a hard time?"

"Detective Hardaway came," Pippa said with disgust. "What's *he* doing here?"

But before Thomas could respond, the lights dimmed and Mr. Dumfrey took the stage.

"Ladies and gentlemen, boys and girls, children of all ages," his voice boomed out in the room, which had suddenly gone very quiet. "We are gathered here today to say farewell to a man who was known by all and beloved by even more . . . a man as brave as he was handsome . . . as sensitive as he was brave . . . and as generous as he was beloved."

The children exchanged a look. Potts had never, to their knowledge, shown even the slightest evidence of being any of those things.

Mr. Dumfrey whipped a handkerchief—also black—from his suit pocket and began dabbing his eyes furiously. "And now, to say a few words, I present to you the bereaved brother of our poor, lost friend . . . Mr. Ernst Potts."

"I didn't know Potts had a brother," Pippa whispered.

"Neither did I," Thomas whispered back.

The brother who came shuffling on the stage was

nearly identical to the brother who had passed away. His mouth was set in a deep scowl, and he was wearing the same outfit of heavy work boots, gray trousers, and a floppy cap pulled low over watery blue eyes. Dumfrey retreated from the podium and gestured for Ernst to take his place. For a moment there was total silence. Then Ernst coughed.

"I didn't like my brother all that much," he said. "To be fair and straight with you, he was a mean little turd." The audience began to murmur, and Ernst raised his voice to be heard. "But he didn't deserve the ending he got." He fished a flask out from his jacket and raised it high. "To my brother, Dervish. I hope wherever you are, the floors are spotlessly clean."

"Beautiful!" Mr. Dumfrey stepped forward again, dabbing his eyes with his handkerchief. "Magnificent! Well said! To Potts! May your eternal cup overfloweth! And now—please join us for light refreshments in the Hall of Worldwide Wonders. You'll find sandwiches to the right of the largest collection of fossilized dinosaur eggs in existence, and cookies just past the display case containing the world's biggest hairball, disgorged from the belly of an Asian water buffalo. Please—take a pamphlet! Remember, tomorrow it's back to business as usual, opening at ten a.m., closing at seven p.m., and nothing but wonder and magic in between. But today we reflect! We remember! We—ah, yes, Mr. Mayor, I'd *love* to pose for a picture."

The gears of Thomas's brain had finally become unstuck. He turned to Sam. "Dervish Potts," he said. "D. Potts. Do you know what that means?"

"He had a terrible name?" Sam ventured.

"Hardaway told Dumfrey that Mr. Anderson had an appointment the day he died. *Appointment with D.*," Thomas said. "What do you wanna bet he meant Dervish?"

"But where does that get us?" Pippa said. "Even if Potts did meet with Mr. Anderson, we can't prove it. And we still don't know what happened to that head."

"Children!" Mr. Dumfrey was gesturing to them frantically from the stage. "What are you doing back there? Come here! This instant!"

They emerged cautiously out of the wings. Instantly, Dumfrey threw his arms around them and ushered them to the center of the stage. "That's right, that's right. In the spotlight, where you belong. You're my star performers! Max, get that toothpick out of your mouth. Remember to smile. I said smile, Sam. You look like you're about to have a tooth extracted."

There was a sudden explosion of camera flashes, and Thomas was blinded. Spots of color swam in front of his eyes. Disembodied voices called out: "Over here! Look over here!"

Suddenly, Thomas saw a monstrous bird bearing down on them. No. Not a bird, but something much worse: Andrea von Stikk, wearing a feather hat.

"Mr. Dumfrey," she said with a look of distaste, as if the name were a dirty word. "Up to your usual tricks, I see. Parading these poor children in front of the crowds like little lambs offered up for sacrifice."

"Miss von Stikk." Mr. Dumfrey greeted her with a stiff bow. "What a pleasant surprise. I didn't expect to see you here. I rather thought you were too busy torturing children with their multiplication tables."

She smiled thinly. "Education is never torture, Mr. Dumfrey," she said. "And I'm here on official business." She withdrew from her large purse a stack of papers and slapped them in Mr. Dumfrey's hands. "A court petition," she said, as he fumbled for his glasses, "for the removal of the children from your custody."

"What?" Thomas nearly choked on his tongue.

Mr. Dumfrey lowered his glasses. His face was white. "You won't get away with this."

"I most certainly will," Miss von Stikk said. Her beady black eyes glittered dangerously. "You may have been cleared by the police, Mr. Dumfrey, but I can assure you the court of public opinion has found you guilty many times over. I will not sit by and let you corrupt these four extraordinary children. These angels belong with— Ahhhhhh!"

As she spoke, Miss von Stikk placed a hand on Max's shoulder. Instantly, Max whipped the toothpick from her mouth and drove it straight into von Stikk's hand. Miss von Stikk let out a blood-curdling scream.

"I told you to keep your hands off me," Max growled.

"Max, that was very wrong," Mr. Dumfrey said, but Thomas was sure he was struggling not to smile. "Miss von Stikk is only trying to help, misguided though she may be in her methods."

"We don't want no help," Max said.

"Any," Pippa said. Max glared at her. Pippa blushed and turned to face Miss von Stikk. "We don't want *any* help. We want to stay with Mr. Dumfrey."

Miss von Stikk was cradling her injured hand to her chest. Her nostrils flared with every breath. She reminded Thomas very much of a bull when confronted by a red flag. "I have no need of further proof," she said in a voice strangled with fury. "You have raised these children to be animals. You are unfit to be their caretaker, and I intend to prove it. Good day to you, Mr. Dumfrey. You'll be hearing from my lawyer."

30

No sooner had Andrea von Stikk swept out of the room than the children received another, secondary shock. Still blinded by the glare of the cameras, Pippa could not immediately identify the source of the commotion. She heard Miss Fitch squeal, then a familiar peal of laughter.

Blinking rapidly, she saw the thick crowd parting. From within them, like two figures carried to shore on a dark wave, came Hugo and Phoebe—flushed, smiling, and holding hands. Thomas let out a cry of surprise, and Pippa gasped.

"Aha." Mr. Dumfrey's eyes were twinkling, and Pippa saw that he, for one, was not at all surprised by their reappearance. "There you are. Just in time to pay your respects. And to receive my respects, of course." Mr. Dumfrey pumped Hugo's hand as he lumbered onto the stage and helped Phoebe up behind him. Phoebe blushed when Mr. Dumfrey leaned down to kiss her hand. "Congratulations, my dearest Phoebe," Mr. Dumfrey said. "Or should I say . . . my dearest *Mrs.* Hugo?"

"What?" all four children said at once. Miss Fitch swooned and was barely saved from toppling backward by the intervention of Goldini, who caught her.

"Married?" both albino twins cried at once.

"'As fair art thou, my bonnie lass,'" quoted Smalls, wiping away a tear with a gigantic thumb. "Robert Burns," he clarified.

Only then did Pippa notice that Hugo was wearing a very dark suit, cut especially to accommodate his monstrous neck and shoulders, and a hat the size of a pumpkin, made to fit over his huge, bulbous head. Phoebe was wearing a voluminous white dress that made her look like a large ball of cotton.

"It's true," Hugo said, removing his hat. His smile was so big, Pippa thought it might split his face in two. "Phoebe is my wife."

"A marriage!" Mr. Evans cried, and cameras began to flash again.

Pippa's jaw fell open. "*That's* your big secret?"

Hugo smiled sheepishly. Phoebe jumped in. "We were afraid to tell anyone at first," she said, squeezing Hugo's arm. "We felt terrible about leaving the act after everything Mr. Dumfrey has done for us."

"Pshaw." Mr. Dumfrey waved a hand dismissively. "I didn't do so much. Still, now that you mention it," he added, turning to a collection of reporters still clustered around the stage, "I suppose that the public will be happy to learn that no showplace on earth treats its performers better than the one-and-only Dumfrey's Dime Museum!"

"You're . . . you're leaving the act?" Pippa said. She remembered the conversation Thomas had relayed. Pippa had assumed Hugo and Phoebe felt guilty because they were involved in the theft of the head. But all along, they had merely planned to get married.

Hugo took a deep breath. "Do you remember Mrs. Weathersby? Old as the hills with a face like a lemon?"

It was Mr. Evans who spoke up. "Mrs. Weathersby? She was the very first victim of the curse!" His voice echoed through the Odditorium. "I went to interview the old girl myself. She kicked the bucket not fifteen minutes later. I broke the story. You can read all about it in the *Screamer*." He raised his voice even louder, to be heard above the murmuring of the crowd.

"That's the one." Hugo looked at Phoebe. Phoebe nodded at him. "She . . . she was my mother."

Mr. Evans looked about ready to swoon from joy. He began scribbling furiously in his notebook.

"Your *mother*?" This time it was all the residents of the museum—except Mr. Dumfrey—who spoke the words at once.

Hugo nodded. "She didn't like to tell anyone about me, of course," he said. "Because of . . ." He gestured to his oversize head and his nose the size of an onion, and Pippa's heart ached for him. Poor, kind Hugo. She couldn't believe they had ever suspected him of murder. "She told everyone her son was dead. But she came to see the show sometimes. Never said a word to me, but slipped me a ten-spot every now and then. And she remembered me in her will."

"She remembered you very well," Phoebe said. Her face was flushed with pleasure. "Hugo can retire. And I can open a little bakery, like I've always dreamed."

Hugo ducked his head. "It didn't seem right to ask her to marry me when I didn't have an extra nickel," he said. "But now . . ."

"Ah, yes. But now," Mr. Dumfrey said, "you can live happily ever after."

"You knew," Sam said accusatorily. "You knew all along."

Mr. Dumfrey spread his hands as if to say, Of course.

"But you were there," Max said, "the day Thomas was pushed under the train."

This time, it was Hugo's turn to look stunned. He turned to Thomas. "You—you were pushed under a train? When? How?"

Thomas looked uneasily at the group of newspaper reporters, standing with their pens hovering over their notepads. "It was an accident," he said quickly. "It happened yesterday."

"Yesterday." Hugo continued to look bewildered. "Yesterday was the day I went to settle my mother's affairs with her lawyer on Center Street in Brooklyn. Phoebe and I met at the courthouse."

Another mystery solved. They must have caught him leaving the lawyer's office on his way to get married.

"Well, well." Mr. Dumfrey opened his arms as though to embrace the entire crowd. "A wedding and a funeral! How absolutely remarkable. I really couldn't have planned it better myself."

But the way his eyes twinkled made Pippa wonder if *planning* it was exactly what Mr. Dumfrey had done.

* * *

Potts's memorial service, which turned into a celebration of Phoebe and Hugo's wedding, lasted well into the evening, and Pippa was exhausted by the time everyone had at last cleared out and all the exhibit halls had been swept of debris. Her cheeks ached from smiling for photographers. Her teeth ached from all the soda she had consumed.

And her heart ached when she thought of the hideous Andrea von Stikk.

She couldn't sleep. Every time she did, she drifted down into the same dark nightmare: a long black tunnel, lined with cages, and human hands reaching for her, whispering her name, begging for help. Finally, she sat up. Max's bed was already empty. She must have gone to the bathroom.

Pippa shoved her feet into her slippers and reached for the robe she kept near the bed. Mr. Dumfrey had given it to her for her last birthday. She was headed to the stairs when she heard a rustling and a soft muttered curse from the common area. Peeking over the bookshelves, she saw Thomas pressed to the ground, fishing for something underneath the armchair.

"What are you doing?" she whispered.

He sat up quickly, banging his head on the underside of the chair. "Ow," he said, and rubbed his head.

He held up a small wooden eyeball; she knew from watching him that it was a critical piece for some of the more complicated strategies of DeathTrap. "Found it."

"You can't sleep, either?"

He shook his head. "I've been awake for hours. I've played three games already."

"How're you doing?" she whispered.

"I won," he said. He made a face. "And I lost."

"Hey."

Pippa spun around, startled. Sam had appeared behind her, his face shadowed by the curtain of his hair.

"You, too?" she said.

He shrugged. "I'm not tired."

"*Shhhh*." Several people said simultaneously from the dark.

Pippa gestured to the stairs. Thomas stood up, nodding, and he and Sam followed her out into the hall and down the spiral staircase. Pippa's slippered feet slapped loudly on the steps. There was something delicious about the museum after dark: cool and vast and *theirs*, like a secret vault full of hidden treasure.

The light was on in the kitchen, and Max was standing at the stove.

"It's about time," she said, when they entered. "I

thought you'd be down sooner."

There were four mugs centered in the middle of the table. Max turned away from the stove, holding a steaming pot, and carefully ladled hot chocolate into each of them.

"You're the best, Max," Sam said, with sudden emotion.

Max tossed her hair. "No need to get all gooey about it," she said, but Pippa noticed she couldn't quite conceal a smile.

They sat together in quiet for a bit, sipping the hot chocolate, which was surprisingly good. Max had even remembered to froth the milk. The kitchen was warm and bright, and Pippa found herself wishing that they could stay there forever, together, with the darkness held at bay behind the windows; with the nightmares safely trapped upstairs, among the shadows.

"What is it, Pip?" Thomas said gently. "You're shaking."

It was true. Pippa had spilled a bit of hot chocolate on her thumb. She set down her cup and took a deep breath. "I've been having these . . . *dreams*," she said. She avoided Max's gaze; Max would only laugh. "Awful dreams."

"Everyone has nightmares," Thomas said. "Statistically, one out of every seven dreams is actually—"

"Lay off the math lesson," Sam said. Then he turned to Pippa. "What kind of dreams?"

She dug her fingernail into a knot in the wooden table. She was embarrassed, now, that she had brought it up. But she couldn't stop the words from tumbling out of her mouth. "There's a tunnel," she said. "And—and cages. Like the kind you see at the zoo. Only there aren't any animals. There's only—"

"People," Thomas finished for her. She looked up, astonished. He was staring at her, wide-eyed. "I've—I've had the same dream," he said.

Pippa felt a sudden thickness in her throat. "That's impossible," she croaked out. "People don't dream the same things."

"They must," Sam interjected. He had pushed his hair out of his eyes; his gaze was sharp and alert. "Because I've had the same dream, too."

There were several long moments of silence. Pippa felt as if her brain was wrapped in a slow, sticky syrup. What did it mean? What could it mean?

Thomas was staring off into space, as though he could decode the answer there. "The probability of three people dreaming the same exact thing," he murmured, "is one in three billion eight hundred and seventy-five."

"What about the probability of *four* people dreaming the exact same thing?" Max said in a shaky voice. Pippa looked up. Max wasn't laughing after all. She was gripping her mug so tightly her knuckles had gone white.

"Impossible," Thomas whispered.

Pippa's chest felt tight. She remembered the conversation she had overheard backstage just after Max's arrival. What had Mr. Dumfrey said, exactly? *Now I know all four of them are safe.* Almost as if they were connected . . .

In the silence, Pippa heard it: the faint tinkle of shattered glass. Max jumped to her feet.

"Did you hear that?" Sam whispered, and Max hushed him. In one fluid movement, Thomas vaulted over the table and crept silently up the stairs, pressing his ear to the door.

Pippa held her breath. Her heart was drumming in her chest. She strained to listen. Someone was moving swiftly across the lobby.

Thomas eased the door open and gestured for the others to follow him. Max grabbed the weapon nearest at hand—in this case, a spoon, which wasn't much of a weapon at all. Pippa moved up the stairs, pausing only to kick off her slippers. The floor was cold against her bare feet. Sam followed behind her, moving on his tiptoes.

Together, they emerged into the darkness of the special exhibits room, and Miss Cobble's chambers, now empty. They slipped into the hallway, moving silently past the grand central staircase, and skirted two Indian totem poles that stood like sentries next to the ticket desk. Max's spoon glittered in the moonlight coming through the windows. Pippa's heart was in her throat. Long shadows lay like liquid across the floor.

Thomas held up a hand, and Max stopped walking. Pippa stepped on her heel, and Max turned around and poked her sharply with her spoon. Pippa swallowed back a cry of surprise and instead settled for pinching Max's elbow.

They listened. The grandfather clock ticked on in the quiet; there was a sudden sweep of bright light, as though from a flashlight, at the end of the hall. The light disappeared again, and footsteps creak-creak-creaked into the Odditorium.

They moved forward again, but so slowly that Pippa had the sensation they weren't moving at all, as if the darkness were tar and they were floundering in place. But eventually they were there, at the entrance to the Odditorium.

The beam of light—definitely a flashlight—was moving quickly up the aisle toward the stage on which Potts's coffin had been placed for display by Mr. Dumfrey. A feeble blue light illuminated the dead Potts, lying with his hands folded, looking just as ill-tempered as he had in real life.

As they watched, a shadow broke free of the dark and stepped onto the stage. Crouching, the man—Pippa thought it *must* be a man, because of the loose pants and coat he was wearing—pocketed the flashlight and bent over the casket.

Everything happened very quickly. Thomas and Max slipped off toward opposite sides of the stage, and Sam and Pippa charged down the central aisle, shouting, "Stop! Freeze!"

The intruder whipped around and cried out. Backlit by the dim blue light, his features were indistinguishable. He tried to run toward the wings, but Max charged him and barreled him backward, holding the spoon to his jugular, roaring fearsomely. Then Sam was there, restraining him, and Pippa heard someone calling, "Lights! Turn on the lights!" before she realized that she was the one yelling.

The stage lights came on, suddenly dazzling. Dazzling, too, was the intruder's extraordinary clothing:

purple pants, a bright-red shirt, and a billowing purple coat, all of it clashing awfully with the boy's thatch of shock-red hair.

They had found Reginald Anderson.

31

"P-please," Reginald Anderson blubbered. "I can explain."

"Then start explaining," Max growled. She was still holding her spoon menacingly in Reggie's direction, as though she intended to scoop his brains out with it. They had seated Reggie in one of the narrow folding chairs used by the audience.

Reggie opened his mouth, then closed it again. All at once, he buried his head in his hands and began to sob loudly into the fabric of his hat.

"I'm sorry," he said in a choked voice. "I never shoulda come . . . but I didn't know what else to do. . . ."

"Slow down and start from the beginning," said

Pippa, who with every second was doubting more and more that he might have been responsible for the attack on Bill Evans or Potts's murder. Even the sight of a spoon made him tremble. On the other hand, he had broken into the museum—and he had been rummaging around in Potts's casket.

Reggie took a deep breath and raised his head. His lower lip trembled. "I'm in a real tight spot," he said. "But I'm no killer. I swear I'm no killer."

"What did you want with Potts?" Max jabbed her spoon closer to his face.

"I—I didn't even know his name before today," Reggie said quickly. "I saw his picture in the paper. I knew his face. He'd been to see my uncle . . . once or twice." He mumbled the last words quickly.

"Mmm-hmmm." Thomas crossed his arms. "And was *once* the day your uncle died?"

He nodded miserably. Pippa's breath caught in her throat. She caught Thomas's eye. So they'd been right about Potts—he had been dealing with Mr. Anderson behind Dumfrey's back. And Potts had been in Anderson's shop the day he died.

Reggie worried his thin woolen hat between his hands. "I didn't think anything of it at first. My uncle had lots of clients. Lots of people going in and out. I'd had a fight with him that morning, you see. I phoned him up to tell him—to tell him I wasn't coming back. To tell him I was running away with my girl, Betsy. Betsy Williams. She lives in Boston—"

"Get on with it," Max said impatiently.

"Well, that morning I phoned up but he hardly let me get a word out. Gotta go, Reggie, I got Scarface coming over. That's what he said."

"Scarface?" Sam repeated.

Reggie gestured to the casket where Potts was lying, his acne scars inexpertly concealed under heavy makeup. "That's what my uncle called him. He called me Red most of the time. Or Dummy." Reggie blushed.

"That doesn't explain what you're doing, poking around here in the middle of the night," Thomas said.

By now, Reggie's face was the exact same shade of crimson as his hair. "I'm broke," he said. "Betsy won't marry me unless I get some money together. . . . I tried gambling for it but . . ." He trailed off.

"Now you owe money all over town," Sam finished.

Reggie looked at him. "How did you know?"

"It doesn't matter," Thomas cut in quickly. "Go on."

He was working the hat so hard, Pippa feared he would tear it in two. "My uncle always carried a lighter," he said, in a choked voice. "It was my grandfather's. It was made of pure silver, and there was a real sapphire in the catch." Reggie's voice began to tremble. "It's terrible but I—well, I knew my uncle couldn't miss it now. I was going to use it to pay off my debts. But it's gone. My uncle always had it on him, always. I thought Scarface—er, Potts—might have taken it. It seems silly but . . . I was desperate."

Pippa noticed that Max's spoon had begun to tremble. Pippa looked at her questioningly, and Max quickly crossed her arms.

"Now Betsy will never marry me," Reggie said, and swallowed back a sob.

Max turned suddenly and bolted out of the room. Thomas raised an eyebrow.

"I'll go talk to her," Sam whispered.

"What's got into them?" Reggie turned around to watch Sam go.

"Stay focused." Thomas snapped his fingers in front of Reggie's nose. "Tell me what you know about Bill Evans."

Reggie's eyes widened. "The newspaper man?"

"So you know him," Thomas said.

Reggie shrugged. "Only from the papers."

"He was nearly killed two days ago," Pippa said,

watching Reggie carefully for any signs of guilt.

But he only looked bewildered. "I read about it," he said. "He was in a car accident." He looked from Pippa to Thomas and back again. Then, suddenly, realization seemed to dawn on him. "Don't tell me you think I had something to do with it . . . ?"

Now that she had spoken to him, Pippa didn't think Reggie was capable of mowing a man down in cold blood—or, for that matter, of squashing an ant. But she said, "Evans told us the person driving the car had red hair."

"Now just hang on a second." Reggie straightened up in his chair. "You can't pin this one on me. I never even learned to drive. I can't. I'm completely color-blind. The state won't let me ride a bicycle, even."

Pippa and Thomas exchanged a look. So that explained the hideous choice of clothing.

Reggie's eyes overflowed again. "I'm not a crook," he said. "I promise. I got in over my head . . . all because I wanted Betsy to say yes—"

"Yeah, we got that," Thomas said, and sighed. He rubbed his eyes. "All right," he said. "Get out of here."

"You—you're not going to call the police?" Reggie stammered.

Thomas shook his head. Reggie stood up. He took a

step forward, as though tempted to embrace Thomas. Thinking better of it, he settled for pumping Thomas's hand and then Pippa's. His palm was very wet.

"Thank you," he gushed. "I won't forget this. And you won't have any more trouble from me. I promise."

Pippa withdrew her hand from his and wiped it carefully on her pajamas. She was tired, suddenly—an exhaustion in her bones and blood and even the roots of her hair.

Pippa and Thomas saw Reggie out of the museum, carefully locking the door behind him. They carefully swept up the glass Reggie had shattered. Miss Fitch would see to the broken window tomorrow. Upstairs, they found Sam waiting for them on the landing.

"Max all right?" Thomas asked.

He shrugged. "She wouldn't talk to me," he said. Even in the dark, Pippa could see that he was blushing. "She hauled off straight to bed."

"She's always weird," Pippa said, yawning. But even as they passed into the darkness of the attic, Pippa couldn't shake off the feeling that she was missing something incredibly important.

Max was already in bed, as Sam had said. She was snoring quietly into her pillow.

"Max?" Pippa whispered. There was no answer. She

climbed into bed and pulled the covers to her chin. "Max?" She tried again.

Max only snored a little louder. But even as Pippa drifted off to sleep, the bad feeling stayed with her—and the feeling, too, that Max was only faking.

32

Thomas woke just before dawn. In his first confused moment, he thought that the rustling he heard was Reggie Anderson come back. But then he realized Reggie would not have sneaked all the way up to the attic. Sitting up, he saw Max moving quietly between the familiar jumble of furniture and beds. She glanced behind her, as though to verify no one was watching, and Thomas shrank back into the shadows. In the moonlight, her face looked white and worried. Then she turned around again and slipped out into the hall.

He climbed out of bed and padded quickly across the carpet to the door, passing only a few feet from

Danny, who was snoring loudly in an armchair, where he had fallen asleep after toasting Hugo and Phoebe. Thomas eased open the door with two fingers, praying it wouldn't creak, and peeked out into the hall. A thin fissure of light spilled out into the hall from the bathroom. Thomas debated whether to knock and ask if everything was all right, or to wait for her in the hall, or to return to bed and question her later.

Then he heard more rustling and Max muttering, "It's got to be here. . . . It has to be. . . ."

He took a deep breath, approached the bathroom door, and knocked softly.

Instantly, the rustling stopped. "Max?" he said. "It's Thomas."

"Go away," she said fiercely. But instead, he pushed open the door.

Max sprang to her feet, fist clenched, as if she were going to attack him. In a second, Thomas took in everything: her rucksack open on the ground, its contents scattered across the linoleum; Max's expression of fear; the white half-moons of her knuckles. Then he realized she wasn't winding up to punch him. She was gripping something in her fist.

Suddenly, Thomas understood.

"Show me," he said.

For a second, he thought she would refuse. But then her shoulders sagged and she held out her hand and opened her fingers, so he could see the silver lighter in her palm.

The silver lighter with a blue sapphire in its catch.

Thomas stared. "That's . . . that's Mr. Anderson's lighter." He looked up at Max's miserable expression. "The one Reggie wanted."

"I didn't know it was anything special," Max said quickly.

Thomas sighed. "You'll have to give it back," he said. "You know that, don't you?"

"I can't get busted for stealing," Max said. "It was just a game. I didn't mean anything by it. I was dipping in and out of people's pockets, to see if anyone would notice—"

"Wait a second." Thomas suddenly felt very alert. "Slow down. You took the lighter from someone's *pocket*? Not from Mr. Anderson's apartment?"

"I was bored," she said. "Everyone was gabbing on and on about Potts. . . ." She shrugged.

An electric excitement zipped up Thomas's spine. Max had lifted Mr. Anderson's lighter from the pocket of one of the guests at Potts's memorial. Since Reggie said that Mr. Anderson never went anywhere without his lighter, that could only mean one thing: someone had stolen it from Mr. Anderson.

He took a deep breath. "Max, listen to me carefully. This is important. Whose pocket did you pick?"

To his infinite disappointment, Max shook her head. "He was wearing a dark blue suit. You have to move fast, you know, when you're snatching, otherwise—"

"Think," Thomas cut her off. "Do you remember anything about him? Anything at all?"

"I told you," Max said irritably. "I wasn't taking notes."

Thomas massaged the bridge of his nose. There had been hundreds of people at Potts's memorial, most of them strangers. But had he recognized anyone? When he closed his eyes, all he could see was the glare of a dozen camera flashes. All he could hear was Evans telling him to look this way, look this way . . .

And then it was as if the flash was not in his mind but in his whole body, in his whole mind. He opened his eyes.

Evans.

Max was frowning at him. "What is it? What's the matter?"

Thomas's heart was going fast. "Please, Max. Try and remember. Did you pick Evans's pocket?"

Before she could answer, Pippa spoke up from the hall. "What about Evans's pocket?"

Thomas turned around. Pippa and Sam were standing in the hall. Sam was rubbing sleep out of his eyes.

Thomas snatched the lighter from Max's hand.

"Max took this from someone yesterday," Thomas said.

Pippa glared at Max. "I thought I told you—"

Sam gawked. "That's the lighter Reggie was after."

"I didn't mean nothing by it," Max grumbled.

"Anything!" Pippa said exasperatedly. "You didn't mean— Oh, just forget it."

"Listen." Thomas's hand was trembling. "I think Evans might be involved. He's been up to his neck in this case from the very beginning, hasn't he? He's the one who fed us that story of the redhead and the car. He's the one who wrote about the curse of the shrunken head in the first place."

Pippa blinked. Slowly, an awed expression came over her face. "I saw that lighter once," she said, in a hushed voice. "I saw it in his pocket, when we went to the office of the *Daily Screamer*."

"That was just after Potts was killed," Max said excitedly.

Pippa stiffened. Her eyes lost their focus. "The green

fish . . . ," she whispered.

"The green *what*?" Thomas said.

She blinked, and turned to him. "The green fish," she said excitedly. So he had not misheard.

"What are you talking about, Pip?" Sam said.

Pippa made a noise of impatience. "Remember when we tracked Potts to that awful restaurant, Paulie's? That was the first day I ever read a mind. I saw what Paulie was thinking. I saw a blurry green fish." She paused. "Only it wasn't a fish. It was a shark."

"So?" Thomas was getting more impatient by the second.

"So?" Pippa practically choked on the word. "Don't you see? He was thinking of *a green shark tattoo*, just like the one Evans has on his arm." Her face split into a grin. "He said he didn't remember anything about the man who was eating with Potts just before Potts died. But he must have seen Evans's tattoo and remembered it without knowing he remembered it. Get it? Evans was there. Evans had dinner with Potts. And then Potts died."

A chill spread over Thomas, starting in his chest and reaching to the roots of his hair. If they were right—and they had to be right—Evans had killed at least two people. Maybe three. They had only Evans's word for it that Mrs. Weathersby was alive when he left her, and only later plunged to her death.

Thomas's stomach turned over. He'd sat in Evans's office, he'd spoken with Evans, and he'd had no idea.

Max broke the long stretch of silence. "I still don't get it," she said, hugging herself. "Did Evans steal the head, too? What's he going to do with it? And why'd he go bonkers and start killing people?

Thomas took a deep breath. "There's only one way to find out," he said.

Pippa, Max, and Sam stared at him.

"How?" Pippa said.

"We ask Evans," Thomas said.

33

They went straightaway, after changing in the darkness of the attic out of their pajamas and into street clothes. When they emerged into the brisk air, the sky was just beginning to lighten in the east, like a large blue blanket whose corners had caught flame. Max had always loved the city at this hour, when the buildings were like tall black stakes against the sky, and only a few lights flickered in the windows; when the streets were empty; when the whole city felt like a large, slumbering monster, and she could pass unseen in its shadows.

But now that they were on their way to catch a real-life monster, Max felt different. She imagined that the shadows were full of people waiting to reach out and grab her. The wind felt like an alien touch and lifted the hairs on the back of her neck. She was glad that she wasn't alone. Sam spent the subway ride in silence, chin down, almost as if he were asleep, although Max knew better. Thomas, on the other hand, couldn't stop moving. He stood up and sat down again. He drummed his fingers on the seat. He jogged his knee. And Pippa stared out the window, her breath fogging the glass.

Max would never have admitted it, but she was even—even—glad for Pippa.

They knew from the newspaper reports of Bill Evans's accident that he lived on Ludlow Street, between Hester and Canal. Thomas trusted they'd be able to find it, and it turned out they shouldn't have worried. As soon as they reached the corner of Canal and Ludlow, Evans's apartment building was easy to spot: bouquets of flowers, get-well cards, and even soggy teddy bears were clustered in front of the gate at number 12.

"Looks like Evans has a fan club," Sam said.

"Not for long," Thomas said.

Max's stomach knotted up. She shoved her hands in her pockets and reassured herself that her knives were still there.

All the windows of the apartment building were dark; it must have been just after six o'clock. Down the street, a man wheeled a fruit cart toward Canal, whistling softly. Soon the city would open its eyes.

Thomas navigated the piles of flowers and gifts and pushed open the gate. He gestured for the others to follow him.

"Are you going to ring?" Pippa whispered as they clustered together at the top of the stoop. To the right of the front door were several doorbells. BILL EVANS was written in block print next to the middle one, apartment 2A.

Thomas shook his head. "No ringing. We want to catch him by surprise."

"You think he'll try and run for it?" Max asked.

"We can't give him the chance. Sam? Will you?" Thomas gestured to the door.

Sam repressed a small sigh and shuffled forward. Max fingered her knives impatiently. Her palms were sweating. Would that affect her ability to throw, if she had to? She thought of Evans's toothy smile, and all of the stuff he'd written about them in the papers. She'd love to stake him straight through the head.

But she knew she could never really hurt someone, as much as she pretended. That's why the thought of confronting Evans made her mouth go dry and her palms go wet. People thought she and Pippa and Thomas and Sam were the freaks. But the real freaks were people like Evans—people who could hide their true selves completely, as if all their lives they were wearing Halloween masks.

Sam leaned carefully into the building door. There was a click. He turned back to the others, a look of confusion on his face. "It's unlocked."

That made Max even more nervous. It was as if Evans was expecting them. And maybe he was.

Inside, the hall was dark and smelled like fresh paint. A narrow staircase led up to the second floor. Thomas took the lead. Pippa followed him, then Max, then Sam. Max could hear his quiet breathing in the dark and was comforted by it. The stairs squeaked awfully, and at any second she expected Evans to materialize from the darkness. But they reached the landing without incident and stood clustered in front of the door to 2A. There was not a rustle of sound from within. Evans must still be sleeping.

Sam leaned into the door. And once again, it opened at the slightest pressure of his hand, swinging inward with a faint groan. Sam looked bewildered. "This one's unlocked, too," he whispered.

Max's heart was flapping like a salmon in her chest.

Inside Evans's apartment, all of the curtains were drawn. It was as dark as night, especially after Thomas had eased the door shut behind them. Max had the sudden, frantic urge to run. Surely Evans would hear her heart drumming, and Sam's rapid breathing, and the faint rustle of Pippa's jacket.

But one second passed, then two. Nothing happened.

Gradually, Max's eyes began to adjust, and she saw that it wasn't completely dark. There was a faint light coming from the next room, as if there, a curtain had been left open a crack. They were standing, she saw, in a small kitchenette area. Directly ahead of them was a wooden table and beyond it, a partially open door.

Thomas was already moving toward it. As Max passed through the doorway, she felt Sam jostle her, but she was too afraid to speak out loud and tell him to watch out. The fear was everywhere now, like being squeezed inside a sweaty palm.

The next room was a study. Against the far wall were two windows. The curtains were parted a little, revealing a view of another apartment building and allowing a little daylight to penetrate. In front of the windows was a large desk, empty except for a silver letter opener. In front of the desk was an armchair.

And in the armchair, his back to them, was Bill Evans.

"Turn around." Thomas reached out and turned on a lamp. Instantly, the colors of the room were revealed: Evans's thatch of brown hair, the navy-blue curtains, the scarlet rug.

Evans didn't move.

"Stop playing games," Thomas said again. But still, Evans said nothing and remained facing the windows.

Sam lost patience. He crossed the room in two quick strides. "You heard what he said—"

The words died on his lips as he spun the chair around. Pippa screamed.

Evans's eyes were open, and there was blood on his lips. He wasn't breathing.

Suddenly, the door slammed shut behind them.

Max, Pippa, Thomas, and Sam whirled around. A very tall, very thin man was standing in the corner, where he had been concealed from view by the open door. His skin was an unhealthy gray, like the sky just before it rained, and his eyes, behind his glasses, a very pale blue. When he smiled, Max saw his teeth were unusually long and very yellow. He looked vaguely familiar, but Max couldn't think where she had seen him.

"Hello, my children," he said. "I've been waiting for you."

"Who—who are you?" Pippa stammered.

"My name"—the man removed his hat with a flourish—"is Professor Rattigan."

34

"Professor Rattigan," Pippa repeated in a whisper. "We—we heard about you on the news."

"You're the crazy man who escaped from prison," Max blurted out.

Professor Rattigan replaced his hat. "Yes and no. I did escape from prison. I am not, however, crazy."

Max noticed Thomas glance quickly at the telephone on the table. But Professor Rattigan noticed, too.

"No use, Thomas, my boy," he said cheerfully. "The line's cut. I took care of that myself."

"How—how do you know my name?" Thomas's face was very white.

"Half of New York knows your name." Professor

Rattigan chuckled. "You're a celebrity! Thanks to our friend Bill Evans over here." He gestured unconcernedly at Mr. Evans, still staring, unseeing, into the air. Max wished that Sam would turn his armchair around again. She felt at any second like Bill Evans might blink and stand up.

"I've enjoyed reading about you very much." Professor Rattigan moved over to a second armchair, drawn up close to the fireplace, and sat. He peeled off his black gloves, pinching the fingers, removing them one by one. Max was disgusted to see that his fingers were long and very white, like something dead in the water. "Of course, I've been waiting to meet you—all of you—for a very long time. Or shall I say—I've been waiting to meet you *again*. You've turned out even better than I'd hoped."

The children exchanged a look. No matter what he said, he was obviously bonkers. Max reached quickly for the knives in her coat pocket, but Professor Rattigan clucked his tongue.

"It's no use, Mackenzie." He reached into his overcoat and withdrew all three of her knives. "I took the liberty of removing them from you when you entered the room."

"But . . ." Max's mouth fell open. She remembered

how she'd felt Sam bump against her. But it must have been Professor Rattigan, fumbling in her coat pockets. She couldn't believe it. She—Max!—had been pick-pocketed. She felt a flare-up of rage. "Those are *mine*."

"You'll get them back." Rattigan popped open her switchblade and began picking his nails. "*If* you do as I say. Now, now—" He held up a hand as Max started to protest. "Enough about *me*. I want to hear about you! How did you figure out that Evans was responsible for stealing the head? That's why you're here, right? About the head and all the murders? Poor Potts. Poor Mr. Anderson. And poor Mrs. Weathersby."

"Mrs. Weathersby's death was an accident," Thomas said cautiously.

Rattigan waggled a finger. "I'd expect better from you, Thomas. Think! Use that remarkable brain." He settled back in his chair and steepled his fingertips. "Evans goes to speak to an old lady about the shock she's had at a run-down museum. It's a decent story, per-haps, but it won't light up the front page. And Evans, who has been canned from almost every major news-paper, is desperate for a story that *will* light up the front page." Rattigan paused, as if to ensure that the chil-dren were listening. "It's a very warm evening. They step out onto the balcony to talk. Before long, they begin to argue. Weathersby doesn't want to discuss the museum. She won't even admit she's been! You know why, of course . . . ?" His eyes clicked over to Thomas.

"Hugo," he said. "She didn't want anyone to figure out about Hugo."

Rattigan looked delighted. "Excellent! Precisely. Mrs. Weathersby, respectable, ancient Mrs. Weathersby, was worried Evans might nose around and discover her son was a *freak*. Don't jump down my throat, Mackenzie, those are Mrs. Weathersby's thoughts, not mine."

Max clamped her mouth shut. She had, in fact, been about to seize on his use of the word *freak*.

Rattigan went on, "She gets angry, tells him to leave, and threatens to call the police. He loses his temper and comes at her. She screams and tries to back away, and goes straight over the balcony. Splat." Rattigan paused for dramatic effect. "Evans was scared, at first. But then he saw a tremendous opportunity."

"The curse of the shrunken head," Thomas whispered.

"Precisely!" Rattigan thumped his fist down on the armrest. Pippa jumped. "The chance to break a story that would put Bill Evans back on top. Once he got started, he had to find ways to keep the story going. He had every detail because he, Evans, was responsible: for hiring Potts to steal the head and bump off Mr. Anderson, so no one would discover that the head was merely a cardboard fake; for poisoning Potts's dinner, when Potts got cold feet and wanted to confess; for burning down the restaurant to eliminate every last shred of evidence. He even staged his own accident when *you* started sniffing a little too close to the truth. It was the scoop of a lifetime!"

"How do you know all of this?" Pippa asked.

"He confessed," Rattigan said, flicking an invisible speck of dirt from his pants, "just before I killed him." He said it casually, as if he were saying *just before I took him out for ice cream.*

"But why?" Thomas said. "Why did you kill him?"

Rattigan spread his palms. "I didn't need him anymore. He had served his purpose. I was only using him, you see."

"Using him for what?" Sam said.

Rattigan smiled, revealing his long, yellow teeth. "To get to you, of course."

Max swallowed. She felt like there was a whole cat stuck in her throat. "Why?" she said, hoping she sounded angry and not afraid. "What do you want with us?"

Rattigan chuckled. "I don't want anything *with* you," he said. "You *belong* to me. I've been watching you for a week now, and you are every bit as extraordinary as I'd hoped."

Suddenly, Max knew where she had seen him before: outside Anderson's Delights, rooting through the trash, and wearing a pair of aviator's goggles. And then again, on the subway ride back from Bellevue after Thomas had stolen the report on Potts's death. He'd been following them, *spying* on them, all along.

Rattigan went on, "I've even given you some little . . . tests. Just to make sure that my experiments had turned out well."

"It was you," Thomas said hoarsely. "You pushed me under the train."

Sam balled up his fists. "And you tried to clobber me with concrete," he said.

"Water under the bridge, I hope," Rattigan said cheerfully. "You performed admirably well. Oh, yes. You far exceeded my expectations." He beamed at them, and for just a second, he reminded Max of Mr. Dumfrey congratulating them on a show well performed. But the impression quickly passed.

Outside, distantly, Max heard the wail of a police siren and felt a surge of hope. Maybe if they kept Rattigan talking, someone would miss Evans and call the police.

As if reading her mind, Rattigan withdrew a pocket watch from his vest pocket and frowned. "My, my. How time flies, especially when you're catching up with old friends. This has been fun, hasn't it?" He stood up, suddenly businesslike. "But we can talk far more comfortably elsewhere. If you'll just follow me . . ." He gestured to the door.

Nobody moved.

Thomas said, "We're not following you anywhere."

"You can't make us," Max said.

"It's four to one," Sam said.

"Quite, quite." Rattigan smiled again. "I certainly would never think of going up against *you*, Samson. Nevertheless, I'm sure you'll all come along quietly. Unless, of course, you'd like something very bad to happen to your friend Dumfrey."

"What's Dumfrey got to do with this?" Thomas said in a growl.

Rattigan blinked. "He's got everything to do with it! Surely you wouldn't want to be responsible for his death?"

"His death?" Pippa squeaked, and leaned heavily against Bill Evans's desk, as if she might faint. But then Max saw Pippa slip the silver letter opener into her pocket. Max swallowed a cry of disbelief—perfect

Pippa, grammar-loving, rule-following Pippa, was actually stealing. Pippa met her gaze and, for just a second, the ghost of a smile passed across her face.

Rattigan, fortunately, noticed nothing. He was busy polishing his glasses. "Terrible. Most unfortunate. An accident of the cruelest kind"—he returned his glasses to his nose—"*unless* you come along with me. If you do, I'll make sure that Dumfrey stays safe as a kitten."

"How do we know we can trust you?" Max said.

"Ah." Rattigan turned to her. "I'm afraid you don't. But you have no choice, do you? It's an awful thing, to gamble with someone's life."

"He's right," Thomas said quietly, in a strangled voice. "We have to go with him."

"I knew I could count on you to be logical." Rattigan smiled again. "*Especially* you, Thomas. Of course, you were *designed* to be the brainy one. Shall we?"

And with another flourish, Rattigan ushered them out the door.

35

In the time they had been inside Mr. Evans's apartment, the sun had broken free of the buildings and the streets had woken up. A woman in a housecoat was sweeping a stoop across the street; a baker smelling distinctly of fresh bread and butter hurried past them, cradling a large bag of flour in his arms; and all down the street front doors opened and closed, and men in suits consulted wristwatches and hurried off toward the subway.

To Pippa, it all felt as distant as a dream. She could think of nothing but escape. She had the letter opener in her pocket, but she had no idea what to do with it. Could she bring herself to stab Rattigan? Could Max?

What would happen if she shouted and waved her arms to any one of the strangers passing by? Would they help her? Would they think she'd gone nuts?

Would Mr. Dumfrey die?

She prayed that someone, anyone, would notice Professor Rattigan from the news and contact the police. But it was hopeless. No one paid him the slightest bit of attention. He kept his hat pulled low and he walked quickly, whistling, as if he were taking the children to an excursion at the zoo. Pippa wondered how far they would walk and felt a brief surge of hope—they must surely pass a policeman at some point. But immediately, her hopes were crushed. As though in response to a secret signal from Rattigan, a dark sedan with tinted windows turned the corner and pulled up next to a fire hydrant. She knew that once they got in the car, they were lost.

"I don't trust him one inch," Thomas whispered. The children were all hanging back together, moving as slowly as they could without being accused of delaying. "Who's to say he won't kill Dumfrey even if we do go with him?"

"You really think he rigged an accident for Dumfrey?" Max whispered.

Thomas nodded. His face was white. "I wouldn't put anything past him."

Pippa swallowed. "Then we've got no choice," she said. "We've got to make a run for it, and save Dumfrey ourselves."

"But by the time we get back to the museum, it may be too late," Sam said gravely.

"If we get in that car, we're done for," Pippa said. She felt a desperate panic clawing its way up her chest. Rattigan had reached the car and opened the back door. The interior was dark and smelled like new leather.

"Come along, come along," Rattigan said in a singsong. But Pippa could tell he was getting impatient. His eyes darted back and forth, as if he was scanning the crowd for potential danger. "Time waits for no man, the early bird catches the worm, and so on and so on."

Pippa felt like her limbs were rooted to the ground. She could not—she would not—get into the car. Thomas, Max, and Sam had stopped beside her.

Rattigan lowered his voice. "Remember our agreement," he said, showing his teeth again. "Let's have no unpleasantness, now."

"Sorry, Pip," Sam said. And, sighing, he started to climb into the car.

Then—a miracle. Across the street, Pippa saw a heavyset woman wearing a large feathered hat and gloves trimmed with fur.

Andrea von Stikk.

Pippa had never, ever thought she'd be happy to see the horrible woman—but in that minute, she would have dropped to her knees and kissed the toes of von Stikk's leather shoes.

"Miss von Stikk!" she called, frantically waving her arms. Sam straightened up instantly, and Rattigan let out a sound like a dog's growl. "Miss von Stikk!"

"Pippa!" Miss von Stikk's voice pierced the thin air. She instantly changed course. "How amazing. I was on my way to see you—well, to see Mr. Dumfrey."

"That was very stupid," Rattigan spat out, seizing Pippa roughly by the arm.

"Let her go," Thomas said.

"Very convenient." Andrea von Stikk barreled into the street toward them. A car had to swerve to avoid her, and the driver leaned on his horn and shouted something rude out the window. "You see, we have much to discuss. I spoke to my lawyers yesterday. . . ."

At that moment, a police car, perhaps attracted by the noise of the honking, turned from Grand onto Ludlow. Rattigan and Pippa spotted it at the same time.

"Sam!" Pippa hissed, jabbing a finger toward the fire hydrant.

Sam didn't hesitate. He sprang forward and gripped

the hydrant with both hands; then, with a grunt, he pulled. The fire hydrant snapped out of the pavement, and instantly, a huge geyser of water shot up from the ground.

It was as though a fountain had been opened in the sidewalk. Suddenly, everyone was shouting and pointing fingers. Andrea von Stikk, drenched from head to toe, stood spluttering and pushing limp feathers from her face. Children hung out the windows. And the police car skidded to a halt.

Rattigan released Pippa and straightened his tie with his long fingers. "How disappointing," he said, and climbed into the backseat of the waiting car. "No matter. We'll meet again. Say good-bye to Dumfrey, children."

He slammed the door and motioned for the driver to go.

Thomas spun toward Sam, who was still holding the torn-off fire hydrant, and shouted, "Stop him!"

Clutching the hydrant in one hand, Sam cocked his arm like a quarterback and took aim at Rattigan's car, which had pulled away from the curb and was picking up speed.

Pippa tossed the stolen silver letter opener to Max. Max didn't even blink. Turning gracefully, she raised the letter opener, squinted, and took aim at a tire.

Just then, the doors to the squad car flew open and two policemen jumped out: Sergeant Schroeder and Officer Gilhooley.

"Drop it!" they cried at Sam and Max.

"But he's getting away!" Pippa cried.

"I said drop it!" Gilhooley yelled. "Now!"

Sam hesitated for an instant, then let the hydrant fall with a heavy clang to the sidewalk. Max muttered a bad word and tossed the letter opener at her feet.

"Now put your hands up," Schroeder commanded. "All four of you."

They had no choice. Like outlaws in a cowboy movie, the four children raised their hands while the gushing water continued to rain down on them.

By then, Rattigan's car had turned the corner and disappeared.

36

"You don't understand." Thomas was trying to be heard over the murmurs of the gathering crowd and static from the police radio and the continuous gushing of the water. Time was pouring, pooling away. "That was Rattigan. You should be going after him."

"Slow down, slow down." Gilhooley, now soaked, looked like a rat that had been dragged up from the sewer. Water was running down his long nose.

"Start at the beginning," Schroeder said, pointing his club threateningly at Thomas's chest, "and don't even think of stopping till you get to the end."

"There's no time!" Thomas felt panic building up

inside him, a deep well of it. With every passing second, Dumfrey was in danger.

Would Rattigan make good on his threat? Had he already? "Aren't you listening to me? You're letting Professor Rattigan get away!"

"Rattigan?" Gilhooley scratched his head. "The kook from the news?"

"He was trying to kidnap us," Pippa broke in. "He killed Bill Evans."

Schroeder's lips thinned to a skeptical frown. "That's quite a story."

"I'm not making it up," Pippa cried. "It's the truth."

"You see, officers?" Andrea von Stikk was shaking. Thomas didn't know whether it was because she was wet or outraged or both. She flicked the feathers out of her eyes. "You see how these children have been hopelessly warped? It's all because of that monstrous caretaker of theirs—Dumfrey. If you release them to my care—"

"Hold up, lady. Who are you, anyway?"

"Who am I? Who are you, sir?"

As Andrea von Stikk and Schroeder began to argue, the crowd around them grew even denser, until they were hemmed in on all sides. Some were carrying umbrellas. Others were craning their necks to see what the excitement was about. One woman had even brought out a box of Raisinets, as if she were at the movies.

Thomas was getting desperate. They would never get out of here at this rate. He had to do something. They had to get back to the museum before Rattigan could get to Dumfrey.

"Now you listen here, lady—"

"That's Miss von Stikk to you!"

Thomas moved. Sensing a slight shift in the pattern of the crowd, a momentary break, he slipped into the narrow space between two bodies while the cops' attention was distracted. He sucked in a breath, making himself as thin as possible, pretending to be invisible—a speck of dirt, a floating dust mote. He spun and ducked and slid and broke through the crowd at last. In the street, the cop car was still sitting with its doors open, radio crackling, as water rained down on the windshield.

The car.

Thomas slipped into the passenger seat and released the safety brake. He sprang back as the car began rolling— slowly, at first, then with increasing speed.

"Look!" someone cried out.

"The car! It's getting away!"

"It's going to crash!"

Then the crowd was turning, and surging around him, and everyone was pointing and laughing as the cop car, unmanned, barreled down the street. Sergeant Gilhooley hurtled past Thomas, one hand gripping his hat, long legs pumping. Sergeant Schroeder huffed after him, shouting instructions, wet shoes slapping on the pavement. Like magic, the crowd followed them, flowing like a stream down Ludlow Street. Even Andrea von Stikk hurried to keep up, holding her skirt up to her knees as she sloshed through the gutter.

Thomas, Pippa, Sam, and Max were forgotten.

"Let's go!" Thomas said. But the others were already moving, turning instinctively in the direction of the subway station that would carry them uptown and to the museum. They had no time to lose.

If they weren't already too late.

37

The ride back to Forty-Second Street had never felt so long. The subway seemed to be inching, crawling, *oozing* through the darkened tunnels, as if its wheels were coated with molasses. Thomas knew that on average, subway trains took three minutes to move from one station to the next, but it felt to him like three hours. Anxiety was crawling through his whole body, as if a thousand ants were marching under his skin. Every time the train stopped at a station and the doors slid open to admit a shuffling mass of passengers, Thomas had the urge to scream. Max bit her nails to shreds and Sam gripped one of the handrails so hard, he left an enormous dent in the metal.

Had they done the right thing by running away from Rattigan? He didn't know. He couldn't think clearly. For once in his life, his brain could produce not a single useful calculation or statistic. He couldn't imagine what Rattigan wanted with them in the first place.

All he knew was that he would never forgive himself if anything happened to Mr. Dumfrey.

Finally, they were only one stop away. But halfway to Forty-Second Street, the train gave a jerk and a groan and shuddered to a stop. The lights flickered and then went off; the car was plunged into darkness. The passengers in the car began to mutter.

"Last week I got stuck right here for forty-five minutes," someone said with a sigh. "Engine problems."

"You gotta be kidding me," Max said, but her voice was high-pitched, nearly hysterical.

"We're running out of time," Pippa whispered. "If Rattigan got to Dumfrey . . ." She didn't finish her thought. She didn't have to.

"Follow me," Sam said. He pushed his way over to the side of the car, wedged his fingers into the little crack between the doors, and, with a grunt, pried them apart, grateful for the darkness, which meant that nobody could gape. "Come on!" He held the doors open as Thomas, Pippa, and Max slipped past him and jumped down onto the tracks.

Thomas could hear the sound of rats scurrying out of the way. Pippa was whimpering behind him. He kept one hand on the wall for balance, moving as quickly as he could along the tracks, careful to avoid the third rail, heart leapfrogging in his throat. He felt each passing second as if it had a separate taste and texture, flaking away like snow, dissolving.

Then he saw the glimmer of lights from the subway station ahead of him. Relief broke in his chest. Almost there.

Please, he thought. Please, let us be in time.

They came out of the darkness, panting. They hauled themselves up onto the platform and dashed up the stairs into the street. They sprinted to the museum, shoving past people on the street. Thomas scanned every face, half expecting Rattigan to jump out at them, leering, triumphant. But he saw nothing but strangers: men nose-deep in newspapers, children hurrying to school, women calling to one another from windows and stoops. Sam plunged past a display of vegetables at the corner of Eighth Avenue, upsetting an entire tray of bruised tomatoes to roll into the street.

"Hooligans!" the vendor cried, waving his fist.

"Sorry!" Sam called back.

Finally, they arrived. They burst through the front doors and skidded through the empty lobby. It was quiet and very still. Thomas thought his heart might rocket out of his chest. Through the Hall of Worldwide Wonders; up the spiral staircase to the third floor.

They burst through Mr. Dumfrey's office door together.

"Children!" Mr. Dumfrey was sitting behind his desk, wearing his scarlet robe and a pair of felt slippers, sipping from a steaming cup of hot chocolate. "Where have you been? I'm afraid we've had a bit of a slow start this morning. But what a glorious triumph last night was! What a brilliant success!"

"You . . . you're all right," Thomas panted out.

"Of course I'm all right." Mr. Dumfrey removed his glasses and squinted at Thomas. "What's the matter with you? What's the matter with all of you? You look paler than Quinn and Caroline."

"Mr. Dumfrey, you're in danger," Max said between gasps.

Mr. Dumfrey frowned. "Don't tell me *you* got into the champagne last night," he said sternly. "You're far too young. Much better to start on beer. Kidding!"

"It's true, Mr. Dumfrey," Thomas said. But even as the words escaped his mouth, he wasn't sure. Dumfrey's office looked the same as it always did—no booby traps or trip wires or knives dangling from the ceiling, just stacks everywhere, piles of boxes and papers and Cornelius hopping around his cage, squawking. Could Rattigan have been bluffing?

Then Pippa stiffened. "Your pocket," she said. "There's a note in your pocket. For a delivery."

Mr. Dumfrey sighed and returned his glasses to his nose. "What have I told you a thousand times, Pippa? It's rude to read people's pockets without their permission."

"Did someone send you a package?" Thomas asked.

"Not ten minutes ago," Mr. Dumfrey said. He withdrew the note from his pocket and smoothed it on the desk, then read aloud: "'Dear Mr. Dumfrey. I believe this belongs to you. Sorry for any trouble I've caused.' Wonderful, isn't it? The thief must have had a change of heart. And now the shrunken head has returned!"

"Who brought you the head?" Thomas said. He was gripped by certainty now: Rattigan. Had to be.

Mr. Dumfrey continued to stare as if the children had lost their minds. "Nobody *brought* it to me," he said, frowning. "The doorbell rang. When I opened the door, I found the note and the package on the doorstep. I imagine the thief was ashamed to show his face."

"Oh no," Max muttered.

"Mr. Dumfrey." Thomas was struggling to breathe.

"Where's the head now?"

"By Barnum's britches, what's going on?" Dumfrey straightened up a little. "You're acting very strange."

"The head, Mr. Dumfrey!" Thomas's throat was tight with panic. "Where is it?"

"Right over there." Mr. Dumfrey pointed to a small cardboard box, open to reveal mounds of tissue paper. "And looking not much worse for the wear, I'm happy to say. Now will someone explain to me—"

But Thomas was no longer listening. He dove toward the box and hefted up the head from its bed of tissue paper. It looked roughly the same. But it was too heavy. Much too heavy.

And Thomas could hear a faint mechanical ticking, coming from somewhere directly behind the head's glass eyes, getting faster and faster.

The head began to vibrate in Thomas's hands. Dumfrey sprang out of his chair, overturning it. Suddenly, everyone was shouting.

"Max!" Thomas shouted. "The window."

She understood him at once. There was a small window fitted high in the wall. As Thomas vaulted up Dumfrey's bookshelves, and hurtled himself into the air, Max grabbed a fountain pen from Dumfrey's desk and shot it straight through the window. Glass shattered outward, and Thomas felt a blast of wind just as he released the head, hurling it as far as he could.

There was a thunderous blast as the head exploded in midair, bright as a second sun. The walls shook. Sam and Max ducked, and Dumfrey pulled Pippa out of the way as a massive stone bust of Benjamin Franklin fell from its pedestal, shattering in heavy pieces directly where she had been standing.

Thomas landed badly, grunting, and an avalanche of books thunked onto his head. The room smelled like smoke and singed paper.

For a moment, Thomas thought he might be dead.

"Thomas!" Then Dumfrey's face appeared above him. As Dumfrey unearthed Thomas from the mountain of books encasing him, more faces came into view: Pippa and Max and Sam, all of them wearing identical expressions of concern.

"I'm all right." Thomas sat up, groaning. "At least, I think I am."

"You did it, Thomas," Sam said. A slow grin spread over his face. "You saved Mr. Dumfrey's life."

Thomas tried to smile, and winced. He'd accidentally clunked his jaw when he fell. "*We* did it," he corrected. And, extending a hand to Pippa, he allowed himself to be helped to his feet.

"I still don't understand what Rattigan wanted with us," Thomas said, sitting up in bed with a blanket draped around his shoulders and a hot-water bottle steaming by his feet. Miss Fitch had insisted on both of these measures, as if he were dying of pneumonia.

Sam, Pippa, Max, and Mr. Dumfrey were gathered around him. Sam was sitting on his bed, and Thomas couldn't help noticing that Max had chosen to sit next to him, slightly closer than was necessary. Pippa was sitting cross-legged on the floor. And Mr. Dumfrey was standing, polishing his glasses with his handkerchief. They had just finished telling him everything: their realization that Bill Evans had bribed Potts to steal the head; that he was responsible for the murders of Potts, Anderson, and Weathersby, their visit to his apartment, their discovery of his body, and their encounter with Rattigan. Mr. Dumfrey listened quietly and didn't even lecture the children about how many rules they had broken. His face was more serious than Thomas had ever seen it.

Finally, when they were finished speaking, he sat down heavily on the end of Thomas's bed.

"I'm going to tell you a story now," he said. "I'd been hoping—praying—that you might never have to know. But I see now that it's time."

"Know what?" Max said, her dark eyes glittering.

Mr. Dumfrey looked up at the ceiling. "Professor Rattigan was a brilliant biologist—the best, perhaps, who had ever lived. When the war broke out, he enlisted, as so many promising young men did."

Thomas settled back against his pillows. He didn't know where the story was going, but he had a sense of something momentous about to be revealed.

"War does things to people. You have to understand. Many men came back broken. Not in their bodies, but here." Mr. Dumfrey tapped his heart. "And here." He tapped his head. "Rattigan hated the war. Who wouldn't? An idea began to form. What if he could make soldiers so perfect, so strong, so smart, that they couldn't be defeated or killed by ordinary means? We would never have to go to war again. No one would risk it. Eventually, there would be no point in waging war at all.

"His idea grew into an obsession: when the war ended, he would create a team of individuals so extraordinary as to be invincible."

Thomas tried to swallow and found that he couldn't.

"During one of the bloodiest battles, almost every single member of his platoon was wiped out. Only Rattigan and two others survived. Rattigan was awarded the Medal of Honor for bravery and discharged." Mr. Dumfrey closed his eyes. "But he came back from the war different. Obsessed. Convinced that his way was the *only* way. He wanted to create an army of his own— the most powerful army in the world. To that end, he got hold of four orphaned children, and began his experiments on them."

Mr. Dumfrey opened his eyes. His gaze traveled slowly over the four of them: Thomas, Sam, Max, and Pippa. Despite the blanket and the heat of the attic, Thomas felt goose bumps pop up all over his arms.

"He was eventually arrested. The children scattered.

They were placed in foster homes and orphanages. One of them escaped and spent many years on the street." Dumfrey's eyes ticked to Max. "The other three found their way into my care. It was not an accident. I admit I was looking for you—for all of you. I knew you were extraordinary, and I wanted to make sure that Rattigan would never get to you again. Even after Rattigan was locked away, I was scared. I'm still scared."

There was a long moment of silence. It took Thomas several tries before he could find his voice.

"How?" he croaked out. "How do you know so much about Rattigan?"

Dumfrey let out a heavy sigh. "He's my brother."

EPILOGUE

"Next!" Mr. Dumfrey called out, drumming a pen against his clipboard. He made a large *X* next to an entry labeled "The Amazing Sword-Swallowing Seth." He turned to Pippa and murmured, "I thought the poor fellow was going to choke on his own blade! Most unconvincing. And what kind of name is Seth for a performer? That's the name of my dentist!"

It had been two weeks since Thomas had saved Mr. Dumfrey from certain death—two weeks since Pippa and the others had learned of their true origins. For several days afterward, she had not believed that she would ever feel the same, that she would ever get over what had happened and what she had learned.

She was a bona fide freak. They all were.

She didn't think she would ever look at Dumfrey the same way again, either. Not after what he had told them about his past. At last she had made sense of the two conversations she had overheard. Miss Fitch, Mr. Dumfrey confessed, was the only other person at the museum who knew the truth about Rattigan and his experiments, and Pippa found herself feeling unaccountably affectionate toward the sour-faced seamstress, who had kept their secret all these years. Pippa understood, too, about the telephone call Mr. Dumfrey had received from the police after Rattigan's escape, which at the time had struck her as so mysterious.

And slowly things *did* return to normal, or as normal as they ever got at Dumfrey's Dime Museum. Now she was sitting between Thomas and Mr. Dumfrey in the dark, in the front row of the Odditorium, watching a parade of aspiring performers looking to fill Hugo's and Phoebe's places. It was nice to be in the audience for once.

"She calls herself a fat lady?" Phoebe whispered, from the row behind Pippa's, as the next act toddled onto the stage: Felicia, the Fat Lady of Lansing, Michigan. "I was three hundred pounds before I was a teenager!"

"There, there, Phoebe," Hugo whispered back. "No one can take your place."

"It's insulting," Phoebe responded. "She's barely round."

"Next!" Mr. Dumfrey hollered. "And please, Felicia—consider adding more carbohydrates to your diet. You're looking a little trim."

Felicia nodded and stomped off the stage. Mr. Dumfrey sighed and rubbed the bridge of his nose. "This is difficult—truly difficult," he muttered. "So far we've seen an incompetent sword swallower, a fat lady who's too thin, and a thin man who's too fat. And that so-called giant! Why, Smalls could pick his teeth with him."

"Don't worry," Pippa said, patting Mr. Dumfrey's hand reassuringly. "You'll find someone."

"I hope so," Mr. Dumfrey said darkly, as the next performer took the stage: Freddy the fire-breather.

The first trick went very well. Freddy lit a long torch and brought it close to his mouth. The flame was extinguished momentarily; then, as he exhaled, a blast of fire roared from his mouth.

"Cool," said Sam.

"I could do that," sniffed Max.

Everyone applauded, and even Thomas looked up,

closing his book at last. He had been strangely quiet since the explosion. Pippa saw that he had once again been reading a book about probabilities.

"What are you thinking about?" she whispered as Freddy the fire-breather, encouraged by the applause, ignited three torches and began to juggle.

"Rattigan," he admitted.

Pippa kept her eyes on the stage, on the swooping circles of flame, orange and blue, passing inches from the fire-breather's face. "Do you think he'll try again?"

"Probably," Thomas said, his fingers tightening momentarily around the book.

Pippa knew she should be afraid. But sitting there in the dark, in the home she loved, with the people she loved, she wasn't—not then.

It happened in an instant. The fire-breather lost his footing. He slipped, and one of the torches shot out of his hands, catching the hem of the curtain, which promptly began to smoke. Quinn shrieked; Caroline screamed; the torches fell with a clatter. Fortunately, Danny was prepared and appeared instantly on the stage, carting a bucket of water, which he reversed onto the smoldering curtain.

"Oh, dear," Mr. Dumfrey sighed. "Will someone go fetch Miss Fitch? I'm afraid we'll need another curtain for tonight's performance. Thank you, Freddy. That was very—erm—illuminating. Next!"

Thomas coughed. Then he began to laugh. Pippa started laughing, and soon Max and Sam were laughing, too.

"I don't see what's so funny," Mr. Dumfrey said. "It's appalling. Truly appalling. Very hard to find good talent nowadays." But he cracked a smile.

Pippa settled back in her chair, her stomach aching, her cheeks sore from smiling. Maybe things would never exactly be normal. But to Pippa, just then, they were perfect.